The Lost Sister

The Lost Sister

Megan Kelley Hall

KENSINGTON BOOKS
http://www.kensingtonbooks.com

KENSINGTON BOOKS are published by

Kensington Publishing Corp.
119 West 40th Street
New York, NY 10018

All Kensington titles, imprints, and distributed lines are available at special quantity discounts for bulk purchases for sales promotion, premiums, fund-raising, educational, or institutional use.

Special book excerpts or customized printings can also be created to fit specific needs. For details, write or phone the office of the Kensington Special Sales Manager: Kensington Publishing Corp., 119 West 40th Street, New York, NY 10018. Attn. Special Sales Department. Phone: 1-800-221-2647.

ISBN-13: 978-0-7582-2680-8
ISBN-10: 0-7582-2680-2

First Kensington Trade Paperback Printing: August 2009
10 9 8 7 6 5 4 3 2 1

Printed in the United States of America

To my rock star,
My movie star,
My wish upon a star come true;
Piper Elizabeth Hall,
This is for you.

Acknowledgments

First of all, I'd like to thank my husband, Eddie, not only because he's my best friend, most ardent supporter, and the love of my life, but also because he noted that I put him on the last page of my acknowledgments in *Sisters of Misery*. So, right off the bat, I want to say, thank you, Eddie! Thank you, thank you!

The members of my family, Gloria, Jocelyn, Connor, and Jim Kelley, have been so incredibly helpful. I am forever indebted to you for all you've done for me and my career as a writer: from giving me moral support, to helping me with the daunting task of raising an incredibly willful and spirited six-year-old while attempting to write books; from giving sage advice, to being there when I needed you—always.

To Kelley & Hall Book Publicity, thank you for taking a debut young adult novel and getting it onto the pages of *USA Today*, *Publishers Weekly*, *Boston* magazine, and *Family Circle*. No easy feat, for sure! You do an amazing job for all of your authors and are the hardest-working people I've ever known.

To Elisabeth Weed, agent extraordinaire, thank you for supporting and encouraging my work, and for giving me wonderful advice when I needed it most.

To the most amazing editor anyone could ever ask for: Danielle Chiotti. I feel so lucky to have had the opportunity to work with you on my first two books.

I'd like to thank the members of the GCC—the Girlfriend's Cyber Circuit: a fabulously talented group of women writers who are so supportive and generous. Thank you for bringing me into your circle of friends. You've all provided so much encouragement and help during the stressful and sometimes painful process of writing and promoting books. You girls help make it a blast!

To my in-laws, Shirley and Fred Hall, thanks for the encouragement and enthusiasm throughout the years. And Fred, I'm so happy to have made my way onto your signed, first-edition, debut-author bookshelf.

Thanks to all the incredible book bloggers, reviewers, and teens out there who championed *Sisters of Misery* and gave me such wonderful reviews.

And, most of all, I have to thank Piper Elizabeth, my little movie star. Who could have predicted that you would be in your first movie the same year that my first book came out? I know that you wish I wrote "real" books (i.e., books for six-year-olds) and that I would spend less time on e-mail, on the computer, and doing "book stuff." But I want you to know that you provide constant inspiration, a wonderful reprieve from my work, and that your energy and excitement about the world around you is truly magical. You are my best friend and my whole reason for being. I promise in the future to try to stop saying that I'll play with you "in a minute," spend less time working on the computer, and more time playing with my little fairy princess.

Prologue

THE MORNING AFTER MISERY ISLAND

Cordelia took off her shoes. She walked slowly up the side of the giant rock that lurched into the water, picking her way along the jagged edges, not noticing the rough barnacles as they dug into her feet. Her hands were still bloodied and filthy from the horrific events from the previous night. She looked out across the water as the sun made its ascent into the sky and looked out at Misery Island. The daylight made the place seem harmless, almost tranquil. There was no evidence of the violence and the cruelty that she'd endured the night before. The hatred that was bestowed upon her by the girls made the bile rise up in the back of her throat, but Maddie's involvement—her own sister!—made her want to cry.

And Abigail! Abigail hadn't even let her shower—hadn't let her say good-bye to anyone. What was the point now? Everything had been a lie. Her real father wasn't the one she'd always believed him to be. Her aunt hated her. Her sister had betrayed her. Her own mother—her best friend—had lied to her. She only had one person she could count on in this world—herself.

Cordelia knew that she would be leaving Hawthorne forever. And she wanted to get one final glance before she headed out of town. With the money given to her by Reed and Finn burning in her pocket, it was enough to get her away and give her a new start. The blood that snaked down her leg convinced her that if she ever had been pregnant, it was all lost now. The harsh blows and kicks she received out on the island had put an end to a situation that she didn't know how to handle. But she couldn't bring herself to tell Finn. She could barely look at him—what must he think of her? She was humiliated and betrayed and lost.

But she could change all that. She could begin again someplace new. Somewhere she could just hide out, remove herself from the lies and the stories and the torture. She could just disappear.

Once on top of the rock, she stood and looked out over the horizon. She rocked back and forth on her feet, assessing the distance from where she stood to the sharp and jagged rocks below. It was a good ten to fifteen feet into the angry swell below her. She resisted the temptation to dive in and cleanse her grimy clothes, allow the salt water to lick her wounds and melt away all the signs of the terrible night. Even though Cordelia was an expert swimmer, the tide was rough and she could easily be thrown back against the rocks, knocking her unconscious and drowning her as dawn broke over the harbor. In that eerie half-light between day and night, Cordelia considered her fate for just a moment. It would be so easy just to take one step forward and let all of the pain and betrayal stay behind her forever, wipe it all into oblivion.

She delicately raised one leg in front of her, pointing her toe in an arabesque pose. Teetering for a moment, Cordelia felt the thrill rush through her body as she considered what it would be like to just let everything drop away: all the pain, all the confusion, all the heartbreak. She would be with her father—her real father, the one who raised her and who died too early, not the biological father that she had only just learned about, Malcolm Crane, the man who made Cordelia and Maddie sisters by cheating on his wife, Abigail, with her own sister—Cordelia's mother. She could be lulled into an everlasting sleep underneath the gentle waves and wouldn't have to deal with the betrayal by Maddie, by Abigail, or—more importantly—by her own mother, Rebecca. Cordelia closed her eyes and imagined the salty waves reaching up to her and caressing her skin, pulling at the strands of her hair, coaxing her forward. She started to hum as her body swayed back and forth, keeping time with the rhythmic lapping of the waves. It would be so easy, she thought again. Who would really care?

Just as she started to sway forward, a large gust of wind knocked her off balance, sending her tumbling into the wide fissures of the craggy rock. The pain that shot up her back and down her legs woke her from the dreamlike trance she'd been in. Horrified at how close she was to doing something tragic, Cordelia scurried down the rock, away from the dangerous whispers of the sea—the calls that tried to lure her into an everlasting swim.

She had to leave this moment. She could almost hear Tess— her wise and thoughtful grandmother—whispering in her ear that it was time for her to go. She was desperate to say goodbye to the old woman whom she'd grown to love so much in her short time in this town, but she knew that if she stayed, she might be unable to resist the temptation to let it all slip away.

Chapter 1

JUDGMENT

The card signals great transformation, renewal, change, rebirth, resurrection, making a final decision. You cannot hide any longer, face what you have to face, make that decision. Change. Time to summon the past, forgive it, and let it go, begin to heal.

Dear Diary,

If it weren't for the little baby boy with the Coke-bottle glasses, I would have killed my father by now. The poison would be seeping into his veins effortlessly with every sip of the herbal tea concoction that I made especially for him. But the moment I saw that little boy, my stepbrother . . . half brother . . . whatever—I couldn't do it. It's not because I want Malcolm Crane to live, not after what he's done to me and the lives of all the women in my family, but because he has another life dependent on him: the life of an innocent little boy. And so, for that reason, I'll let him live.

For now.

No one knows me here. Even those I've left behind in Hawthorne couldn't recognize me now. Besides, no one would ever think to look for me up in the boondocks of Maine. My hair, once a brilliant shade of red, my most striking feature, has been dulled to a mousy brown, courtesy of a sable-brown henna.

I often wonder if anyone has even noticed that I'm gone, not that I really care. Everyone I trusted,

*everyone I loved has lied to me or let me down.
I've always felt like I was on my own. Now I know
that to be true.*

*All I know is that I have to get back home to
California where I belong, and find some way to
make it back there by myself. But first things first.
Someone needs to be taught a lesson. And I'm not
leaving until everything—and everyone—has been
taken care of.*

"One cup of passion fruit-lime green tea," Cordelia said
softly to the man behind the newspaper. She poured the tea
carefully, watching the leaves swirl in the bottom of the cup.
Rebecca had taught her to read the messages in the leaves,
not only once the cup was finished, but also as they swirled
into the delicate teacup. She tried not to read the warning in
the leaves. Once you knew where to look for certain signs, it
was hard not to see them in everything. And she could read
this message as clear as day: *Kill him.*

She looked at the little boy sitting across from his father.
He peered up at her face, which was half hidden behind her
long sheath of brown hair. She winked at him, causing him to
erupt into giggles. He couldn't be more than three or four.
Cordelia wondered where his mother was, who his mother
was. What would become of this little boy if she went ahead
with her plan: to pay Malcolm Crane back for all of his wrong-
doings? For deserting Maddie and Abigail, for impregnating
her mother and never taking responsibility for any of his children back in Hawthorne, Massachusetts, and then simply running off to Maine to start all over again. Cordelia wondered
if he would desert this little boy as well. Maybe she would be
doing him a favor by stopping Malcolm Crane—the father
she'd only known of for a very short time—from hurting
anyone ever again.

"And for the little man?" she asked quietly. She waited for

a glance from the man she now knew to be her father. The man that up until only a few minutes ago she had planned on killing in cold blood.

After leaving Hawthorne, she quickly made her way up to Maine where she knew that Malcolm had been living for more than a decade. Once she found him—which wasn't the hardest thing to do, since he was known for being not only the town drunk, but also one of the professors in the tiny community college—she shadowed his every move. She knew about all of the girls that he was sleeping with—students, assistant professors, barmaids. This was something that she was able to figure out very quickly. She crept into the back of his lectures, studying the man that was her biological father.

She noticed some similarities in their appearance. Although everyone always said that she was an exact replica of her mother—the fair, porcelain skin, the copper hair, the delicate features—she detected some traits that she inherited from her father. The husky, butterscotch voice, the intense, lavender-blue eyes, the lean, athletic build. These were all things that she—as well as many of the dreamy-eyed girls in his classroom—noticed right away. The only two places that he frequented besides his lecture halls and his home were the town pub and the coffee and tea shop across from the college.

She had watched Malcolm Crane in between his classes. She'd managed to get a job at the Maine Tea and Coffee Bean— the only place he frequented during the week—and served him almost daily, but he never showed any sign of recognition. He was flirtatious and friendly, but it was all on the surface. She truly believed that if there was anything good in him, he would recognize his own daughter. But then, sadly, he probably wouldn't even recognize Maddie and he had watched his little girl grow up and knew her to be his own. But even that didn't give him reason enough to stick around in Hawthorne, to stay with his wife and young daughter.

Everything that Cordelia had done up until this point had

been meticulously planned. She had taken the rat poison from the storage room—there were so many boxes, she was sure that no one would miss it. By the time anyone realized that Malcolm Crane had been murdered, she would be long gone. They didn't even know her real name. Over the past few months, she'd made sure not to leave a mark. She lived like a ghost among mortals. She felt like she had died that night out on Misery Island and could only be brought back to life once she'd exacted her revenge. And the first one on her list was Malcolm Crane. But then this little boy had to come along and change everything.

"Danny, you heard the lady, did you want something to drink?" The little boy looked up and smiled at her and the toothy grin broke her heart.

"Milk, please," he lisped.

"Sure, right . . . milk," she stammered, backing away from the counter, feeling the rat poison burning in her apron pocket. She couldn't do it. Not with this little boy. No matter how much she blamed Malcolm Crane for everything that had gone wrong in her life up until this point—the lies from Rebecca, the return to Hawthorne, even the death of the man she believed to be her real father up until a few months ago, even though deep down she knew he had nothing to do with Simon LeClaire's death—she couldn't make this little boy, Daniel Crane, go through the pain of losing a parent. It was still too real and raw for her—too hard for someone her own age to deal with, let alone a little boy.

She backed up into another table and practically knocked over another waitress. "Hey, watch it, CeeCee." Cordelia steadied herself and turned to apologize to her coworker. She'd gone by CeeCee, a nickname given to her by the man she grew up thinking to be her father—the man that up until his untimely death from cancer was her true father. The man who cared for her as if she were his own flesh and blood, and who, a few horrible months ago, she discovered was not her real father. Her biological father was this man sitting in front of her. This waste of a human being. This horrible, selfish narcissist. He finally looked up at her. After months of her serving him his morning coffee and his afternoon tea, he actually made eye contact with her.

"Are you all right, darlin'?" A look of concern crossed Malcolm Crane's face, the lines around his eyebrows deepened. Despite his weather-beaten face, she could see why some girls in his classes hung on his every word and the waitresses at Maine Tea and Coffee Bean cooed about him looking like Robert Redford. Yet instead of the lusty feelings that his gaze seemed to evoke with everyone around her, she only felt nausea.

"I'm fine," she clipped. "I'll be back with the milk for your son."

He winked, rolled his newspaper up, and lightly bonked the little boy's head. "Say thank you to the pretty lady, Daniel."

"Thanks, pretty lady," the little boy whispered, and then giggled.

Cordelia knew in her heart that she couldn't go through with it. She couldn't take away this little boy's father. But that didn't mean she couldn't stick around long enough to make Malcolm Crane wish he was dead.

From behind the Formica counter, she saw a look of concern wash over Malcolm Crane's face. He scrunched up his forehead and peered more closely at the newspaper. Then he sat back and stared straight ahead for a few moments, looking as though he were very far away, while little Daniel busily colored the paper place mat with the café's crayons. Cordelia walked hesitantly back to the table, curious of what had caused this sudden shift in his mood. She placed the plastic cup in front of the young boy and tried to see what paper Malcolm had been reading.

It was the *Hawthorne Gazette*. Odd that he was still receiving news from home all the way up here in the boondocks. She prayed that it wasn't another article about her disappearance. By now she had managed to avoid the second glances and the quick looks of recognition, people trying to place her face, knowing that she looked familiar, but not quite sure from where. When she first left Hawthorne, she had chopped what was left of her hair and dyed it brown so that she could slip away easily. Redheads often commanded more attention than brunettes. But she couldn't change her features. People often called her beautiful, ethereal, even exquisite. She wondered how they'd describe her after she'd become a murderer.

Cordelia watched as Malcolm gathered up his son and left the coffee shop in a hurry. She rushed over to the empty table and grabbed the newspaper that was left behind in haste. Her eyes flicked down the page and a jolt of shock went through her body. There was an article about an ongoing fight between the Endicott family and the historical society of Hawthorne. Other neighboring towns of Salem, Marblehead, Beverly, and Swampscott were weighing in on the historical importance of the building. But that wasn't what caught Cordelia's attention. The article was written about all of the tragedies that occurred at Ravenswood Asylum throughout the years, especially the most recent one that took place only months ago.

Cordelia's fingers trembled as she read the story entitled "Bloody Night at Ravenswood Remembered." She skimmed the story, picking out the most disturbing phrases.

> Rebecca LeClaire, one of the last inmates before the closing of the asylum, apprehended after apparent suicide attempt . . . Witnesses at the site were sister, Abigail Crane, niece, Maddie Crane, and local teen Finnegan O'Malley. Tess Martin, 82, passed away in her sleep that same night, unaware of the tragedy that had overtaken her family.

Cordelia inhaled deeply as she continued reading about what had happened in the wake of her disappearance. Since that night, there had been an ongoing fight over the property—how the Endicotts wanted to turn it into a luxury resort, capitalizing on the fright factor of its proximity to Salem, Massachusetts, and the witch trials, as well as all of the tragic legends that surround the place. The historical society had tied up any future projects with enough red tape until they could declare it a historic property.

Cordelia was hit by a wave of vertigo. The world spun around her, almost knocking her from her feet.

I have to go back, she thought. Something she thought she would never do.

"Easy there, CeeCee. Take a load off. You look like you're going to be sick." Her manager, Chris Markson, had come up behind her and noticed the color drained from her face. "Sit down, I'll get you some water."

Cordelia was used to getting this attention from the guys in her life. She knew that the girls were probably in the back gossiping about how she was being a drama queen and how unfair it was that she got a break in the middle of her shift. But Cordelia didn't care. All she could think about was what her family had gone through—all of the pain that she had brought upon them by running away—and all that she had missed while she was gone. How long had it been? How many months had she made them suffer in her absence? Could it really be almost a year? A year of hiding her past, her true identity, her intentions. Keeping everyone at an arm's length, not letting anyone in and trying desperately not to think of all the people she'd left behind.

In her attempt at starting a new life and seeking vengeance on the one person who, in her mind, was responsible for destroying all of their lives, she had done even more damage by leaving than she could ever have thought possible.

In her attempt to cut herself off from everyone and everything in Hawthorne and create this new life, she never realized all of the destruction she caused in her wake. Why would she do that to herself and her family?

"Water?" the voice called out. And then again, "Water?"

Cordelia looked up and saw her coworker holding a glass of water in front of her.

"Yes, water," Cordelia said in a daze, remembering the ritual hazing events that took place on Misery Island—Fire, Water, Air, and Earth—the degrading and painful events that forced her to leave it all behind. The pain and humiliation she endured. The betrayal. The lies.

"Thank you, Chris," she said, taking the glass from his hand, ignoring his perplexed expression.

As she gulped down the water, she allowed herself to think about what had happened that night. Since she'd moved to Maine, she had managed to put those memories aside, choosing not to think of that night, but instead to channel her anger and energy toward the man she believed was at the root of all of her suffering: Malcolm Crane.

"Uh . . . CeeCee?" Chris hesitated. "You need to lie down or something? Do you need a break?" She could hear her female coworkers snickering behind the coffee bar. Cordelia was uncomfortable with this kind of attention. She had managed to fly under the radar for so long, she wasn't about to let anyone get too close to her. Not even a handsome and sweet college student like Chris Markson. When she looked at him and his perfectly sculpted features, all it did was make her miss Finn and his crooked smile even more. She couldn't imagine facing Finn again. For all he knew she had taken off carrying his child. He must hate her for not letting him know if he was a father or not. The truth was that even though she might have been pregnant, she couldn't even be sure that the baby was his. It could just as easily have been Trevor's. A bastard child from a bastard rapist.

"Yeah, I just need some fresh air," she managed. Standing up, she tucked the newspaper under her arm and rushed past him and out into the crisp autumn air. She walked across the street to a bench and sat for a few minutes staring at the paper folded on her lap.

What's happening? Everything was falling into place and then that little boy came out of nowhere, and then this newspaper shows up with the article about Tess and my mother's attempt to kill herself. What have I done? she thought miserably. She knew what Tess and her mother would say, that she should pay attention to these signs, that they were pointing her in a new direction. Maybe killing her father wasn't the answer. Maybe she had unfinished business to deal with in Hawthorne instead. True, she had been betrayed and lied to and hurt and deceived, but her family needed her. Finn and Reed needed her. Rebecca needed her. And Maddie . . . she didn't know what she felt about Maddie.

My sister, my cousin? she thought. It didn't matter what relationship they had—Maddie had had the chance to save her when she needed her most, and she didn't. She was too weak and scared. But Cordelia really couldn't blame her. Hawthorne and those girls were all she ever knew. She aimlessly thumbed through the pages until she noticed something fall out of the paper onto her lap.

She looked at the glossy tarot card that had fallen out of the paper. It looked brand-new, right out of the pack. Suddenly she felt like someone had known all along where she was and what she was planning. Someone was trying to scare her by letting her know that there was unfinished business. Someone was out to get her.

A man on a horse marched triumphantly over fallen bodies. He was holding a large black flag. But instead of a face, there was only a skull. And the eyes of the horse were bloodred.

It was the Death tarot card.

∞

Reed Campbell lifted the brown glass bottle to his lips, letting the liquid fill and burn the back of his throat. The cool salty air rubbed his throat raw, forcing him to indulge in his preferred medication. He caught a glimpse of himself in the glass window of his boat—the only place he felt at home these days.

He was the bastard son, all right.

While his baby brother, Trevor, had somehow become the golden child of Hawthorne, Massachusetts—the fair-haired prodigal son who could do no wrong—Reed occupied the role of town drunk, screwup, alleged murderer, and pedophile. On his sober days, he realized how the drinking was becoming a problem, which was why he'd made sure that those days were few and far between. It had already cost him his job, his dignity, and countless friends.

But thanks to Great-grandfather Campbell and the little oil company he started decades ago, Reed no longer felt the need to be gainfully employed. His bank account remained healthy thanks to the thousands of people who needed to stay warm on shivering New England nights. Reed often reminded himself of that fact on nights when he careened down to the waterfront after last call at one of the local taverns. Even though he was personally a failure and unable to support himself, the oil company that bore his family name kept everyone in town warm, and by default, lined his own deep, albeit threadbare, pockets.

He drowned out his sorrows in bottles and bars. He knew that his feelings for Cordelia and Maddie could be seen as inappropriate—that his actions could be called into question. Cordelia just blew him away with her love of literature and her free spirit. He knew that her time in Hawthorne would be short-lived, but he just couldn't understand why people would think he had anything to do with her disappearance. If anything, he was more enthralled and enchanted by her than anyone else in town. Perhaps that was his downfall.

And Maddie. Ever since she left for boarding school, he realized how deep his feelings ran for her. There were hundreds of reasons why he should stay away from her and keep her out of his mind. But he couldn't get over the way that she looked at him—like he was a knight in shining armor. She saw past all the flaws that his family and the town of Hawthorne held over him. She made him feel like a man. And even though he was in a relationship with someone new—someone his own age, someone more appropriate—he couldn't get Maddie out of his head. Which was why he kept the liquor flowing and the nights endless so he was never faced with the harsh light of the dawn.

ॐ

Finnegan O'Malley didn't believe in ghosts, but he swore on his great-grandmother's grave that he saw one. And not just any ghost. Not the random specters known to wander through the historical properties he took care of, the ones who seemed to have no awareness of their ghostly state, but just continued their daily activities in the same manner that they had done centuries before. Not Deacon Knott, who was believed to still take up residence on the top floor of the Knott Cove Inn, his heavy boots famously echoing throughout the Victorian bed-and-breakfast. Curls of smoke from his pipe hovered in the air of the grand parlor, his shadow loomed over the pretty women who dared to stay overnight as guests. Some even claimed to have been pinched rather viciously in their sleep, the purplish bruising on their backsides or upper thighs the only physical proof.

No, this ghost was a familiar one to Finn, or at least, she had been in life. This was a girl who continued to haunt Finn equally in his dreaming and wakeful states. A girl whose voice still rang out as clear and lyrical as it had when she first swept into town. She was a misfit and an outsider, not unlike himself. Someone whom he'd admired and even loved (though he'd never admit it to anyone—hardly even to himself), and ultimately had lost. But Cordelia LeClaire hadn't slipped away easily. He couldn't let her go—his heart wouldn't allow for it.

He'd loved her from the first moment he'd laid eyes on her. He loved her even more when he observed her midnight swims and watched as she danced through gardens in the early morning hours. He didn't know why he felt the need to watch over her. It just came instinctually. It was like watching over a beautiful rainbow fish in a sea of sharks. He still remembered their first kiss. It was just as important—if not more—than the night that they first made love. He'd secretly watched her midnight swims with Maddie, and he knew that she would return on certain nights alone. He knew she would need protection, even if she didn't believe it herself. And knowing the rough treatment she'd received upon her arrival in town, that there would be some people who would take advantage of her solitary swims if they ever found out. Which was why he was determined to never let her out of his sight on those hot, humid nights when the ocean beckoned to her like a siren's song to a sailor.

One stifling night at the end of August, he watched from behind a rock as she dipped in and out of the ocean like a mermaid. He was afraid to take his eyes off her for fear that she'd slip beneath the water and swim away forever—taking his heart with her.

He watched as she cocked her head to the side and spun around in the water. She looked right over to where he was crouched and he slunk backward, afraid that he'd been caught as a sort of Peeping Tom.

She came right out of the water—letting the heat of the night burn the water droplets off her skin, her long red hair clinging to her wet skin—and instinctively moved over to his hiding spot.

Before he could come up with a plausible excuse, she smiled widely and put her hand on his cheek.

"My own personal bodyguard," she said brightly. "My valiant knight, I know that you've been keeping watch over me. I can feel your eyes on me."

He stuttered, trying to come up with an explanation. Wanting her to believe that he wasn't some kind of a stalker. Before he could say anything more, she quieted him with a kiss. At first it was tentative and sweet. And then he reciprocated with a longer kiss, embracing her and not minding that her wet body was soaking his clothes. It was a kiss that he'd remember until his dying day.

He knew her intimately and he knew her secrets. He'd once heard his grandfather say that if two people shared a secret—one that nobody else knew about—it bound them together until the secret was finally revealed. He swore on his life that he'd never reveal it, not when she went missing, and not even when he'd been suspected of being involved in her vanishing. He gave his word—and his heart—to Cordelia.

And now, with no warning, in the bright light of day, he saw her. She'd come back to him. It was only for a moment and could be blamed on the dehydrated and overtired state he was in after doing the landscaping in the Old Town Hall's courtyard. He knew it was Cordelia because he caught her familiar scent of apples and lavender. He knew it was her from the look in her eyes. It was the same look he saw in her pale, watery blue eyes that she had the last time he saw her. Those eyes were forever etched in his memory. They were wide-set, haunted, shimmering, and most memorably, they were filled with fear.

Kate Endicott didn't believe in coincidences.

She was not superstitious, and wasn't really concerned with improving her luck, which was why Kate still wasn't sure what had compelled to her ask her mother, Kiki, to bring in a feng shui expert to enhance the flow of their house, and ultimately, their lives.

Maybe it was due to the Ravenswood debacle. The fact that Finn had royally screwed over Kiki Endicott's plans to turn Ravenswood Asylum into the luxury hotel, the Endicott. Well, it wasn't just him; it was that entire historical society.

Whatever.

They had screwed everything up big time and now millions of dollars were at stake. Investors were getting angry. And Kate saw the look of pity in her friends' eyes. Nobody pitied Kate Endicott. No one!

Kate and her mother were always on top of new trends. Always the first in line for the new yoga club or Pilates classes that had sprung up around Hawthorne. And when the topic of feng shui cluttered the pages of Kate's favorite magazines and lifestyle journals, she knew that she would have to improve her family's chi by renovating their house.

Perhaps she was just restless.

She could feel the change in the tide that was upsetting the smooth sailing of her life. Something had floated into the harbor of her perfect life and was threatening to capsize her carefully guarded vessel. Kate Endicott wouldn't let that happen; she refused to go down with the sinking ship. That was something that Kiki had taught her long ago, and she wasn't about to let it happen to them now. Not now, not ever.

&

Abigail Crane pinned her hair up carefully as she looked at her reflection in the low light of her bedroom. She tried wrapping her mind around what the doctors had told her—chemo was the only course of action to stop the spread of cancer in her body. Toxins placed in her body to seek out and destroy other deadly toxins. It was like sending in a black widow spider to take care of a venomous snake. The goal was for them to destroy each other—her body would end up as the ravaged battlefield.

She had just placed the call to Maddie at Stanton, asking her to come back to Hawthorne for winter break. It wasn't too much for a mother to ask of her own daughter, but there were plenty of reasons that Maddie would want to refuse. True, most children would want to take care of their sick mothers, but most children hadn't been betrayed in the same way that Abigail had betrayed Maddie. She realized that not telling Maddie the truth about Cordelia—that they weren't cousins, but really half sisters—was the wrong thing to do, but she couldn't take it back now. What else could she do to make it up to her? When Maddie left Hawthorne, she left with her own baggage—guilt about her treatment of Cordelia and over Rebecca's mental state that had nothing to do with Abigail. She had her own demons to fight.

Abigail had been visiting Rebecca for months—trying to make up for own failings—for causing Cordelia to run away, for not telling Rebecca about their confrontation. If she'd told the truth sooner, perhaps that night at Ravenswood and Rebecca's attempted suicide could have been avoided. She had her own ghosts to put to rest. But she needed her daughter now; perhaps tough times would help to mend their broken family. She didn't think her request of Maddie was too much to ask.

But the horrified reaction from Maddie made her think otherwise. Madeline had made it clear that she didn't want to return to Hawthorne until she had successfully tracked down Cordelia—a means of assuaging her own guilt. But it was too late for that. Abigail's cancer wouldn't wait for a flighty teenager who could be anywhere in the country to be tracked down. She had made her amends with Rebecca—or was at least trying to. Now it was Maddie's turn to come home and put things to rest. No matter how painful or uncomfortable it would be—for all of them.

Chapter 2

THE FOOL

A blank slate, infinite possibilities, new start, change, renewal, and a brand-new beginning, movement, a fresh, exciting new time.

It's funny how one phone call can completely change your life, Maddie thought angrily as she packed her bags for winter break.

She'd made her peace that she was finally done with Hawthorne—the past, the betrayal, the pain—and then one day Maddie got a call that changed everything. Maddie's mother, Abigail Crane, the strongest woman she'd ever known, was diagnosed with cancer. While helping her mother—a woman whom she couldn't even recall the last time she hugged—was one of the last things Maddie wanted to do, her school therapist suggested that going back to Hawthorne, helping her mother through her chemo treatments, checking in on her aunt Rebecca in the new facility, and finally coming to terms with what had happened to Cordelia, would help with the nightmares. Maddie might finally begin to move on and let go of the weight of it all.

Maddie thought it strange when people whom you expect to be around forever suddenly are at risk of being taken from you. Like Cordelia, her grandmother, Tess, and now, inevitably, Abigail. Even though Maddie made the decision to leave Hawthorne and its secrets and curses behind without thinking twice, now that Maddie knew she only had a limited amount of time with her mother, it all suddenly seemed unfair.

"Come with me, Maddie," said Luke Bradford as he grabbed

a handful of her neatly folded clothes and promptly removed them from her worn duffel bag. "I'll give you a raise."

"I don't work for you." Maddie laughed.

"But you could," he said.

"You know I can't."

"Come on, Maddie! It'll be a blast!" Luke insisted. Maddie looked at Luke, wondering how she was ever going to survive without her constant companion. Ever since they were lucky enough to room across the hall from each other in Eaton Hall, sixth floor, since she transferred, Luke Bradford and Maddie had been inseparable. And since he was one of the most sought after guys on campus, Maddie became the instant "best friend" to girls who wanted the inside track to the sandy-haired athlete who could easily pass as a close relative to Brad Pitt.

Maddie swatted him and started putting her clothes back into the suitcase, allowing her long, straight brown hair to fall over her shoulder, shielding her sad smile.

"I have a place all set for you on the ship," Luke insisted. "It's easy money. Basically, we get paid to have a monthlong booze cruise in a beautiful tropical paradise. Isn't that much better than going to a freezing wasteland like Hawthorne, Massachusetts?"

"Not a wasteland, a winter wonderland," she retorted.

Luke Bradford's father—a permanent fixture in the Fortune 500 list year after year—decided that his only son and future heir to his empire needed a good dose of corporate work ethic. Plus, he knew that it would enhance and effectively pad his résumé, allowing him to move one step closer to getting accepted at one of the Ivies. Unfortunately, Luke's grades weren't helping to clinch the deal, so a Bradford library might be in order.

"I would love it, really," Maddie moaned. "I'd rather do anything than go back to Hawthorne."

"Thanks." Luke collapsed into a chair by the window, staring outside at the snow-covered quad. "That makes me feel special. Spending Christmas break with your best friend is just barely more appealing than going back to a place you hate. No, really, that makes me feel great."

It hit Maddie then, how much she was going to miss Luke. She'd taken for granted all of the things that had carried her through the past few months and kept her mind off Hawthorne: his unannounced drop-overs when he'd show up balancing a bag of Chinese takeout in one arm and stacks of horror movies in the other. At times she'd had to remind herself why they never got together. Boyfriends come and go, friends are forever was what Maddie told anyone who asked why they weren't a couple yet.

Instead, Maddie sat back, watching him go through girl after girl, always returning back to her to relay all the unpleasant details of each relationship, describing how he felt trapped or bored. And then it was just the two of them again, starting with his knock on the door, pizza, and Red Bull, preparing for a night filled with dirty jokes, mindless movies, and uncontrollable laughter.

It was better than any real relationship either of them had ever had, and they were both terrified of tampering with perfection. Deep down Maddie knew the real reason that they hadn't gotten together. Luke respected that she was one of the last few virgins left on campus. Or at least that's what he said.

"You know that I love you," he said earnestly. Just then he rose from the seat, made his way over to her, and dropped down on one knee. "If I asked you to marry me, Madeline Crane, would you reconsider?"

Maddie raised an eyebrow, waiting for the punch line.

"Is that a no?"

Laughing, Maddie pulled all six feet two of him to his feet

and he embraced her in a deep, bear hug. He was one of the few people that made her feel small and protected—at five foot ten, Maddie was used to being the giant in the room.

"You know that if you marry me, you'd have to get rid of all your other girlfriends."

"Oh, damn, I didn't think of that."

Maddie pinched his arm hard.

"Ow," Luke cried, cowering. "I take it back. I'm not into abusive relationships. I watch *Oprah*—I know how to deal with people like you."

Again, Maddie took a swipe at him. He laughed, retreating just out of her reach.

It's strange how life can get better simply by changing your surroundings, Maddie mused. A few months ago, she had been dealing with so much loss and unhappiness. But now all she had to worry about was what classes she should take or what party to attend. She had made a new life, one that she was in control of; not one that was predetermined years ago by families and people she'd never known, but whose blood ran through her veins. People who constantly let her down, like her mother and father. Or those who terrified her, like Kate, her aunt Rebecca, and, now, Cordelia—wherever she was. The other girls were guilty of hurting her that night out on Misery, but Maddie was even more so. She had betrayed her own sister, an act she wasn't sure was forgivable—under any circumstances.

"Luke, you know that I need to help my mom right now. I've already made all the arrangements. . . ." Maddie's voice trailed off. She honestly didn't know what Abigail needed anymore. What any of them needed these days. Closure? Support? Forgiveness? Or the ability to forget and move on? All of it seemed a pipe dream.

Maddie had successfully trained herself—her mind, her body—to become numb. After Cordelia disappeared and Rebecca was institutionalized, Maddie's emotions sort of turned themselves off.

The truth was that Maddie was terrified of going back, afraid of what she'd find, afraid of facing the truth, afraid of the consequences. Maddie left that world far behind when she started at Stanton Prep. How could she possibly return to Mariner's Way—even if it was only for a short school break— constantly being confronted by old ghosts and shadows of her former life?

Luke nodded his head, becoming uncharacteristically sympathetic. "I know, Maddie, really I do. Just don't get any ideas about moving back there, transferring to Hawthorne and joining the water polo team or whatever the Christ they do out there," he needled, his goofy, lopsided grin returning.

Luke was born and raised in New York, and the idea of a small New England town was so foreign to him. But then again, his life—growing up wealthy in New York City—was just as much a mystery to Maddie as her life was to him. Sure, she'd told him stories about growing up in a small-minded, puritanical society. And he knew about Cordelia—the way she was treated and the night she disappeared. He knew bits and pieces of what had happened out on Misery Island. But she could never let him know her own involvement in the horrific events of that night—that she was too afraid to stand up for her own flesh and blood. That she was just as guilty, if not more, for the treatment Cordelia was forced to withstand. She couldn't imagine what he'd think of her if he knew the truth. "I was actually thinking I might do a little more digging to see what I come up with on Cordelia," Maddie offered lightly, curious to see his reaction.

"Maddie, come on!" he said, exasperated. "Seriously, you don't need to bring up that shit again. Whatever happened to your cousin was not your fault. She obviously was happy to leave that town and your family behind. And you should think about doing the same, okay?"

"Luke, come on," Maddie persisted, remembering how angry Luke used to get at her on the nights they'd stay up late talking and she would tell him about the hazing rituals that took place out on Misery Island.

"It wasn't your fault," Luke would say over and over.

But he wasn't there; he didn't know the whole story. And if he did know, would he still look at her the same way? Or would he look at her with the same amount of disgust that she felt she deserved?

Cordelia continued to haunt her dreams as a shadowy figure, her face shrouded in the thick fog that often rolled onto the island of Misery. In her dreams, Maddie would try to get a clear look at her face, hungry for a clue—any hint as to what had happened to Cordelia after that night.

But nothing ever came.

And in the mornings, Maddie's dreams of Cordelia and that horrible time in their lives would shuffle backward into the subconscious realm of her cluttered mind, taking a backseat to her daily problems. But still her guilt remained constant, lurking in the corner like a cat ready to pounce on its prey. How could she do that to her own flesh and blood? Her own sister?

Cordelia would never forgive her.

Would she even forgive herself?

Luke's cell phone suddenly started beeping. He looked down at the flashing lights, his blue eyes squinting at the number that came up on the screen. He shrugged his shoulders, indicating that it wasn't familiar, and put his finger out, signaling that he would only be a minute.

"Luke Bradford . . . Hey, doll, I was just thinking about you."

Luke used names like doll, baby, freckles, honey, sweetness, brown eyes, when he couldn't remember the girl's name.

For some guys, it could come off sounding cheesy, like they were using a line. But Luke had the sincerity to really pull it off. Even Maddie let herself get sucked in once in a while. Anyway, it must have been a recent conquest because he didn't immediately blow the girl off.

Maddie felt her heart make what could only be described as a sigh. Despite their better intentions of staying friends and not letting a relationship mess up what they had, Maddie realized that she'd been completely kidding herself.

She'd been desperately in love with Luke since they first met—even before his transformation from a too-skinny, long-legged boy to the Abercrombie & Fitch model look-alike he'd become, and each time a new girl came along, it only made her feel worse. Worse than worse, it made her feel invisible, unloved, and unimportant. Sure, she'd noticed the looks from other guys, the sideways glances, the winks. But the closest thing to a compliment that Maddie had ever gotten from Luke was when he jokingly compared her to a racehorse— long legs, big brown eyes, and a chestnut mane. Not exactly what a girl wanted to hear from the guy she adored.

It was then that Maddie realized that she needed this sepa-ration from Luke just as much as she needed to find Cordelia. Maybe putting these nagging questions to rest would allow her to take her mind off Luke and their "just friends" rela-tionship; mend her heart . . . just a little bit. The trip on his father's cruise ship sounded like a dream come true, but watch-ing the parade of tanned and beautiful model-wannabes go in and out of his cabin would drive Maddie insane.

She didn't know which was worse: loving someone who was too old for her and unattainable, or caring for someone who could easily break her heart. Loving Reed Campbell, her former teacher, was safer, because she knew if nothing ever came of it, she could just chalk it up to their age difference. But with Luke, there was nothing keeping them apart—noth-ing except for his wandering eye.

Maddie listened to him go on and on in his smoky "I'm going to get lucky tonight" voice, and continued packing her suitcase—trying not to let her annoyance with him show as it ate away at her.

Lifting his legs up off her bed to pull her jewelry pouch out, Maddie noticed something drop to the floor. She bent down onto the floor, something that would have prompted a lewd comment from Luke had he not been otherwise engaged, and poked her head under the bed.

An onyx rune stone—one that came from Cordelia and Rebecca's old store—had tumbled onto the hardwood floor. Maddie grabbed hold of it and turned it to look at the symbol etched onto the other side, but both sides were blank. She hadn't come across one of these stones since she first got to school. Maybe it was some kind of sign that going back to Hawthorne was a bad idea.

That's the understatement of the century, Maddie thought wryly.

Closing her eyes, Maddie went through the runic alphabet in her mind. Cordelia and Rebecca could recite the stones and their meanings effortlessly, but Maddie never was able to keep them all straight. Maddie always had to fall back on a little book of rune stone meanings that she came across in a secondhand bookshop.

Tess had once told Maddie that all the women in their family possessed a gift. It was a sort of knowing, a special extrasensory perception. Before that night on Misery Island, Maddie had just started to become more in tune with her abilities, but ever since she left Hawthorne behind, the door to those abilities had slammed shut.

Just then, the name came to Maddie—as if someone had whispered it in her ear.

Wyrd.

The Wyrd stone. *That's right,* Maddie thought. *Now, what*

does it mean again? Blank . . . blank slate? A new beginning? No, that wasn't the right definition.

Maddie picked it up and carried it with her as she moved across the room, checking to make sure that all her belongings were packed up. Maddie already shipped most of it yesterday, the big things. But the rest would be traveling with her by train.

Wyrd . . . *Wyrd* . . . *Wyrd.* Maddie ran it through her head a couple of times.

Standing at the window, Maddie watched as bundled-up students made their way across the icy quad. She dropped her head to the side, closed her eyes, and tried to will the meaning into her head.

"Now, that looks like an invitation if I ever saw one," Luke said. Before Maddie realized what was happening, his lips were drifting lightly across her neck. He whispered in her ear, "Do you really have to go home, darlin'?"

Maddie laughed, stepping just out of his reach, angry at the rising swell of her heart and annoyed at his teasing. When she turned to face him, however, Maddie noticed his face held no sign of humor. He simply stared into her eyes. So intensely, in fact, that Maddie could swear she felt trembling in the back of her knees.

"Luke . . ." Maddie let the word hang between them for a few moments, not quite sure what he wanted from her. She wasn't planning on being one of his "girls," and he couldn't— or wouldn't—give Maddie the type of relationship that she wanted.

"Aw, Maddie. You know I love ya," he said, dimples deepening as he lightened the awkward moment. "Come here and give me a hug good-bye."

He pulled her into his arms and squeezed tight, too tight. Maddie could feel him inhale deeply, as if trying to identify her brand of shampoo, and then he sighed heavily. They held on for a few moments, a little longer than normal, when his cell phone went off again.

Damn phone, Maddie thought. Probably some beautiful, airheaded, rich girl without a care in the world. *Who am I kidding? I'm the girl with the sick mother, the crazy aunt in a psych ward, the deadbeat dad, the disappearing cousin—right now, I don't even want to deal with someone like me.* Talk about depressing. Only Cordelia could get away with having such a crazy life and still have guys falling at her feet.

"Well, gotta go. You know how I hate to keep the girls waiting," he joked, and pulled her away from him by her shoulders. Maddie didn't want to look at him, couldn't look into his eyes. She didn't know if she hated him or loved him; if she was going to laugh or cry.

Luke tilted her chin up with his finger. "I'm gonna miss that face."

Maddie gave him a half smile. "I'll miss you, too, Luke. I—"

He dragged his finger up to her lips, shaking his head. "Uh-unh. I hate saying good-bye just as much as you do."

Maddie smiled beneath his finger and he leaned in and kissed her cheek, whispering, "Call me if you need me. For anything. Anytime. Seriously."

Before he headed out the door, they hugged one last time and he murmured something about staying a good girl during her time in Hawthorne. Maddie heard his phone ring persistently as he made his way down the dorm hallway. She rolled her eyes, sighing audibly as she scanned the room, eyeing the packing that still needed to be done.

She dropped down onto her bed, burying her face in her pillow, and squeezed her eyes shut.

Leaving Maine was going to be difficult, Maddie thought as she rolled over and gazed out the dorm window, but going back to Hawthorne . . . well, now, that would be murder.

ಜ

As the train moved through the beautiful New England landscape, Maddie knew that she'd never be able to focus on the books or magazines she'd packed for this trip.

"Would you like something to drink?" A woman's voice jolted her from her thoughts. She had a rolling tray of canned sodas and bottled water. Maddie reached into her travel bag, digging around for some money to get a Diet Coke, when she felt something cool, round, and smooth at the bottom of the bag.

Maddie pulled out the Wyrd rune stone. She didn't remember packing it. And she still couldn't remember the meaning.

"Ahem." The woman coughed to get her attention. "Whaddya want, hon?"

"Oh, sorry," Maddie stammered. "I guess I'm all set, thanks."

The woman made a sighing noise as she lumbered past and Maddie closed her eyes, trying to remember the meaning.

She stared out the window, her vision growing blurry as the trees whizzed by. *Oh, never mind,* Maddie thought. There were more important things to think about. Like what she was in for when she returned home to Hawthorne. Everything she'd been able to avoid for the past year.

Maddie realized she had been squeezing the rune in her hand so tightly that it left a deep red indentation inside her palm. She traced the red line with her free hand, as if it held a deeper memory. Something that was familiar in the darkness of that night . . .

The Wyrd stone—the meaning suddenly jumped into her mind—was something that could not be known or controlled. Something that could only be determined by fate.

Ironic, Maddie thought as she looked out the window, contemplating her trip home as the outside world deepened to a purple under the darkening sky.

She shoved the stone into her backpack and got a paper cut on her hand. The delicate inner part of her finger had scraped across an envelope that had been left at her door right before she left for Christmas break. She hadn't had time to read the corny card that was obviously from Luke, so she stuck it into her bag to read on the train.

The thin line of blood ran quickly across her finger and she shoved it in her mouth as she fished the envelope out of the backpack. She was sure it was going to be a hokey Christmas card or a picturesque postcard of some exotic location with a comment from Luke saying, *Look what you're missing.*

But it wasn't any of those things. She pulled the card out of the envelope and immediately she felt sick. It wasn't a holiday card or a postcard or a silly letter from Luke. It couldn't have been from Luke at all.

It was a tarot card. A picture of the Grim Reaper adorned the front of it and underneath it was a single word.

Death.

Chapter 3

QUEEN OF SWORDS

One who is austere, stern, unforgiving, and vindictive.
Grief, sorrow, and loss can make us wise and insightful,
or it can make us emotionally barren, clinging to the
rules of what is "right and wrong" without tempering
our judgment with compassion.

As she waited for her daughter to arrive home from prep
school, Abigail Crane peered into the mahogany mirror
hanging in the hallway of the old Victorian on Mariner's
Way, trying to imagine herself bald. She pulled her graying
hair back severely, away from her forehead. Cupping the top
of her head, she squinted in an attempt to make her hand
blend into the rest of her skin.

This will never do, she thought bitterly.

Abigail wasn't so concerned with her health, but rather,
how she'd be viewed by the other women in town. Bald women
made people feel uncomfortable, guilty even. She was already
getting the odd stares at the farmers' market or when she went
into local shops. She heard the whispers, she could feel the
stares. Everyone wanted to know what had happened that
night in Ravenswood. So once she started the cancer treatments, people would stare at her because of not only what
they had heard about her, but also what they saw. It was bad
enough that Cordelia had turned their family into a freakish
side show, but Rebecca's suicide attempt and institutionalization had pushed her to the limit. No wonder Maddie transferred out of town and now she was forced to return on her
mother's behalf.

Chemotherapy would have to wait, at least until the Misery

Island Gala—the last event of the season. She envisioned her mother, Tess, rolling her eyes, scolding Abigail for being a ridiculous vain fool. Even though Tess had passed away many months ago, her presence was still very palpable within the walls of the house.

Getting rid of the cancer was more important than the way people saw you, Tess would have insisted. At least, before the dementia had taken over her mind. Once that happened, it was like living with a little girl. Two girls, including Maddie.

Foolish girl, Tess would have snapped at her if she were still alive. She could almost hear her wise voice in the groans and shudders of the house, in the lapping of the ocean at the base of the street. *You'll never understand what's important in life. And when you finally do, it will be too late.*

Abigail sneered at the imagined voice. She furrowed her brow and abruptly turned from the mirror in disgust. Yet just before she had turned completely away, something in the reflection captured her attention. It was only a wisp of movement by the cellar door, quick as a minnow, but she caught it at the edge of her vision just the same. The door had been nudged open again. No matter how many times she locked it up, barricading the blasted portal, it seemed to find a way to open itself up again. The objects she placed in front of the aging door were always neatly moved to the side, allowing it to swing freely once more. Someone or something didn't want to forget what had happened down there in the early hours of the morning last Halloween. The time she had told Cordelia the truth about her father. The last time she had ever laid eyes on the girl. Something just wouldn't let her forget her sins.

Abigail narrowed her eyes, making a mental note to get someone from town in to fix the thing, maybe even hire someone to plaster over it—board it up once and for all. That's what she'd do. Abigail Crane was too sick to battle any more demons, too tired to quiet restless spirits.

It was time for her to end it once and for all. But with Maddie back in the house, that would at least make the time she had left bearable. But at what cost? Abigail contemplated this as she reached into her pocket and felt the well-worn tarot card she'd received a month ago. It was the Death card and it was slid under the front door in the middle of the night. There were only two people who would have left that card for her, and one of them had been locked up in a psychiatric ward. The other one was a mystery.

Even when she lived here, Cordelia LeClaire was a mystery. And since she'd disappeared on Halloween night, she'd grown into a local legend. The beautiful temptress who calls men to their destruction. The free spirit that dances through the town by moonlight, bewitching and beguiling. The siren that wails by the ocean, causing havoc and chaos among those who love and are closest to her. All of these descriptions were adequate, but none quite matched up with the vision that Abigail was left with the last time she saw her niece, bloodied and enraged. She saw a beautiful but fierce young woman. A caged animal that had been taunted and provoked and angered. Her eyes were filled with hatred. It was the face of someone driven to the ends of her sanity. Someone who was capable of anything.

Revenge . . . destruction . . . murder.

∞

As Madeline Crane walked through the town upon her return, every new face, every car seemed unfamiliar and ominous. The trees that lined the historic streets clumped together and stretched upward in a wiry, tangled mass. Like the witches in Grimms' fairy tales, they pointed their bony fingers in an accusatory manner at those who passed by. The clouds in the sky were a vast, pillowy assortment of grays and foamy whites, hovering above the town preparing for its hibernation during the long cold winter months ahead. A sense of despair and loneliness echoed inside everyone in the town of Hawthorne. Spring couldn't come soon enough to chase away the dreariness that would soon settle over the townspeople throughout the coldest season.

Maddie once again was reminded of the constant ache and edginess that comes with the disappearance of a loved one, keeping her uneasy and depressed. It was in the low, soulful caw of the crows, the desperation in the call of the swallows. She and her beloved aunt Rebecca always held out hope, even in the face of all the doubts and nightmarish images that threatened to plunge them into all-encompassing despair.

After everything that had happened, it seemed impossible to Madeline how the world kept moving on, indifferent as air. Cars sped down the one-way streets, trucks grumbled by, joggers continued along their morning route. It was as if Cordelia LeClaire never existed. She was just one of the many stories that linger around old fireplaces and curl into children's nightmares.

Don't run away or you'll go missing like that Cordelia LeClaire. . . .

It seemed obvious to Maddie now that Cordelia and Rebecca never would have been accepted into Hawthorne society, or any of the other wealthy North Shore communities. The girls of Hawthorne were similar to the rest of the adults in town: very judgmental and not inclined to welcome anything or anyone different. It was as though the water from the local wells had poisoned their minds, perhaps in the same way it had affected their strict puritanical ancestors.

As Maddie walked past the town post office, she noticed a familiar face grinning at her. The picture was dirty and curled at the edges, but she remembered blanketing the town with those flyers right after Cordelia's disappearance. She and Rebecca had worked tirelessly stapling them to every phone pole, bulletin board, and wall in town. Most of them were probably long gone by now. That was before Rebecca's breakdown—perhaps she, too, was now long gone, lost in her own mind. Her attempted suicide that night at Ravenswood had been the final straw—cementing the fact that Rebecca would never be the same, at least until Cordelia's return. Even then, Maddie wasn't so sure she'd ever fully recover.

Madeline always wondered about the photos that were used in "Missing" flyers. The eyes of the victims were always so innocent and unknowing. Even before Cordelia had come and gone from her life, Madeline would search the eyes of the missing children on posters and flyers. She'd look at the yellowing, curled pieces of paper tacked up on the walls of the post office or the local convenience store and try to see if there was any hint of what was to come in their lives.

Did they know in that shutter speed of a second that this would be the photo used to tell hundreds and thousands of people that they had disappeared? That this was what they looked like in a happy, unknowing point in their lifetime, and that if anyone should ever come across this face in an altered form—a bloated, waterlogged version after a drowning, or a cold blue version on a morgue slab—then they would at least know what beauty was once there?

Madeline walked through the town and finally came to her home on Mariner's Lane. She sadly looked up into Tess's window, still half expecting to see her grandmother's crinkled face watching for her return. The house hadn't changed much since Madeline left it behind. The stark Victorian sat high up on the hill, aloof and untouched by its surroundings. Only now it lacked the sense of welcoming that it had when Tess was alive, the lack of excitement that buzzed through the weathered clapboards when Rebecca and Cordelia breathed life into the house that now was an empty shell.

Aunt Rebecca's store, vacant for over a year now, still sat across the street from the old Victorian where she grew up. The sign, REBECCA'S CLOSET, hung from the wrought-iron hanger. The windows and doors were boarded up. The word WITCH was scrawled in large sloping letters across the rotting boards. No one wanted to rent it since Cordelia disappeared, and Rebecca went crazy and got locked away like a witch from an old fairy tale.

Maddie pushed the heavy door open.

"Mom?" Maddie called into the dark Victorian. She was met with a chilly burst of air. Old houses near the ocean always held on to some of the coolness of the salty nights, but their house always seemed unnaturally cool. Tess once told her that cold spots were a sign of spirits, and Maddie was sure that Tess was still lingering around the house, bustling about and watching over Abigail. Not even death would stop Tess from watching out for all of them. Maddie could almost hear a faint chuckle as she called again to her mother. "Anyone home?" Typically, Tess would be the first one to greet her at the door, and it kind of felt like she had.

It wasn't clear who was more surprised at seeing the other. Maddie tried to take in her mother's frail appearance, shocked at how the cancer had visibly taken its toll on her. Abigail had never been large, but now she was barely a wisp of a woman. Somewhere deep inside Maddie came the urge to instinctively care for her mother, to wrap her arms around her and take away any pain. Her eyes filled with tears until her mother's razor-sharp tone snapped Maddie back into reality.

"Don't they feed you at Stanton? You're all skin and bones!" her mother said with a judgmental tone. "And that hair? Were you ever planning on getting it cut or are you going to let it grow down to your knees?"

Maddie self-consciously tucked her mid-back-length hair behind her ear and steeled herself for the onslaught of criticisms. That brief moment of closeness they had shared after the night at Ravenswood and before she left Hawthorne seemed never to have happened. Her mother was back to her old bossy, scrutinizing ways—no matter what the sickness was that currently plagued her. Any hint of softness and ca-maraderie was now long gone.

Abigail barely recognized her own daughter as well. How could such a short time away from Hawthorne have changed her so much? She wondered if the transition had been taking place before Maddie transferred to the new boarding school. *Who is this confident, stubborn young woman? Where is the shy, quivering mouse of a daughter who took off months ago?* Abigail wondered. Maddie appeared to have shot up overnight. She seemed taller, but perhaps that was just because she stood straighter and with more confidence. She had a defiance in her eyes that shook Abigail to the bone.

This new version of her daughter seemed very different from the one who took off last June. The girl who could be startled and thoroughly shaken by the most common of oc-currences: the tickle of a spider, the wail of a loon at dawn, the flutter of a bat or bird overhead. She was a girl who always looked over her shoulder, but now it seemed that she looked at life with her chin thrust forward, as if daring you to take one step closer, tempting fate to throw one more hurdle in her path. She had become more like . . . her. Like Cordelia. And that worried Abigail more than anything else.

"So, how does it feel to be back?" Abigail asked tersely as she shuffled Maddie's bags farther into the hallway. Madeline Crane misjudged her mother's illness. She knew that Abigail had been diagnosed with cancer—the silent killer that had worked its way through many of the women in town—the re-sult of a town too close to a faltering power plant. Madeline always found that morbidly ironic. Most people from this town were too afraid to leave—scared of the evils that ex-isted beyond the boundaries of Hawthorne—and yet the biggest threat came from staying too long in this town and being ex-posed to the harmful leakage from the power plant. Abigail Crane was dealing with a form of cancer that required bed rest. Maddie should have known that her mother wouldn't listen to the doctor's recommendations. Even though she was a sick, frail woman, not even cancer could stop her from doing things on her own terms.

"How are you feeling?" Maddie said, looking around and noting how nothing had changed at all in the house since she'd left.

"Never mind that. I'm fine. Now, let's get your things upstairs so your bags don't clutter up the hallway. When you unpack your clothes, you can put the empty suitcases in the guest room."

The guest room was actually Cordelia's old room, and yet Abigail still couldn't bring herself to say Cordelia's name out loud. It was as if the brief time that Cordelia had spent in Hawthorne was just a bad dream . . . a nightmare brought to life. And her mother would never forgive her cousin for all the unwanted attention on the family.

"Fine, I'll put my bags in Cordelia's old room," Maddie said firmly, not just to hear her cousin's name out loud again in this house, but also to gauge her mother's reaction.

She turned back to Maddie, holding her gaze for a few beats, as if she was not quite sure what Maddie's intentions were, and then continued up the staircase, spine perfectly straight, head held high.

"It would still be Cordelia's room if she hadn't run off the way she did," she said sternly over her shoulder.

Okay, here we go, Maddie thought. It would be an interesting visit.

Later that evening, after they had eaten dinner, Abigail steered the conversation to the local gossip. She filled Maddie in on the big debate over Ravenswood and how the Endicott family was fighting the town to have it made into a hotel. The red tape that was expertly set up by the historical society was suddenly coming under scrutiny, and it seemed, as usual, that the Endicotts would end up winning in the end.

"You know that Kiki Endicott," Abigail clucked. "She's a

pit bull, that's for sure. She never gives up until she gets what she wants. Well, you know that with Kate. 'Apples don't fall far, my dear.' You remember Tess was fond of that expression."

Abigail smiled softly at the mention of Tess. Though the women never seemed to get along in life, now that Tess had passed on, Maddie wondered if Abigail regretted her treatment of her mother.

Maddie felt as if she would start to cry if she spoke about Tess, yet she chose that moment to broach an even more delicate subject.

"Speaking of Tess, did she—had she known about . . . about me and Cordelia? That we were sisters?"

Abigail's face hardened. "That you were *half* sisters? Yes, I'm sure that she knew. We never spoke openly about it. Rebecca and I made a pact to never discuss it. It was something that we all regretted. An unfortunate predicament, that's for sure. But when Rebecca left with Simon, I thought it best to leave it all alone. After that, your father and I—well, let's just say that some fences were never meant to be mended." Abigail's face soured at the mention of Malcolm Crane. "But you know your grandmother, she always seemed to know things that she'd have no way of actually *knowing*. Tess was a smart woman. She must have known. But she was wise enough to let it stay silent."

Maddie remembered her mother's philosophy and said dryly, "If you don't talk about it, it's not real, right, Mother?"

Abigail held her daughter's gaze, lifted her chin, and then nodded firmly. Maddie sighed. Some things would never change.

Maddie decided to excuse herself, knowing that the conversation would only go downhill from there. She'd only been in Hawthorne for a few hours and already her stress level was rising.

After unpacking a few of her clothes, Maddie got ready for bed. Nothing had changed in this room. Her old oak dresser still contained the Crabtree & Evelyn scented drawer liners, making the room smell faintly of spring rain. It didn't show the signs of all that had transpired over the past year.

Already irritated with her mother, Maddie collapsed onto the bed. Why wouldn't Abigail accept her part in Cordelia's disappearance? Why was she acting like nothing had changed when their entire world had been flipped upside down? Cordelia was gone. Rebecca locked up. Tess had passed away. And Maddie had started a life far from Hawthorne. Things couldn't be more different, and yet Maddie started to feel that familiar sense of dread.

Chapter 4

THE HANGED MAN

Loss. Lack of commitment. Preoccupation with selfish and material things. Despite drawbacks, a preference for the status quo. Oppression. Apathy in pursuit of goals. Failure to act with an inability to move forward or progress.

As the sun spread lithe and steady across the pink-hued morning sky, Madeline sat up and looked at herself in the old vanity mirror that hung directly across from her bed. She imagined herself peering into the mirror before she left many months ago—younger, softer somehow. *I guess that's what losing people you care about does to you,* she mused.

Maddie flopped back into the covers and stretched catlike in the bed before pushing back the covers and getting up. She pulled a silver-plated brush from the vanity table and started delicately brushing the pillow-kinks out of her hair. It was the start of a new day in Hawthorne and Maddie Crane had no idea what to expect.

She headed downstairs, surprised at the silence that filled the house. Abigail was still in bed. This was something that completely rattled Maddie. In her entire life, she'd never been the first one awake in the house. Maddie couldn't remember a time when she hadn't come downstairs to a brightly lit kitchen, filled with the smell of breakfast cooking and coffee brewing. It was like a ghost house.

A list of groceries was waiting for her on the kitchen table. *Mom and her lists,* Maddie thought.

But Maddie was happy for an excuse to get out of the house—the quiet was too much for her to bear. Getting out and seeing people—even Hawthorne people—was better than the funereal silence that was all around her.

∞

"That'll be one hundred and sixty-four dollars," the cashier said in a monotone.

"What? Are you feeding an army?" came a voice from behind her. It took Maddie a moment to realize that the comment was intended for her.

"Looks that way, doesn't it?" Maddie laughed politely and turned to leave, angling her head toward the door so that she wouldn't get caught up in a conversation. *Not now, not this early,* she thought. She was pushing the carriage toward the exit when a hand reached out and grabbed her firmly by the arm.

"Not even a hello. Well, I guess a semester away makes you too cool to talk to me," said the guy in the harbor patrol uniform standing behind her.

Maddie had to blink her eyes before she could believe what she was seeing. *Trevor Campbell?* The last time she'd seen him was at Tess's funeral. She'd managed to avoid him for all these months, and now here she was face-to-face with one of the many people responsible for Cordelia's disappearance from Hawthorne. Trevor had raped Cordelia last year before she left; just one in a long line of indiscretions the town of Hawthorne managed to sweep under the rug. Not surprisingly, he didn't seem the slightest bit self-conscious or guilty.

"How've you been, Crane?" he asked, beaming as he proudly wore his harbor attire. While in other towns being a harbor cop may have been looked at as a blue-collar position, it was a highly coveted position in Hawthorne, reserved for only the coolest and wealthiest kids. It was really just an excuse to hang out on the harbor all day in the sun and get paid for it. It came as no surprise that Trevor Campbell's family had bought his way into this cushy position, because he was widely known as a troublemaker. Yet she had no idea why he would commit to the job over Christmas break. He must have done something to piss his parents off for them to make him actually work during his vacation. He definitely had some ulterior motive, yet she couldn't figure out what it could be. In any case, he was the last person Maddie wanted to see. "I know, I know, I'm hard to recognize in uniform."

"No, I could recognize an asshole even when he's all cleaned up and in uniform," Maddie said through clenched teeth. Trevor was Kate Endicott's boyfriend and the boy who used to taunt Maddie and Cordelia mercilessly at Hawthorne Academy. He could even be the father of Cordelia's child and it didn't seem to affect him in the least.

"Ouch!" he said, laughing. "Is that any way to treat an old friend?"

"I'll let you know when I see one," Maddie said. "So, working for the harbormaster, hmm? What prompted the switch to the other side of the law? I didn't know that assholes were given jobs to serve and protect."

He smirked, shaking his head. Even in his crisp uniform of white oxford shirt, khakis, and closely cropped hair, he couldn't shake the spoiled, party-boy image that existed in her memory. Maddie pictured him passed out on the floor in a drunken stupor at every party. Unless, of course, he was hooking up with one of the many girls that followed him around the halls of Hawthorne Academy. And yet how he managed to do it right under Kate Endicott's perfectly upturned nose remained a mystery. Luckily, Maddie avoided falling under the spell of his baby-faced, all-American charms.

"Decided to clean up my act," he said. "Fresh start. You should be familiar with wanting to start over. Right, boarding school girl?" he asked smugly, holding her gaze a little longer than what felt comfortable.

"Um . . . yeah," Maddie muttered, "I guess so." She willed

herself not to let Trevor Campbell under her skin—not again. Strangely, Maddie could almost feel the shy, awkward Maddie Crane—the one she thought she had disposed of years ago—gingerly rubbing her eyes and coming back to life.

"So," he chuckled, "what brings Maddie Crane back to Hawthorne? Was Maine life too much for you? Did you get sick of all the maple syrup and mountain climbing?"

"Uh, that's Vermont, Trevor," Maddie said slowly. She could barely stomach sticking around much longer talking to this bastard. She couldn't believe that he was related to Reed, the only person she had had feelings for until Luke came into her life. Yet Trevor was one of the few who knew what she had done to Cordelia on Misery Island—who had witnessed the act that she so regretted when she had thrown that stone at Cordelia's head. And for that, she hated him even more. "Actually, if you really want to know, I came back to take care of my mom for Christmas break." Then she added, "She needs help with my aunt Rebecca."

"Oh yeah," said Trevor. "How could I forget about that crazy aunt of yours?"

My God, Maddie thought, *some people never change*. She was just about to storm off, but not before she told him where he could shove that smug attitude of his, when he caught her off-guard by saying, "It's good that you're here to take care of your mother. Especially after what happened this past fall."

"This fall?" Maddie asked. She had no idea what he was talking about.

"Wow, your mom didn't tell you? That's weird," he replied to her confused look. Maddie wanted to punch that smug look off his face, but her desire for information got the best of her.

"It was the strangest thing. I was at the station, playing a game of poker with the boys. So, it was a Tuesday night, not much really goes on during the week. The bars are empty and the high school keggers don't really happen until the week-end. Do you remember the parties we used to throw out on Misery? Man, those were the days."

"Focus, Trevor," Maddie said impatiently, wanting to physically hurt him for even mentioning Misery Island, but at the same time she desperately wanted to know what he was talking about.

"So," he continued, "this crazy 9-1-1 call comes in. Turns out it's your mom on the phone just crying and screaming and going on and on about someone in the house, and they need everyone, even me, to help contain the situation. That's what this is for." He pulled out a Taser gun and Maddie shivered at the thought of Trevor Campbell, a guy with a drinking problem, a history of assault and rape, and an overwhelming sense of entitlement, being allowed to carry a weapon. "So, Sully—er, do you remember Officer Sullivan? Garrett Sullivan?"

Maddie bristled. Trevor obviously was aware that she knew Garrett Sullivan. He was the one who was a part of that awful night at Ravenswood. Trevor was just taunting her.

"Anyway, he tells her to get out of the house and get to a safe place, and she just kept on screaming 'It's not my fault,' blah, blah, blah. Sully barely understood a word of it, y'know? Then, nothing. Silence. He said it was like the phone's just ripped from the wall."

At that point, Maddie couldn't hide her emotions. Why hadn't anyone mentioned this before? "What happened?" she yelled.

"I'm getting to that," he said, suddenly appearing excited to have such a rapt audience. "So, we pull up to the house and there aren't any lights on. We knock and knock . . . nothing. Then they force entry into the house with backup"—he pointed to himself with a self-satisfied grin—"'cause they didn't know what they were walking into. We were pretty jacked by this time, because nothing really happens around here. Well, at least not in a long time."

Maddie inhaled sharply, painfully, knowing that he was referring to Cordelia and the night at Ravenswood, the night that ended in her aunt's attempted suicide and the revelation that Cordelia and Maddie were tied together by a bond deeper than either of them ever could have imagined—they shared a father.

"Once we got into your house and looked around, well . . . it was a total disaster. The furniture all tipped over, books were everywhere, smashed glass, and that smell . . . like something burning. So Sully called out to your mom. And there's just nothin'. No sounds, no one, nothin'.

"We started picking our way through the mess when Sully stopped short 'cause he heard this hollow tapping sound. It was coming from the basement. So, we go down to the basement, and man, that is one creepy place. Dirt floors, stone walls, it's like a dungeon. Then the tapping just filled the room. It was everywhere, all around us, freakin' us out.

"So, finally, we head back upstairs, and there's your mother at the top of the staircase, actin' like she was half drugged, her hair all crazy and wild. The first thing she asks is, 'Is it gone?'

"Sully asks her, 'Who did this to you, Abigail?' She just stared at us. Man, I've never seen anyone stare like that before—like she just saw the devil himself. . . .'" His voice trailed off and he shifted his gaze over her shoulder for a moment.

He visibly shuddered and then continued. "So we went back into the living room and started picking up the furniture and putting everything back in place. Then your mom walks downstairs like nothin's happened. Sully wanted to take her down to the station for questioning, but she wouldn't have it. She just looked at us for a long time. Said it wouldn't be necessary."

"So they never filed a report? They never found out who did this to her? Trevor, who the hell broke into my house?"

"Dunno. They got nothing," he said, shrugging his shoulders. "Your mom just said she had a bad reaction to the medication she was taking and it caused her to go all crazy and destructive. So we just left it at that. But . . ."

"But what? How could they believe that? There's no way that Abigail could have caused all that damage by herself. There has to be more to it, Trevor." Maddie was getting more and more frustrated—she was squeezing the handlebar of the grocery cart so hard that her knuckles were white.

"That's just it. She couldn't have done it herself. And no one was sure if she wasn't just covering up for someone. Like maybe you or your dad . . . ?"

"Well, I was up at school and as far as I know, my father hasn't set foot out of Maine in over a decade, and my aunt . . . well, obviously, you know she's been hospitalized since Cordelia . . ." Maddie let her voice trail off, noticing the way his eyes bored into her at the mention of Rebecca and Cordelia.

"Sully contacted your dad—his alibi checked out," he said, rocking back and forth on his feet, hands in his pockets. "Then he even went to Fairview to talk to your aunt. Total waste of time, that was. She hasn't talked to anyone since, well, for a long time."

"So it's just another unsolved case, then," Maddie said angrily.

"Yup," Trevor said, smiling in that pampered prep school way. "Pretty much how it is with your family, isn't it? Trouble just follows you around."

Maddie gave him a dirty look.

"That's okay, Maddie," he said, his voice turning husky. "I like girls who stir up some trouble."

"Then I guess you and Kate are still perfect for each other." Maddie wasn't going to let him off the hook. "Or are you with Darcy now? Have you made up your mind yet, Trevor?"

A wave of disgust washed over Maddie as she was pulled out of his story and saw how he was leering at her. She remembered when he attacked her in Potter's Grove. His fleeting interest in Cordelia made Kate so crazy with jealousy that she took the hazing ritual out on Misery Island too far, leading to Cordelia's disappearance. And all of it was because Kate thought that Trevor was into Cordelia. All of their lives irrevocably altered because of one spoiled, bitchy girl's insecurities and one repulsively violent boy who had an overwhelming sense of entitlement. It was all coming back and she suddenly wanted to be nowhere near Trevor Campbell.

"I can always make space for one more in my harem," he said huskily through a stiff jaw. She almost felt violated as he looked her up and down from under his half-lidded eyes. "Especially a boarding school girl. Do they make you wear those cute little outfits?"

"You disgust me, Trevor," she stated.

"Hasn't stopped other girls—didn't stop Cordelia," he said smugly when he noticed her bristle. "You don't know what you're missing. Or are you still pining away for my big brother? Too bad he's found someone else to play house with."

"If you mention Cordelia's name again, I'll march down to the police station myself and have you arrested for rape, you smug bastard."

"Hey, my boys down at the station know that you can't call it rape when you have a willing participant." He then lowered his voice and added, "Besides, who are they gonna believe? A runaway girl with a mom locked up in the loony bin, or one of their own?"

Maddie steeled herself against his taunts. She hated how he was acting, like being harbor patrol gave him the same rights and privileges as a regular town cop. It was obvious that he felt superior to the lowly police force, but at the same time he probably thought it made him look cool to hang out, smoke cigars, and play poker with the police—like they were his boys. He acted like he could get away with anything in this town. Even rape . . . or murder. . . .

Maddie shoved past him, forcing him to spill hot coffee on his hands.

"Ow, Crane, watch it!" he called after her. She heard him mutter about some "crazy bitches in this town."

She'd deal with Trevor and the police station later, Maddie thought. She had her own interrogation to conduct as soon as she got home.

∞

Abigail brushed her off when confronted with the information from Trevor. "It was nothing," Abigail fumed. "A bad reaction to my medication. Made me all jumpy and crazy." She shook her head emphatically. "Stupid doctors and their ridiculous pills. That's why they call it a practice, you know, because they haven't gotten it right yet."

Maddie tried to reason with her that there was no way she could have done the damage Trevor described. Cancer patients usually have less energy, not enough to destroy a house.

Again, she shrugged it off. "You know how those boys are down at the station. Always blowing things out of proportion. You've read the police log in town, haven't you? A squirrel crosses the street and you'd think the town was under attack by wild animals. Nonsense. Utter nonsense. Besides, why would you believe a word from that good-for-nothing Campbell boy? If you recall, his older brother was the one they think was involved with Cordelia before she disappeared." Abigail put an exaggerated emphasis on that last word to remind Maddie of her feelings on the subject.

Abigail continued to mutter to herself as she stormed out of the room. "Just because those Campbells have all that money from that oil company doesn't make them any better than the trash they are."

Maddie heard her stomp up the stairs and the bedroom door slam. And she knew then that the discussion was permanently over.

Consumed by anger and frustration, Maddie left the Victorian to walk down the street to the beach. This was where she and Cordelia used to sneak off to when they went for midnight swims. The wintry night air felt good on her skin and helped to cool her down.

For some reason, the streets of Hawthorne had never scared Maddie until Cordelia's disappearance. Nights never held any devilish secrets, except for those nightmarish unearthly creatures born out of her cousin's wild imagination. Real people never scared Maddie the way that things that went bump in the night did—and the stories that Cordelia spun about the ghosts that curl around bedposts and sit upon a young girl's chest while she sleeps, attempting to steal her breath and soul. Or the headless banshee that wails and shrieks beneath your bedroom window, heralding a death that will soon claim a family member.

Maddie was quite certain that Cordelia never frightened easily, which was what enabled those frightening tales to trip and fall from her tongue without any hint of trepidation or reluctance of speaking about such dark things, no matter if they were in a darkened room or passing by a cemetery bathed in moonlight. And even after all of the horrible things were done to her by the girls that night on Misery Island, Cordelia never showed any fear.

Questions raced through Maddie's head as she looked out at the dark churning waters. *Will I ever get the chance to apologize to Cordelia for everything? For remaining friends with girls who tormented her since her arrival in Hawthorne? Will I get the chance to tell her how sorry I am for standing by and letting the events on Misery Island take place? For being too afraid to stand up for her, to save her?*

She knew she had to go home. Her mother was the reason she came back to Hawthorne—the only reason. And she needed to be there for her, to support her and help her through this difficult time. But as she turned to leave, something caught her eye. She swore she saw a girl standing on top of the jagged rocks. Her body bent like a dancer's in an arabesque pose, leg lifted as if about to go into flight. A shock of red hair against the inky night. Yet when she looked again, there was nothing there—no one standing on the rock that sank into the deep waters. It was just a trick of the eye, she reasoned. And despite her unsettling feelings, she turned back toward her home, willing to put the past behind her and deal with what was yet to come.

☙

Later that evening, Abigail paced the well-worn floor of her bedroom, listening to the noise and movement coming from Madeline's room. It seemed so strange to have activity and any form of life within these walls again. She didn't want to think about that night. The one where she lost control. The night that she saw things that couldn't be real—couldn't possibly occur. She'd known about the hauntings in Hawthorne and the lengths that Tess had gone to keep restless spirits at bay. But without the old woman in the house, the activity started up in the house. The unfinished business, the secrets, the lies—all of it would unravel in a way that no one could control. She wondered if the medication was just making her see things—things that weren't there, that couldn't be real. Or if the spirits that haunted her were always there and she just chose to shut them out. Perhaps she was so close to death that the veil between the living and the dead was being drawn aside, allowing her a peek into the afterlife.

Soon, though, Maddie would leave her, leave Hawthorne, and when she did, Abigail would be leaving this house as well, feet first and finally at peace. *God willing,* she thought. *God willing.*

Chapter 5

THE HERMIT

A card of introspection and analysis. Solitude, contemplation, and thought. You have grown wise from past experiences, and must follow the path slowly but steadily.

Despite her time away from Hawthorne Academy, as Maddie pulled up to the school, all the old emotions slid back into place: self-doubt, frustration, anger, loss. And fear. Fear was a constant these days. Of what, she wasn't exactly sure. It had been a year since she left Hawthorne Academy and they had been sending her notices that if she didn't pick up her records, they would be tossed. Maddie didn't really care one way or another, but Abigail was adamant that she retrieve her records. It was as if she needed physical proof that Maddie had once been enrolled within the hallowed halls of Hawthorne Academy—something Abigail always desired, but never could afford for herself.

Maddie passed through the double doors of the elementary school wing and made her way across the linoleum floors marred with a spattering of small footprint decals, and she peered into classrooms.

"Maddie? Oh my God! How are you!" squealed a blond girl as she rushed across the room looking like a giant among a village of tiny desks and multicolored chairs. "Trevor told me that he ran into you and I just, well, I should have picked up the phone right there and then."

As Darcy Willett chattered away in front of her, Maddie tried keeping a smile plastered on her face. Darcy was an exact replica of her mother, with white-blond hair pulled back tightly in a headband, and a Lilly Pulitzer dress.

So Darcy's a teacher now? God help those poor kids, Maddie thought.

"Can you believe that I'm working at Hawthorne Academy's day care this winter? Am I a dork or what?" Darcy beamed. "I even worked as a counselor over on Children's Island over the summer. Kate said it was just an excuse for me to work on my tan—being outside on the island with a bunch of rug rats all day."

"Better you than Kate," Maddie said.

Kate hated kids. Even when Kate Endicott was younger, she always preferred to hang around with the older girls. Maddie remembered the few times that Kate was required to babysit her young cousins, Annie and Mary, and the torturous games she would put them through. One time during a mock game of hide-and-seek, she locked the young girls in the toolshed, threatening their lives if they ever mentioned it to their parents. When Kate's aunt forced Annie, the younger of the two cousins, to explain the grease-stained clothing and flea bites she had acquired during their absence, she finally gave in and told on Kate. Madeline never doubted for a moment that Kate was responsible for the death of little Annie's beloved rabbit. The girls learned their lesson, too, and would feign sickness whenever they were supposed to go over to the Endicotts' house for family events.

"No kidding!" Darcy laughed. "Besides, most of my time out there was spent on overnights, campouts, making s'mores by the campfire. And I just love being with kids. They're just so sweet and innocent."

Maddie watched as Darcy chattered on, wondering how going back to an island, even if it wasn't Misery, wouldn't bring back any bad memories. Maddie ultimately determined, as she listened to the cheerful banter, that Darcy had absolutely no regrets or guilt about what went on that horrific night that Cordelia disappeared. Darcy continued without missing a beat, or noticing that she was under Maddie's watchful gaze.

"Speaking of our dearest Kate, I will have to get all the girls together so we can catch up with you. Maybe we can all head over to Mariner's Way for a visit and see your sweet mother, the poor thing."

Maddie looked at her quizzically. Darcy quickly explained how she knew about Abigail's condition. "Hannah sees her when she visits your aunt Rebecca. Hannah helps out at Fairview now that Ravenswood has shut down."

It seemed as though all the members of the Sisters of Misery, all of the girls who took place in the terrible events of that night out on Misery Island, were doing something to ease their guilt by doing community service. Darcy was working with kids. Hannah was working with mental patients. What was she going to discover next? That Bridget was working with people with eating disorders? That Kate was working at HAWK, the local battered women's shelter?

"I see. So she must have taken care of my aunt Rebecca at some point," Maddie said, expecting to see her squirm for a moment.

"I suppose," Darcy answered distractedly, before turning to one of the kids who appeared out of nowhere and attached himself to her pastel skirt. "You know, we're trying to raise money to turn it into a historic destination. It's such an eyesore, so creepy. And I can't even imagine what it would have been like to actually be a patient there." To make her point, she dramatically shuddered. "Kate's family is behind it. They're throwing some kind of charity event for it."

"Why would they ever do that?" Maddie wondered aloud. It seemed very strange for them to care about the fate of Ravenswood now that her family's plans of turning it into a luxury hotel was halted by Finn, his family, and the historical society.

"Hmmm?" Darcy murmured, trying to wipe off some of the Elmer's Glue that the child had rubbed onto her skirt. "Oh, I don't know. You never know with Kate—she's always getting involved in something these days. The more visibility, the better. Anytime there's a chance of a photo opportunity or a chance of getting her face into the social section of the paper, Kate Endicott's there in a heartbeat."

"Some things never change," Maddie said dryly.

Darcy laughed conspiratorially. She added in a hushed tone, "I'm sure her family is making money off of it in some way. Trying to find some way to cut through all that red tape so that they can get their precious hotel. You know the Endicotts." Her smile froze on her face as she noticed someone behind them in the hallway. God forbid it got back to Kate that Darcy Willett had been badmouthing her.

"Anyway," she continued, "I've got to get the kids ready for pickup, but let's get together soon."

"I've got the rest of the break." Maddie raised her arms awkwardly. *Why am I suddenly turning into a dork now that I'm back on my old stomping grounds?* she thought angrily. *It's as though the old, gawky Maddie Crane is slipping back inside to reclaim my body.*

"Perfect! So then you'll be here for the big gala we're throwing at the end of the month out on Misery Island. Kate will be thrilled!"

The bell rang, and Darcy made a "call me" symbol with her hand, as she backed into the classroom.

&

Reed Campbell threw back another drink; he'd lost count as to how many at this point. His brother, Trevor, had come and gone, and now Reed had to clear his head of all the bullshit that his brother had heaped on him during their visit. Talk around town was Maddie had come back for winter break. Trevor had come to tell his older brother to lie low; the last thing he needed was to get wrapped up in all of that again. It had taken him months to live down the rumors of his alleged involvement with Cordelia and Maddie, and if he took up with her again, it would never go away. *"It'll follow you around like a beer-goggled one-night stand,"* as Trevor put it so eloquently.

"Asshole," Reed muttered under his breath, as he thought about his kid brother's ulterior motives. He didn't give a crap about Reed; Trevor Campbell only cared about saving his own ass. He was worried that if push came to shove, Reed would rat him out about what really happened with Cordelia. If she ran away, it would have been because of Trevor's raping her. Trevor was just a thorn in his brother's side, but unfortunately he was still his brother. The bastard brother.

Reed sighed as he remembered all the newspaper headlines when Cordelia disappeared. *Teen-Loving Teacher. Prep School Pedophile.*

There was never a shred of evidence connecting them, but what did that matter in this town? All they needed to convict him in public opinion was a hunch. Or someone with an axe to grind with the ability to spread a rumor at lightning speed.

Someone like Kate Endicott. Despite her constant attempts at seducing him, there was no way he was going to betray his brother and sleep with Kate: his teenaged student and younger brother's girlfriend. But Kate didn't get what Kate wanted, something that she wasn't used to. So she got her revenge by creating this uproar, and consequently destroying his life. Reed wondered as the whiskey burned its way down his throat if Kate knew the real truth behind the rumors. If she knew that it was Maddie that he had fallen for and not Cordelia. Either way, it didn't matter. He was too old to be thinking about those girls, which was what he told Kate the numerous times she hit on him. But she never let up. Even now with his new girlfriend, Kate was always waiting in the wings (and sometimes even in his bed). Waiting for an opportunity to pounce because he would never give in to her wishes. He remembered the quote that Cordelia told him once at a tutoring session after school. *Hell hath no fury like a woman scorned.* He laughed bitterly as he thought that the darkest demons of hell had nothing on Kate Endicott.

∞

"So she's back," Kate said to Darcy. "Wonder how long it's going to take for her to come visit me? Or maybe her boyfriend Finn won't let her because we screwed up his plans to turn Ravenswood into a shrine to his beloved Cordelia." She laughed as she cradled the cell phone against her diamond-studded ear. Word was quickly spreading to the girls about Maddie's return.

Stretching her legs out on her chaise longue, Kate looked out at Hawthorne Harbor from the windows that wrapped around the house. She pulled her Burberry wrap closer around her willowy body and took a sip of her Baileys-spiked hot cocoa.

Darcy relayed the information about her run-in with Maddie at Hawthorne Academy. Kate wanted every detail—even down to what Maddie was wearing, how she looked, what she said—everything.

"I doubt it," Darcy said. "She's still pissed about what happened with Cordelia."

"Please," Kate said, deftly grabbing a cigarette and lighting it in one swift movement. She inhaled deeply and then exhaled as she spoke. "Like Maddie is so innocent. She was right there with us. If she's going to blame anyone, she should blame herself for trying to force Cordelia onto us. She's the one who should have known better. She knows who's really responsible."

Kate was infuriated. Girls were bullied all the time—and it never hurt anyone. At least not seriously or in any permanent manner. Her parents used to encourage her to withstand her older sister's torments growing up. Kiki Endicott berated

Kate for crying, telling her that she needed to grow a thicker skin and get tough. Her older sister, Carly, sneered at her little sister's tearstained face.

"Suck it up, Katey-Cat," Carly would shout at her younger sister. "Who's ever gonna like a crybaby like you?" And then she would tug at her sister's blond locks, or pull the head off a favorite doll. Kate even woke up one morning with a large wad of gum gobbed up in her long hair.

"It's really Madeline's fault, if you think about it," she said in a hushed tone to Darcy. She didn't want any of the cleaning women to overhear her conversation. She knew how fast gossip flew around Hawthorne. "I mean, it was her cousin that came into town and started all of this. So if Maddie has come back to point fingers, then I think it's our responsibility to give it right back to her—give her what she deserves."

∽

As soon as Finn heard that Maddie was back in town, he went to see her. Unfortunately, no one came to the door at the old Victorian on Mariner's Way when he rang the bell. He knew about Abigail and her battle with cancer and that she was probably right inside the house watching him, maybe even too weak to answer the door. He was going to leave a note, but then decided against it. He'd come back another time. Instead, he took a detour on his way home and visited a place that always brought him comfort and hope. He walked by the faces of the Pickering sisters that had been carved into the wall at Ravenswood and wondered how long this wall was going to last. If the Endicotts had their way, this wall would be demolished along with the rest of Ravenswood in order to build their luxury hotel. And then he would lose his last and final tie to Cordelia.

He had added Cordelia's face to the wall that commemorated his ancestors, and continued the tradition started by his great-great-grandfathers. He brushed the ivy from the faces and some dirt from the crevices around the carvings. They almost resembled the old carvings of gargoyles he'd seen on old churches, but the faces were softer, more cherubic than menacing. He knew that people used to carve gargoyles onto buildings to keep away evil spirits—they were used for protection. But he knew that these women—the ones whose faces were on the wall—were the ones who really needed protection.

The Pickering sisters, his great-aunts, were hunted as witches during the Salem witch trials. And Cordelia was persecuted for being different—for being too beautiful, too wild, untamed. Finn chuckled. Cordelia was definitely a modern day version of a witch and what those girls did to her . . . He stopped because he couldn't bring himself to think about that terrible night that he had witnessed out on Misery Island. It was a night that most strong and able-bodied men wouldn't have been able to withstand, let alone a teenaged girl.

He wondered about her, as he always did. More times than he'd ever admit to anyone. Was she out there with his child? What did she use the money for? Was she pregnant, or was she just using that as an excuse to get out of Hawthorne? Had she ever really loved him, the way that he loved her? He hated pining for her, and was quite sure that if she had the same feelings for him, he would have heard from her by now. He knew it was time to move on, and in many ways he had. But now Maddie was back in town and all the old feelings inside him were starting to come back to life. The constant ache he felt whenever he looked out at Misery Island, or visited the beach where they first kissed, or caught a scent of lavender and jasmine that reminded him of Cordelia's perfume.

He moved closer to the face of Cordelia that was carved into the stone and noticed something a little off. As he peered closer, he saw something crumpled up and shoved into the space that was her mouth.

It was a card or a note.

He gently pulled the note from the stone wall, taking care to make sure that no one was watching him. Did anyone know that he came here each night to take care of these carvings? The only person he'd ever told was Maddie.

The card was folded down to a quarter of its size. Once it was unfolded, Finn held it up to the streetlight to get a better look. It was a tarot card. He wondered if this was intended for him as some kind of a cruel joke, or if this was actually a message from Cordelia.

It was the Lovers card. And the name FINN was scratched hastily across the back in what looked frighteningly like blood.

Chapter 6

THE DEVIL

Addiction or obsession. Uncontrolled energy. A situation
better avoided. A powerful man who is hard to resist. This
card is also synonymous with temptation and addiction.
Lack of control, excess, obsession, and raw ambition.
It is a card that revels in extremity.

SIXTEEN MONTHS EARLIER

Cordelia boated out to Reed Campbell's ship as she had
done many times since they'd made a connection in
class. He knew how hard it was for her to sit and think about
her father—something that would anger Rebecca. Whenever
she'd try to lose herself in a memory of her father, Simon
LeClaire, Rebecca would come at her like a mind reader, as if
she could actually look into Cordelia's brain and see the
memories gathering and swirling about, and reprimand her
for living in the past.

"Every time you think of him, you are only tying him to
this plane of existence," Rebecca would scold. "He's seeking
eternal peace and you keep tugging him back with all of your
memories. Let him rest in peace."

Cordelia knew that her mother was trying to be helpful,
trying to help her move past the death of her father, but there
was something in the back of her mind, a nagging thought,
that wondered if Rebecca was jealous of the bond that
Cordelia had with her father. It was like an invisible cord that
kept them tethered together in life—and now in death. When
Cordelia crawled out onto the rooftop—sometimes even

joined by Tess—and looked up at the stars and listened to the ocean, she felt closer to her father than ever. On the nights that Tess would join her she'd swear Cordelia to secrecy because they knew that Rebecca and Abigail would nail the windows shut to prevent them from sneaking out and having those peaceful moonlit moments together.

Tess said she'd been doing that for years, ever since her husband, Jack—Cordelia's grandfather—was lost at sea.

"I'm never lonely," Tess told her. "As long as I am connected by the stars and the sea, Jack's always with me. People say that the dead don't live among us, but they do. You just have to call out to them. Let them know that you want to keep that connection with them into the next realm, and they'll stay with you forever. Most people are just afraid to do it, and the ones you love—like my Jack and your father, Simon—don't want to scare you off. But if you are open and willing, they'll never leave your side. You just need these quiet moments to connect with them, and they'll seek you out. Never forget that."

Then Tess would joke about how when she passed over to the other side, she'd come and bug Maddie, Cordelia, Rebecca—even Abigail—whether they wanted her around or not.

But she knew that Abigail would never believe it. "I could stand behind her and slam doors, pots, and pans and she'd find some excuse—the wind or termites or the creaking of the old house. She'd never let herself open to the idea of an afterlife."

Cordelia rarely got those moments of trying to connect with her father. When she got a dreamy, sad look on her face at the shop, Rebecca would hoist a broom or a dust rag in her hand, saying, "You can't be sad if you're keeping busy by cleaning, so get to it."

She knew that it was her mother's way of protecting Cordelia, but she didn't need protecting. At least, she never thought she did.

Cordelia mentioned that to Reed one day after class. He offered his boat as an escape and said that if she ever needed to get away—even for a few hours—she could always go out onto his ship, lie out beneath the stars, read, write, have a glass of wine ("Don't tell anyone, or I'd get in some deep shit," he'd joke), and just escape for a little while.

Reed had found a place in her heart. He knew she had a little crush on him. But he'd never cross that line, he told her. "Sixteen could get me twenty," he joked, even when she told him that she was a very mature sixteen-year-old.

Cordelia was lying on the stern of the boat watching the stars blink at her in the inky sky. The sky stretched out clear around her, stars like pinholes backlit in a black canvas. She had found a bottle of wine in the cabin and had helped herself to a few glasses of Merlot. The rocking of the boat, the gentle lapping of the waves, the warmth of the alcohol wrapped her in a gauzy haze. She felt that she could reach out and touch heaven and her father's hand would reach right back and grasp her tightly. She could hear her father's voice, gently warning her about staying out too much longer on the boat.

"I won't fall in, Daddy," Cordelia said, laughing. She could almost see his eyes within the patterns of the stars, looking down on her, concerned.

"Who's your daddy?" a voice came from behind her.

She turned to see that it was Trevor—not Reed—who had joined her on the boat. Perhaps at that point she should have trusted her instincts and left, but she didn't feel any fear. She figured that Reed would be along shortly and she'd only have to tolerate his annoying younger brother for a little while.

He grabbed the bottle of wine she'd been drinking, inspecting it and then taking a long slug. "You've got expensive taste. Does my brother know you're raiding his liquor cabinet?"

She nodded.

"Then you must be something pretty special, because Reed

Campbell doesn't like to part with his liquor very easily. What makes you so special, Cordelia?"

It was said in a lighthearted tone, but Cordelia sensed that there was a bit of anger behind it.

She let the question remain unanswered, as if rhetorical, and said, "Reed lets me come out her to be alone with my thoughts sometimes. If you want me to leave, that's no prob—"

He cut her off and said gently, "Hey, hey, no, that's cool. I wouldn't mind some company right about now, actually." He seemed sad and looked like a little lost boy. A harmless boy. "May I?" he asked, gesturing to the space beside her. She pulled some of the blankets tightly around her and scooted over to make room.

They sat for a while just staring at the moonlit water and the night sky. She could hear kids laughing on the shore. A bonfire had been built on the beach. Every time the wind changed direction, she could hear the voices come to her, carried across the harbor with the wind. Sometimes it felt like they were talking and laughing right behind them on the boat. It was like sharing space with ghosts.

"Did you come from that party?" Cordelia finally asked.

"Ugh, yeah," Trevor said, taking another long swig of wine. He looked at the label with a furrowed brow, as if close inspection of the wine would provide him with some answers. "I don't know if I can handle that scene anymore. Too much drama."

Cordelia laughed. "Well, this is a drama-free zone, so you're welcome to stay."

"Oh yeah? I'm welcome to stay on my own family's boat? Well, thank you very much, Miss LeClaire." He laughed, pulling out a pack of cigarettes. "I think I will stick around for a little while. At least until my brother comes and then I'll leave you two to your 'tutoring.'"

Cordelia sensed a simmering anger beneath Trevor's cool demeanor, so she playfully shoved Trevor, shoulder to shoulder. "Come on, Trevor. You know it's not like that. Your brother is a really great guy and he's been so helpful to me over the past few months." She watched as he nodded, inhaled, and then blew smoke rings into the sky.

"Yeah, he's a cool guy. A great brother. Plus, he's been giving me some good advice lately." Trevor's sharp sarcasm subsided for a moment.

"Really?" she asked earnestly. She was having a hard time picturing a bonding session between the brothers, especially since Trevor always seemed like he was above asking for anyone's help. "On what?"

"Aw, I don't know. Shit with Kate, I guess," he said, staring intently at the glowing orange ember at the end of his cigarette. "It's practically like an arranged marriage. Our families pretty much decided that we were going to end up together when we were in preschool."

"Haven't you ever dated anyone else?" Cordelia asked.

"Oh yeah, I mean, we both have. But, still," he growled. "My parents are so gung-ho about us getting hitched, I'm pretty sure they already have the wedding invitations filled out—all we need to do is give them the date."

"Wow," Cordelia said, grabbing his cigarette and taking a long drag. "That's messed up. It's almost medieval."

"Tell me about it," he laughed, finally seeming to loosen up, either with the wine or the night or the sharing of secrets. He put his hand behind his head and lay back against the stern, inching a little closer to Cordelia. "They even want me to hyphenate my name. How gay is that? I'll be Trevor Campbell-Endicott. They all say it's so that when we have kids we'll all have the same name."

"But if Kate changed her last name to Campbell, you would all have the same last name anyway, right?"

He looked at her, disbelieving for a moment. "Wow, you really aren't from around here. Giving up the Endicott name for Kate would be like giving up the name Rockefeller or

Cabot. It's old New England. It opens doors for you. You don't just throw a name like that away." His voice was laced with annoyance.

"Jeez, sorry. I didn't know," Cordelia giggled, trying to reclaim the easygoing rapport she'd developed with Trevor—noting how he continued to hover between anger and sadness. He was like a caged dog—his puppy dog eyes made her feel for him, but she sensed if she got too close he might bite. "I'm not aware of these puritanical issues that take place here in New England. My bad."

"Nah, don't worry about it. I'm sure there are a lot of things that you haven't learned about this place. I'm surprised Maddie and my brother haven't clued you in on them yet."

"Well, I'm a learn-as-you-go kind of girl." She took another sip of wine from the bottle. She wondered where Reed was. She was sort of hoping that this was going to be a night of bonding between them, and not with his little brother. "So, won't you get in trouble with Kate if she knew you were out here with me?"

"Kate can kiss my ass," he said angrily. "She's a first-class bitch."

"Whoa, don't hold anything back, there, Trevor. Tell me how you really feel."

"No, seriously," he said, turning to her. "The way she's been treating you. Shit, she doesn't even know you and she hates you. I mean, it's not like she hates you—"

Cordelia put her hand up and shook her head. "No need to backtrack. She hates me. She's made that pretty clear. I just don't know why. I mean, I haven't done anything to make her hate me. I've barely even spoken to her. Maybe she's pissed at all the time that I've been spending with Maddie or something."

"Nah," Trevor said vehemently, flicking his cigarette butt over the edge of the boat. "She doesn't give a crap about

Maddie. She doesn't care about anyone but herself. Kate does what Kate wants and she doesn't care who she hurts along the way."

His voice was harsh and tinged with pain. Cordelia wondered if they had broken up recently and if he had come out here to talk about it with his big brother.

They sat in silence for a little while. Cordelia took another sip of wine and looked back toward the dock, hoping to catch a glimpse of Reed heading out to meet them. She suddenly wished that she was sharing this moonlit night with Finn and wondered what he was doing at that moment. The slight buzz of the wine made her warm and sleepy. She closed her eyes and imagined Finn by her side. "She screwed her sister's boyfriend," Trevor said flatly.

"What?" Cordelia was pulled from her dreamy thoughts about Finn and realized that Trevor was opening up to her. "When? Why?"

"Last summer or the one before that, I don't know for sure," he said angrily. "Sully told me about it. It happened at one of the parties at Fort Glover. I had my wisdom teeth pulled and I couldn't go. Kate's sister Carly had the flu or something. So that left Kate and John Clarke the time and opportunity to hook up. She always said that I was going to be her first." He laughed—a dark, almost sinister laugh—and added, "She still tells me I'm her first."

Cordelia wasn't surprised at all. But she felt obligated to comfort Trevor just the same, even though she could feel the anger burning from within him. Rebecca had tried to teach her how to read people's auras, and she never thought she would be able to accomplish it. But here in the dark, still night Trevor Campbell's aura was a dark, monstrous green. Her uneasiness grew, yet she tried to calm him. "How do you even know it's true? How does Sully know? He could just be trying to stir up some trouble, you know?"

"Nah, I know it's true. There were others who saw them . . ."

His voice trailed off, not needing to finish the statement. "Besides, that just lets me off the hook if I ever want to be with someone other than Kate, right?"

"Absolutely." Cordelia patted him on the back. "Seriously, don't worry about it. Maybe she's not even the one for you. No matter what your parents say. Don't let them dictate your relationships."

"I'm not worried about it," he snapped at her as he shrugged her hand off him—the caged dog suddenly come to life. "I don't need permission to screw who I want. Not from my parents, not from Kate, not from my brother, and not from you!"

Cordelia was taken aback and didn't understand this sudden turn of emotions. Maybe he thought she was pitying or talking down to him. No matter what had transpired, she could feel a growing sense of dread in the pit of her stomach. The sense of peace and connection with the universe had shifted and she felt like it had tipped off its axis.

Get off the boat, she heard her father say clearly, as if he were whispering in her ear.

"Trevor, you know, I was supposed to meet your brother, but I'm feeling a little seasick, so could you let him know that I'll catch up with him another time?" She had started to rise to her feet when Trevor's hand pulled her back down onto the boat, a sharp pain shooting up her spine as her butt slammed onto the wooden deck.

"Why are you taking off so fast? We haven't even finished this wine. You go and open up a hundred-dollar bottle of wine and don't even stick around to finish it. Now, that's just rude." His entire demeanor had changed from when he first arrived on the boat. His breath was ragged and his eyes narrow. He avoided looking her in the eye and was growing restless. She'd pissed him off somehow and he wasn't going to make it easy for her to leave. She needed to get away from him and from that boat as soon and as seamlessly as she could.

"Trevor, I'm sorry. Reed always said I could help myself to whatever was on the boat. I didn't know it was so expensive. Can't you finish it?" Her eyes darted around the deck. The wind changed direction and the voices on the mainland were slipping farther away.

"Can I finish it? Can I *finish* it?" he laughed. Cordelia didn't realize that he was already very drunk, probably wasted before he even got to the boat. "I'll finish what I want, when I want." He gulped down a few last sips and then hurled the bottle into the harbor. "The question is, can you finish it?"

A wave of panic came over Cordelia and she realized that she needed to get away from Trevor, away from the boat, back home as soon as possible. She needed Finn. Silently she cried out to him, as if he could read her mind and would come to her defense.

"I don't know what you're talking about, Trevor. I don't know what you want me to finish, but Reed—" she stammered.

"Isn't coming tonight. Sorry to burst your bubble." He shifted closer to her. "But I can think of a few ways to make it up to you." Trevor lunged at her, pinning her to the boat. His tongue and mouth were slobbering all over her neck. She could feel the spit dripping down into her hair.

"No, Trevor!" she screamed, and tried to wriggle away. Despite his slight build, he was deceptively strong. She remembered he was the captain of the wrestling team. She was pinned and wasn't going anywhere.

"Easy, easy, you're gonna love this, baby," he hissed in her ear, smiling down at her like she was having the time of her life. "It doesn't have to be this way. Just relax. Shhhhh."

He tried quieting her screams by kissing her, thrusting his tongue down her throat.

She felt like she was drowning. She continued to kick and fight and even drew blood when she bit his lip, but he remained undeterred. It wasn't until she felt the sharp pain inside her that she realized what had happened. As he moved on top of her, the fight in her drained and she stared up into the stars. Her submission made Trevor believe she was enjoying it.

"Yeah, you love it. Yeah, you little slut. Don't feel sorry for me, you stupid bitch. Don't you pity me. You're mine now," he said sharply in her ear in between thrusts. And Cordelia simply slipped away—away from Trevor, away from the boat, away from Hawthorne, away from the pain. She knew, the way that Tess always told her she'd be able to know such things, that it was the beginning of the end of her time in Hawthorne.

Chapter 7

THE HIGH PRIESTESS

Intuition and the inner voice of wisdom. She represents spirituality as opposed to the religious conformity, initiation, knowledge, instinctual, supernatural, secret knowledge. All secret knowledge is hers.

THE DAY CORDELIA DISAPPEARED

After the horrific night on Misery Island, Cordelia knew there was no way she could stay in Hawthorne. When she returned to Mariner's Way, Abigail made it clear that she was unwelcome. Her life was filled with lies and deceit and pain. This town held nothing for her anymore. Cordelia needed to escape—to disappear.

Once she had made the decision to leave, everything seemed to be a sign to point Cordelia in that direction. At first she stole away into the neighboring town of Marblehead, into the Jeremiah Lee Mansion. Finn had taught her a way into most of the historic places in Hawthorne and the surrounding towns. This knowledge would come in handy while she made plans for her escape.

The town of Hawthorne went into its charade of actually caring about what happened to Cordelia. Her name and face were plastered all over the television, Internet, and newspapers. This made her escape even harder. She realized that her nocturnal instincts would come in handy and that she'd have to lie low during the daytime and travel by night.

She was actually considering going back to Rebecca—going home—when she overheard one of the tour guides at the mansion discussing Rebecca and the beautiful array of flowers that were at the center of the mansion.

The floral arrangements had made Rebecca somewhat of a local celebrity. It was a status symbol to have a floral creation from Rebecca LeClaire—mother of the "missing girl." No dinner party or cocktail gathering was complete without a centerpiece courtesy of Rebecca's Closet. It became a conversation item for all of the Hawthorne elite—people who only a few weeks earlier had shunned Rebecca and her unusual daughter. All across the North Shore, people were talking about Rebecca and her magical flowers, as if all of the pain and suffering she experienced made the brilliance of each arrangement so much more enticing.

That evening, Cordelia crept out of her hiding space beneath the massive mahogany staircase and looked at the hauntingly beautiful creation. It looked like a creature springing to life— as if it were a monster that had been lurking beneath the surface of the ocean and had sprung up fully formed—gruesome and exquisite at the same time. Her mother had worked all types of flowers into the centerpiece, but had also included coral, sea spray, and starfish into the base of the flowers. It was beautiful and scary and awe-inspiring. Obviously Cordelia's disappearance had only improved her mother's sales.

"Guess you're not missing me that much, Mom," Cordelia said angrily to the flowers. "I didn't realize that my disappearance would be so profitable for you." She ran her fingers along the flowers, pulling out a bluebird rose—her favorite. It was all one big charade. Her mother had lied to her for her entire life, allowing her to believe that Simon LeClaire was her father. That she was an only child. That she was a California girl. All of it lies. She was just as much a part of Hawthorne as any of the rest of the girls she despised. She had a sister that she barely knew—and up until recently only thought of as a cousin. She had a father—a biological father—alive and well. And now, when she should be tirelessly searching for her only daughter, she chose to spend her time working with flowers? The anger burned inside Cordelia.

"Damn!" she shouted, dropping the flower as she sucked on the bloody spot where the thorn had dug into her thumb. Once the flower was on the floor, Cordelia crushed it angrily with her heel. She started ripping flowers from the arrangement, hurling them across the large foyer. It wasn't until she heard laughter—the slightest tinkling—coming from upstairs that she stopped her destructive tirade.

Spirits of the night, she figured. She had heard that many places on Boston's North Shore were haunted, so it didn't surprise her to come upon an entity. She'd been aware of them before—back when she was living in California. But nothing on the West Coast hung on to spirits the way that the houses and historical properties of New England did. She felt their presence in every area, every nook and cranny of Hawthorne, Marblehead, and especially Salem. Not the parts that everyone flocked to. Not the witches' houses or the dungeons or the supposed "haunted houses." No, the real spirits were in places that nobody expected. The back of a tiny shop, the attic of a local inn, the back porch of a local bar, the aisles of the library, and the basement of a grade school. There was no map of these real ghostly hot spots, no Discovery Channel television special. Because once the "ghost hunters" came out and the spotlight turned onto the spirits, they would just disappear. If they couldn't rest in peace like they wanted, they at least tried to hide in peace.

Which was what Cordelia was planning to do. She would hide in peace along with the restless spirits. If she was planning on "vanishing" the way that the local media had described it, then she'd use these spirits as her guides. She wasn't afraid of them. If anything, she felt protected and guided by them. Simon LeClaire was one of them. She felt his presence with her wherever she went. And if he was trying to find a way to contact her, she would open herself up to his messages in any way that she could.

Cordelia followed the tinkling laughter up the stairs, wondering if it was a spirit leading her to a better hiding spot. Now that she'd destroyed the flowers, the tour guides would be scouring the mansion for any sign of forced entry or burglary. She knew that she couldn't stay there for much longer, but she hadn't thought out an escape route or exactly where she was going.

The laughter stopped when she got to the top floor of the mansion. The Jeremiah Lee Mansion was built in 1768 and had been a bank, a home, and now it was a historic house used as a museum. It showed what life was like in the 1800s, since it was so well preserved. It also seemed to house many residual spirits.

Cordelia had noticed them when she first came here on a field trip while at Hawthorne. Out of the corner of her eyes, she saw women in old-fashioned clothing and children with period costumes peeking around corners and slipping past doorways. It wasn't until she asked one of the tour guides about the actors in period costume, only to receive a blank, questioning stare, that she realized that there weren't any people hired to play old New Englanders. They were the real deal.

Cordelia didn't want to anger any of the spirits that night, so she walked quietly with her head down. The original eighteenth-century mural wallpaper seemed to come alive in the ghostly light. The carved creatures that peeked out from the ornate mahogany fireplace seemed to crane their necks and watch her as she shuffled through the vast, magnificent hallway.

"I just need a place to stay for a night," she whispered, almost to herself. She knew that they could hear her. She felt eyes all around her. "I need a place where no one will find me. I need to escape from this place. If you help me hide, I will be forever grateful."

Cordelia spoke slowly and softly as she walked alongside the banister. A creaking noise came from behind her, and a tapping. They were showing her the way.

Cordelia looked up and noticed that part of the wall was uneven. She had just walked by there earlier and nothing was out of the ordinary. Moving back past the grand staircase, she looked down at her mother's floral centerpiece and noticed that the flowers she had ripped out were put back in place. A chill went down her back, but then she smiled. "Thank you," she called out. "I have a problem with my temper sometimes."

Again, laughter came from the shadows. Not like a person standing next to her laughing, but as if it were playing on a radio or a television set that was left on in an abandoned room somewhere below where she was standing. The laughter sounded tinny and flat, but it had a bit of an echo behind it.

Cordelia moved over to the wall and pressed on it. A secret door! She pulled the door open and discovered a tiny room. The dust within the room was so overwhelming that it was obvious that this part of the house had remained a secret throughout the centuries. She hadn't needed her flashlight while wandering the mansion earlier, because of the bright moonlight filtering through the large glass windows. But now she needed it in this small cloistered spot. Pulling the door closed behind her sent Cordelia into complete darkness.

Once the flashlight was lit, she moved the light around the small room to find a few beds and some old dolls. It was perfect. She lay down on one of the beds that seemed to be filled with straw. She remembered from one of the tour guides that during the American Revolution, they used to hide weapons and gunpowder in the straw of children's beds. Cordelia felt around and realized that nothing was there.

Good, she mused, *the last thing I need is to roll over and set off a shotgun.*

This secret room would give her the whole next day to figure out where she was headed, and give her the rest she needed to get there. California was out. Too expensive. She had the money from Reed and Finn, but it wasn't enough to buy her a plane ticket. Even if she had more money, she knew that her face was plastered all over the news. She'd get spotted right away at Logan Airport.

No, she needed to go someplace rural, someplace where people stayed out of each other's business, someplace where people went when they didn't want to be found. It was then that she thought of the person who was the cause of all this unhappiness. The man who started this game and didn't stick around to finish it. He had disappeared and started a whole new life, letting the rest of his family pick up the broken and jagged pieces of their lives.

Malcolm Crane. The father she'd never met.

Just before she finally drifted off to sleep, allowing her aching muscles and sore, swollen arms and legs to sink into the old-fashioned bed, her mind raced with plans, filling her body with an overwhelming sense of excitement.

She would hunt Daddy Malcolm down in Maine. It would be easy enough to stay out of sight once she got out of Massachusetts. And once she found out exactly where he lived now, it was only a matter of figuring out how to get there. Cordelia didn't know what she'd do when she found her deadbeat dad, but she knew one thing: he would pay for his mistakes. Cordelia would see to that.

&

Cordelia slept all day and into the evening. The cold fall night fell all around her. She heard someone whispering her name and she woke up with a start.

Gently easing the door open, Cordelia was pleased that no one had discovered her hiding spot. She knew she could return here if she needed a place to crash. As she made her way down the grand staircase, she turned when she heard a whooshing sound coming from above. She saw a twirl of skirt as it went around the corner. Her guardian spirits had kept watch over her.

"Thank you," Cordelia whispered into the dark hallway, noticing that her breath suddenly turned to smoke. As the chill went through her, she knew that she would be welcomed back any time she chose to return.

Luckily she had found an oversized flannel jacket and baseball cap in the caretaker's closet at the Jeremiah Lee. Before she left the mansion, she caught sight of herself in an age-crackled mirror. Her hair had been hacked off in clumps and burnt in sections out on Misery Island. She ran to the podium that held information pamphlets about the historic mansion and rooted around through the various office supplies until she found a pair of scissors. Standing before the mirror in the bathroom, she proceeded to cut the rest of her beautiful red curls—what was left of them—to chin-length. With each cut, she felt any lingering ties to Hawthorne being snapped, falling away from her and setting her free. She quickly brushed the hair into a garbage pail. She was free to start over. The old Cordelia was gone. She would be reborn somewhere else—somewhere far from Hawthorne.

Even though it was cut short, her trademark shock of red hair would still give her identity away, so she tucked it under the baseball cap and headed outside, out of town, out of life as she knew it. The streets were quiet and deserted in the early morning hours. She felt more at ease once she had crossed the town lines into Salem. She wasn't sure where she was going, but the more distance she put between herself and Hawthorne, the better.

Now that Halloween was over, the ongoing party that took place in Salem had died down dramatically, the Halloween decorations soon to be replaced with Thanksgiving and Christmas decorations.

As she walked through Salem, she could feel the presence of spirits all around her. They were returning after their long escape during the month of October. She knew what it felt like to be hunted and she felt sorry for the spirits that were trying to peacefully coexist with the living during the crazy festivities. Walking through the deserted streets, she could tell she was being watched. It didn't bother her if the dead were watching her; it was the living that she was trying to avoid.

Suddenly a pair of yellow eyes met her in the darkness. She stepped back in shock, trying to catch her breath. Usually spirits weren't so bold with her. They made their presence known subtly, taking care not to spook her, so to speak. After a few minutes, she realized that it was an animal watching her. Just a dog, she thought, chiding herself for being so jumpy. It wasn't until she got closer that she realized it wasn't a dog at all. The yellow eyes and the massive gray head gave it away. It was a wolf—a wolf lying on a nest of hay in the back of a truck.

Cordelia paced slowly over to the truck to see if it was still warm. It was parked out in front of a tavern that was supposed to close at the same time as the rest of the bars, but occasionally and for a few special customers would stay open. *What would a wolf be doing in the back of a truck?* she thought.

It was then that she remembered hearing about Wolf Hollow, a place farther up the North Shore in Ipswich that was a nonprofit place that cared for wolves.

"Hey there," she said quietly to the majestic animal in the cage. "You don't look that scary to me."

The wolf bowed its head down and peered up at her. It was the look of submission. She blew on her hands, which felt like blocks of ice. Suddenly an idea sprang into her mind. If she could stow away in this truck, she could get as far as Ipswich. And from there, she could hitchhike. She'd be far enough away from Salem and Hawthorne that people wouldn't recognize her and she would be able to save some money to live on until she got settled somewhere.

"You wouldn't mind me curling up next to you for a little while, would you, buddy?" Cordelia whispered through the cage. The wolf made a little whining sound, almost like a puppy. Fear pumped through her chest for a moment, but she pushed it aside because she knew that she needed to get out of town as soon as possible.

The latch on the cage came open easily. The driver must have assumed that most people wouldn't let a wolf out of its cage. However, Cordelia wasn't most people. She counted to three and then jumped into the back of the truck and spoke in a soft tone to the wolf.

"Easy, boy, easy," she cooed. "I'm just going to be your stowaway for a little while. We can both get warm together." She shivered again as the November wind picked up. The wolf watched her with its serene eyes and then dropped its head to its paws, a sign of welcoming and acceptance. Cordelia curled up next to the large beast, taking care to hide herself behind the animal, and cover up her bag with the hay that was in the crate. The wolf was so warm, it was like snuggling up to a cozy hearth. For some reason, she felt no fear with this animal. As she lay silently next to it, looking up at the stars, the wolf sniffed her hair and then licked the side of her face. She had gotten the seal of approval. The hard part was over. Now she had to wait until the driver came back to take her on the first leg of her trip.

The moon made the wolf's coat shimmer and the lazy November stars with the sound of the ocean waves nearby made her sleepy again. It wasn't until she awoke a few hours later that she realized she had left Salem—and Hawthorne—far behind, perhaps forever.

Chapter 8

THE PAGE OF CUPS

A kind, sympathetic dreamer. Imagination. May indicate a time for quiet reflection. A gentle, poetic, quiet, and artistic person gifted with much foresight.

The sun was just about to rise and she was completely engulfed by the wolf. It had wrapped its body around hers, as if she were a pup, successfully hiding her from the driver or anyone at Wolf Hollow. When she awoke, she realized that the truck was now parked inside a barn. The driver must not have wanted to awaken the wolf to put him back into his pen. Cordelia was thankful for that, because she could easily have been discovered—and the authorities most likely would have been alerted.

"Hey, boy, you took good care of me," she whispered. The wolf perked its ears up and then lazily rolled aside, allowing her to move to the back of the truck. She grabbed her backpack and patted the wolf's head.

Cordelia let herself out of the barn and started walking along the country road when several howls floated toward her through the chilly morning air. It sounded as if they were wishing her luck on her journey. Unbeknownst to Cordelia, at that exact moment back in Hawthorne, another howl ripped through the early morning hours as Rebecca, her mother, was taken to Ravenswood; she cried out for the daughter she had lost, and feared she would never see again.

Cordelia walked into the woods surrounding Wolf Hollow, lost in her own thoughts. After learning the truth about her father, her mother, Maddie, everyone, the world seemed changed somehow. Cordelia tried to figure out where to go next. The woods seemed to be closing in. The trees, now half naked, having lost their autumn glory, reached out to her with gnarled fingers. The wind called to her in whispers, beckoning her into its darkened depths.

As the shadows grew long and a chill crept into the air, Cordelia was overcome with an intense desire to leave the dark forest and head back toward the road. She picked her way down a rough and twisting path, not sure where she was headed, but felt a tug in her gut that told her she was going in the right direction. After a little while, she happened upon a tiny house that looked straight out of a fairy tale. A small wooden sign that said THE CROW'S NEST hung from a wrought-iron post. It was just a little house with clapboard shutters and crisscrossed windowpanes—a remnant from the old New England villages, no doubt. The sign had faded, but the large black crow in the center was still freshly painted. A tiny sign on the door frame said FORTUNES READ HERE. For some reason Cordelia felt compelled to enter. Maybe someone could help. Cordelia realized then that she had nowhere else to turn to.

Approaching the bright red door, Cordelia turned the handle and noticed that it was shaped like a claw. Bells tinkled gently as she walked inside. The small room was filled with colors and smells. Candles were burning at every corner of the room, brimming with molten wax. Soft music floated out from the back of the house. Unsure of whose place this was, Cordelia suddenly realized that her face had been all over the newspapers and the television. *What if this person reports me?* she thought anxiously. There was no way anyone could make her return to Hawthorne—at least until she got some of the answers she needed. She had nowhere else to go.

"You've come for help, haven't you?" A lilting voice suddenly broke the silence, interrupting her decision to flee. A grandmotherly woman with a shock of dyed orange hair shuffled out from behind a velvet curtain at the back of the house. Cordelia was used to standing out with her crimson curls, but this woman's hair was so bright it almost hurt her eyes. "Come." She motioned for Cordelia to move away from the door and farther into the house.

"You wouldn't have found this place if you didn't need my help. Now, come on. I won't charge you for this reading. It's on the house." She turned on her heel and swirled her long skirt around her plump body. "I knew you would come around sooner or later."

"Have I met you before?" Cordelia asked, suddenly worried that this woman had recognized her from the news.

"Ah, ah, ah. I don't know anything except that I see a girl in front of me that needs my help," she said, wrinkling her nose. "And maybe a nice warm bath and fresh clothes."

Cordelia sensed that this woman was a kindred spirit, so she relaxed a bit and followed the woman farther back into the cottage.

"Will you help me?" Cordelia asked, not quite sure what kind of help she needed at that point.

She smiled. "Help you on your journey? Yes, of course. Come. Sit."

Cordelia followed her to the back of the room. The woman pushed the heavy curtains back to reveal a small velvet-covered table filled with candles and crystals of every color.

"First things first. My name is Sophie and I am a seer." She smiled widely. She noted Cordelia's confusion and cocked her head to the side. "A teller. A psychic. A medium."

Cordelia continued to look strangely at her. "Are you a . . ."

"A witch. Yes, I'm a witch," she said decidedly.

"I'm—"

"You are a seer as well. I know this just by looking at you. You don't need to tell me your name. The less I know, the less I have to tell. Now sit. I'll get some tea."

Cordelia sat down in mild shock. "How did you know . . ."

Her voice trailed off as she watched the woman bustling around, retrieving a pot of tea and teacups from an ancient-looking cupboard.

"Oh, I know many things. Too much for my own good, if you ask me. Here, drink your tea. It's elderberry. You'll like it."

Cordelia looked down and noticed little tea leaves floating at the top of the steaming liquid.

"Don't mind the leaves. It helps with the reading. They won't hurt you." She smiled.

Cordelia smiled back knowingly. Rebecca had taught her to read tea leaves at a young age. But she was anxious to see what this woman would see when she looked at the swirling tea leaves. Cordelia blew on her tea before taking a small sip. The warmth of the tea spread down inside her body, and she realized for the first time how cold and hungry she was. The fire they were sitting next to also helped her recover her body temperature.

"Now, let's get to business," the old woman said in a matter-of-fact manner, as she settled her bulging body into her chair. She grasped Cordelia's free hand tightly—rings with huge stones covered every one of her fingers.

The woman sagely peered into Cordelia's open palm.

"Don't hold back. You have a strong intuition line in your palms—you should have strength in your beliefs. You are on an important mission," she said gravely. "You have been betrayed many times, yes?"

Cordelia bit her lip. She was unsure of whether or not she wanted to continue down this path for fear of bursting into tears.

"Your mother," the woman said stoically. "She has changed. She has lied to you."

The woman looked deeply into Cordelia's eyes, and then dropped her hand. Sophie turned and grabbed a deck of well-worn tarot cards out of a purple satin pouch and began shuffling.

"It's not your fault that all of this has happened. It seems to me"—she cocked her head to the side, giving Cordelia a long stare—"that your life has been overtaken by some form of an evil spirit—a demon, if you will. But before you can release yourself and your family from this curse, release the spirit, you need to figure out what kind of demon has its sights set on you."

"You mean there's more than one type of demon—er . . . spirit?"

The old woman started shaking in uncontrollable laughter. Her eyes began to water, as she wiped them dry with her wrinkled hands. "More than one? Oh my, you really have no idea what you're dealing with, do you? Well, no matter. I'm here to help you now."

She began laying the cards out in front of her in geometric patterns. As she looked at the emerging patterns, she whispered quietly to herself. Cordelia turned her head sideways to make out the pictures and words marked on the cards. She'd read tarot cards before and sold all sorts in the store, but she'd never seen ones quite like these. The pictures were brilliantly colored and seemed to be handmade, as if the old woman herself had dipped a paintbrush and covered the cards with her own magical artwork. In the orange of the candlelight, the pictures appeared to come alive, glittering and aglow. Sophie dragged her fingers along them as if she were reading Braille.

"You see how there are many Sword cards. This shows me that there are a lot of challenges and difficulties you are trying to overcome," she said, studying the cards intensely. "This one right here," she said as she pointed to the Two of Swords, "tells me that you are avoiding the truth. It makes you unhappy and uncomfortable, so rather than stay and deal with it, you are running away."

Cordelia nodded. So far, Sophie had hit the nail on the head. She waited anxiously for more information, for some type of direction or answer.

"And this card, the Queen of Swords, is where you are right now. It's the card of someone honest and forthright, someone who plays by the rules and faces the truth head-on." Cordelia felt a rush of happiness. Yes, she was the Queen of Swords!

"But don't get too happy, my dear." Sophie shook her finger. "The Queen is reversed. It shows you running from the truth, hiding behind lies and deception, avoiding the heart of the matter."

Cordelia must have been visibly upset because Sophie quickly added, "But you know that this card represents where you are now. You have the power to reverse it and to change your path. This is not what will always be."

"What should I do next?" Cordelia asked.

"Hmmm." Sophie inspected the cards again. She flipped through the deck. Sophie placed a Nine of Swords card on the table. "This shows sleepless nights, feeling trapped and unhappy. It's not a positive card. All of these Sword cards are making me concerned."

Sophie took a deep breath and flipped over the next card.

"The Emperor reversed," she breathed.

"There is a man in your life—or men—who's causing you much pain and unhappiness. A very powerful man, mature and strong, who is in total control of the situation and enforces his views rather rigidly. He has a subconscious expectation that others in his life will go along with his plans, and want what he wants. If he doesn't get what he wants . . ." Her voice trailed off unexpectedly.

"You know," Sophie said, changing the direction of the reading, "you really need to focus on getting these swords out of your path. You need a good night's rest. You need some recuperation."

Sophie looked at the next card and then quickly replaced it on the deck, leaving them spread out on the table. "Let me gather some things that will help you on your quest to deliver yourself from evil—to free yourself from this dark spirit that follows you."

Sophie stood suddenly and walked over to the table filled with dried herbs. She grabbed a ruby-colored velvet bag and began filling it with various things.

Cordelia knew who the Emperor represented. It was the man responsible for all of this: Malcolm Crane. She flipped over the next card—the one that Sophie didn't want to show her. The one that would give her direction and tell her what she needed to do next in order to save herself and those she loved.

It was the Death card.

It was then that Malcolm Crane's fate was sealed.

Chapter 9

THE EMPRESS

A mother, a creator and nurturer, the creation of life, of romance, of art or business. The Empress can represent the germination of an idea before it is ready to be fully born. She is the giver of earthly gifts.

"Let's see. Different spirits are affected by a wide range of herbs. We'll have to try a bunch of them. Rosemary, sandalwood, blackberry, Saint-John's-wort, wintergreen, linden, and heather. Now there, that's a good start. Now, let me think a moment." She tapped her finger thoughtfully against her jutting chin. "The holidays are coming up, which is good, because many of the herbs used this season like clove, frankincense, and mistletoe are quite bothersome to spirits." She spoke in a singsong manner as she filled the satchel with various herbs and flowers.

"Salt. Bells ringing. The smell of burning leather. Wind chimes. Pentacles. Crosses. All of these will help rid you of this spirit."

"But, sweet child," she continued, "I will now tell you the most powerful weapon you can use against this evil spirit."

The old woman walked slowly over to her—her arms outspread. "Its name. You must discover its true name and call it out. Then, and only then, will the spirit release its hold over your life. All the rest of this"—she waved her hands over the table—"are good in provoking the spirits, making them angry. They are useful. But, like vampires, once they are inside—it is almost impossible to be rid of them."

She looked nervously at Cordelia and smiled. "Don't worry, child. Your destiny is ahead of you. You are embarking on a journey. A journey to save yourself, your mother—and your sister."

Cordelia jumped at Sophie's words.

"Now, off with those clothes and into the washroom. You've been keeping company with wolves, I take it?"

Cordelia looked at the woman quizzically. *How did she know?*

"They don't call me Sophie the Seer for nothin'. Now get on into the washroom. There are plenty of towels and soap in the basin. Clean yourself up and I'll find some suitable clothes for you. It's been a long time since I've been your size," she said in a jovial manner as she patted her thick waist. "But I'm sure I'll find something that will do."

Then Cordelia heard the woman muttering to herself as she readied herself for a nice warm bath. "Sleeping with wolves, running away from home, evil spirits. That girl needs my help more than anyone I've ever known."

She continued talking to herself as Cordelia allowed each muscle in her body to soften and relax in the hot water. Over the splashing of the water, Cordelia swore she heard the woman say, "Tess would want me to take care of this for her. I know she will. I owe her that much."

Cordelia snapped to attention, but the only sounds that followed were the whistling of the teakettle and Sophie bustling around the kitchen, preparing dinner. Cordelia shook her head as if to clear it. She needed a good, hot meal. She was starting to hear and see things.

After drying herself off with a plush towel and sliding into the clothes that had been neatly set on the floor in front of the bathroom, Cordelia followed the delicious smells into Sophie's kitchen, where she was met with a huge table filled with a feast.

"Go on and eat as much as you like." Sophie smiled when she noticed Cordelia's excitement. "There's only me in this house and I haven't had anyone to cook for in ages." She pointed a bony finger at Cordelia and said, "Besides, you look like you could use a few good meals."

Cordelia filled herself up with pastries and breads and a hearty vegetable stew. There were all sorts of cheeses and meats. It was a spread fit for a party. And Cordelia ate until she literally couldn't put another piece of food into her stomach. By the time she'd finished, darkness blanketed the little cottage.

Sophie was in a rocking chair by the fireplace, and Cordelia joined her, flopping onto the thick feather bed at her feet.

"So where are you headed?"

"Maine. I need to find someone."

"Mmm." Sophie nodded. The only sounds were the crackling of the fire and the clicking of Sophie's knitting needles. "I've been meaning to get up to Maine for some supplies for this winter."

Cordelia smiled. She knew that Sophie could just as easily stock up for the winter in the local stores. Sophie shot her head up and gave Cordelia a look. "No, there's a certain kind of wood that I always get from the same lumberyard each year. I'm not making excuses just so I can drive you up there myself."

"How did you know—oh, forget it," Cordelia said sheepishly. She wasn't used to having someone read her mind so clearly. She wondered if this was one of the powers that Tess had said she would come into one day.

"Perhaps," Sophie answered, as if Cordelia had asked the question out loud. "But I'm thinking that you have the ability to separate yourself from your own body. Astral projection, they call it now."

"What's that?" Cordelia asked, stifling a yawn. The hum of the wind outside, the snap of the fire, the clicking of the knitting needles, her full belly, all of it was making Cordelia very sleepy. She was happy that she had a warm place to spend the night and even happier that she had someone who would take her where she needed to go. "Astral projection?"

"Your soul and your body are connected by a golden thread. Some people have the ability to escape their body for a little while and let their souls flit around unencumbered, except for the invisible thread. You never want that invisible thread to be jeopardized or else you can't get back into your body."

"How do you know I can do that?"

"How else did you survive that night on Misery Island?"

"You know about that?"

"My dear," Sophie said as she put her knitting down into her lap. "Even if I wasn't psychic, I could have seen the trouble you've been through. It's in your eyes. In your hands. In your aura. You've been put through some hard times and the only way you were able to get through them was that little time of disconnecting from your body."

Cordelia considered this while twirling a strand of her hair around her finger. She remembered bits and pieces of that night, but there were times when she felt like she was hovering above the scene and not actually a part of it. There was the intense pain—that she definitely remembered—but there were parts that should have been excruciating, and somehow, for some reason, they weren't.

"Yes, you've been given that gift of separating from your mortal body. You just need to take care that a spirit doesn't slip inside your body and take over while you're off flitting about. Some spirits that are earthbound are just waiting for the opportunity to see an empty mortal body that they can take over."

"How do they do that?" Cordelia asked, horrified. If the rumors were true about the Pickering sisters out on Misery Island, any one of them could have entered her body during that initiation prank. But then, thinking better of it, she realized that no person—living or dead—would have wanted to trade bodies with her during the terrible and torturous ordeal.

"They simply cut the cord and send you sailing off into the universe. They can do that by slipping right into your body, just in the same way that you slipped into those clothes I left for you. Sure, they won't always fit the right way and it will take some time getting used to, but eventually, they will get used to their new body, their new life. They just need to stay dormant long enough to get their bearings. Once they have it figured out, they can take over someone's life."

"Just like that?"

"Just like that."

"But what does the original soul do?"

"Sadly, they often are forced to sit and watch their bodies inhabited by a new soul. They just pray that someone who loves them will be able to tell the difference and help restore them back into their bodies."

"Has this ever happened to anyone you know?" Cordelia asked, with her tired eyes growing wider for a moment. She wondered if this happened to her mother. Perhaps that was why she never told Cordelia the truth about her father.

Sophie clucked her tongue and looked at Cordelia, not sure how much she should say. "I've seen it happen, yes. To someone I love? No. But it happens. More than you would ever suspect.

"But don't think about that now. You just need to be cautious the next time you try projection. Make sure you're in a safe place where there's no risk of aberrant spirits lurking around. If only others knew the importance of being safe."

Cordelia had so many questions, but she kept nodding off. Sophie stood up and dimmed the lights. She poked at the fire a bit, which had now turned to glowing embers. The color of the embers rivaled the color of the old woman's hair. Cordelia rested her cheek against the downy feather bed, curling into the fetal position. Sophie pulled a thick quilt off the couch and laid it over her, and again, Cordelia was struck by how much the house was straight out of a fairy tale. She almost laughed when she thought about how she was a Gretel—without her Hansel—and had stumbled upon the witch's Gingerbread House. Only she was a willing participant in fattening herself up for the witch to pop into the oven.

Her stomach began to growl again as she thought of jelly beans and gumdrops, gingerbread and frosting. If this were a gingerbread house in the fairy tale, she would eat and eat and eat until there was nothing left. As she drifted off to sleep, she thought she heard Sophie muttering to herself as she shuffled to her bedroom. "Take care of that child. She has no idea what the spirits have done and who've they done it to. Have strength, Cordelia. Have strength. You'll need it."

Just at the very moment Cordelia drifted off to sleep, she realized that she'd never told the woman her name. So how could she know it was Cordelia? The thought stayed with her for a moment before she finally succumbed to deep, deep sleep.

ৰু

Cordelia woke up the next morning to the sun streaming through the windows, the birds chirping, and feeling rested and filled with anticipation. It truly felt as if she had awoken into a fairy tale after a hundred-year nap. And now that the Sleeping Beauty had broken the spell, she knew what had to be done. There was no wicked stepmother to be dealt with, no witches that were going to push her into a cauldron, no evil stepsisters that would push her around, and no knight in shining armor that was searching for her to rescue.

It was just Cordelia. And a king that needed to be dethroned. And after that, perhaps a few princesses that needed a taste of their own poisoned apples. Now that she knew where the path was leading her, all she had to do was take the first step.

The smells in the kitchen were even better than the ones

the previous night. The table was filled with waffles, pancakes, muffins, assorted pastries. Cordelia looked around and waited for her host to start eating. She noticed a piece of paper next to her place setting.

> *Gone into town for some errands. Don't think I'll be able to take you to Maine today. Left you the keys for the old Volkswagen Bug outside. Should have enough life left in her to get you where you're going. Don't worry about bringing her back any time soon. I've got no use for more than one car. Think of it as my gift to you on your journey. And it will keep you from hitching rides with wolves in the future. ☺*
>
> *Take care, Cordelia. Go with my blessings. Have great strength on your journey.*
>
> *Blessings,*
> *Sophie*

The keys were left on the table along with the pastries and breakfast spread. Cordelia poured herself a steaming cup of coffee and began to dig into the food. She could hardly believe her good fortune of stumbling upon this wonderful cottage and this amazing woman. Rebecca would have loved this place, she thought as she looked around. She could almost imagine her mother living like this forty years from now. Just a sweet old lady, living alone with nature, helping wayward strangers as they happened upon her cottage. It was straight off the pages of the Brothers Grimm.

Cordelia noticed that her clothes were freshly washed and folded next to a backpack. As she munched on the corner of a croissant, she walked over to the bag. It had some supplies, canned food, a first aid kit, and an envelope that was marked TRAVELING CASH. Sophie also had placed an unopened pack of tarot cards, an extra sweater, and some matches and bottled water in the bag. Cordelia smiled as she chewed and hunted around in the backpack.

"Where's the tent, Sophie?" she asked. The woman had thought of everything to help her on her journey to Maine. Perhaps the kind, old woman wouldn't have been so helpful if she knew Cordelia's ultimate plan.

What would Sophie think if she discovered that she was unknowingly aiding and abetting a murderer?

80

"I *need* this job," Cordelia begged the handsome man at the Maine Tea and Coffee Bean. "You have no idea how much this would mean to me. I have nowhere else to go. No place to live, no family in the area."

That was partly true. She did have family in the area, it was just that Malcolm Crane didn't know about her—probably wouldn't even recognize her if she plopped herself down on his doorstep. After she had driven the old VW Bug as far as she could into Maine—as far as the old gas tank allowed her—she stopped at a motel to get some rest and to refuel her body and her car. She knew she'd have to do some research to track down her wayward father.

Within a day or two of leaving Sophie's place, she had found herself in a small town library with free Internet access. Looking up Malcolm Crane wasn't too hard. She remembered Rebecca once mentioning that Malcolm was a college professor in Maine, but that was before they'd even moved to Hawthorne—and she still thought of him as her uncle. A lot could have changed since then, but she had to give it a shot. There were no Malcolms listed, but lots of M. Cranes. Fortunately, there were only a few listed in college towns. After placing a couple of phone calls to the college information centers, she learned that there was a Malcolm E. Crane teaching at a small college in Crawford, Maine. After she discovered that, she knew where she had to go and what she had to do. She just needed to be able to support herself and keep busy until she ultimately tracked him down. "Listen," the guy said quietly. "I can tell that you really want this job. But so do half of the students at Bromley College. And most of them have had at least some food service experience."

"But I used to run a store," she insisted, unwilling to take no for an answer. "That should count for something."

He looked at the résumé she'd halfheartedly scratched out.

"CeeCee, look, I see you've listed that you worked in a store, but you didn't put the name of the place, the town, or even a reference name for me to contact. You don't even have your Social Security number on this or a last place of residence. It's like you just appeared out of thin air."

Cordelia couldn't risk being discovered. She knew that as a runaway, she'd be tracked down if she used her real name, real Social, or revealed any of her ties to Hawthorne. When she saw the newspapers in the library she stopped at to research on Malcolm Crane, she realized how much of a big deal her disappearance really was to a small town like Hawthorne.

"I know, I know," she said, her lower lip trembling. "I can't really give you anything but my word. I—I need this job more than you know." Cordelia looked around and nodded at the kids crowding the coffee bar. "I'm telling you. I'm not like these college kids who will blow off shifts for classes and parties. I'll devote all my time to this coffeehouse. I'll work nights, weekends, holidays, Thanksgiving, Christmas, New Year's—whatever you want. Do you need overnight shifts? Done. Dishwasher? Floor washer? Hell, I'll even do your laundry. Just please," she cried as she looked down at his name tag. "Please, Chris. Give me a chance."

"Okay, okay, you've sold me," he said, laughing. "I'm going to stop you before you sell me your soul, for crying out loud." He stopped laughing when he noticed her eyes brimming with tears. She hoped he could tell she wasn't like the other college kids in town. She really wanted to work—needed it to survive and not just for some extra pocket change for nights out on the town or shopping sprees in Kittery.

"The job is yours. You've got it, okay?" he said, dimples deepening. Cordelia could tell that she was winning him over. "And if you need a place to crash until you get back on your feet, we have a small room in the back. Uh, it's not much. No windows or anything. But it's cozy, there's a nice bed. I've slept there a few nights when I've had to stay late and do accounting work. You'd have access to all the food here after hours. Plus, it'd be nice to have someone here watching the place overnight."

Cordelia couldn't believe her good fortune. She almost kissed him. She was nodding her head vigorously as he spoke. She was sold as soon as he said "small room in the back." "Yes, yes, yes!" she said, almost unable to contain herself. She threw her arms around him, thanking him profusely.

He pulled back, blushing a little, and then said, "I can only offer you a little more than minimum wage, but I won't charge you rent or anything."

"Great! Amazing! When can I start?"

He handed her a washcloth and said, "You can start wiping down these tables and then I'll have one of the other girls show you the ropes."

With that, Cordelia floated from table to table, wiping them so well that they gleamed. Everything was falling into place. And she had all the time in the world to track down her father—and to make things right.

Chapter 10

THE HERMIT
(Reversed)

Caution. Discretion. A time to stand back and reflect upon circumstances. Isolation from others. A negative resistance toward help. Groundless suspicions about the motives of others. Imprudent actions or decisions. The continuation of bad habits or unproductive lifestyles. Foolish obstinacy.

Hawthorne Academy had just closed for winter break, but Kate didn't feel like she was going to have much of a vacation, not with Finnegan O'Malley around. He was continuing to make problems for her and her family and she had reached the end of her rope. Ever since Cordelia disappeared last year, he'd become more and more of a thorn in her side. And now that Maddie had come back from Stanton for winter break, Kate realized that Finn would have one more person on his side when it came to Ravenswood.

Especially when it came to that creepy wall with the faces.

Finn warned what would happen if the wall was destroyed. He brought it up at the historical society meetings, the town council meetings, and at the construction site where workers were preparing to turn Ravenswood into the Endicott Hotel.

But no one would listen. Kate wondered why he wouldn't give it up.

He tried to appeal to their sense of historical preservation and then he tried playing on their fears, reminding them of the curse that had allegedly been set upon the town and whoever caused the destruction of the edifice. But it was no use. The Endicotts had cut a deal with the state. They would keep a portion of the asylum intact, erecting a museum that honored the countless patients that passed through Ravenswood like ghosts, as well as a tribute to the architectural genius of Samuel McIntyre. In the original plans for the Endicott Hotel, the seventeenth-century fortress wall with the faces of the Pickering sisters was incorporated into the new construction. But as soon as Kate Endicott discovered the more recent addition to the wall—the one that looked eerily similar to Cordelia LeClaire—she was determined to smash the wall into pieces.

"That piece of trailer trash will have no place at the Endicott. Why should we be reminded of that crazy bitch and everything she put us through?" Kate scoffed to her friends as they sat around the table at Crestwood Yacht Club, going over plans for the Misery Island Winter Gala. The charity event would help the Endicotts' case when they needed to swing the town council's vote in their favor.

"Do you really want to risk it?" Darcy asked as she stuffed the elegant cream invitations, obviously frightened by the ramifications. Kate laughed at Darcy's fearful question.

"Risk what?" Kate snapped at the girls, her voice echoing against the vaulted ceiling of the empty club's ballroom. "Risk pissing off a bunch of ghosts and legends? Or risk pissing off the lawn-boy-turned-historical-activist and his skanky girlfriend?"

Darcy turned red and looked down at the invitations. She winced as a paper cut spread blood onto her thumb and then onto the invitation. Kate noticed the smear of blood and whipped the invitation out of Darcy's hand. Bridget and Hannah held their breath wondering what Kate would do next.

"Do you really think that we're risking the wrath of Cordelia or the spooky Pickering sisters? Please," she said snidely. "Isn't it time you stopped believing in creepy legends and fairy tales?"

Kate wasn't aware that Finn was actually the one responsible for the faces on the stone wall, but she had seen him mooning around the carving that most resembled Cordelia—the missing girl that she and the Sisters of Misery had treated so cruelly prior to her disappearance. It became more evident when Kate learned that Finn was the rallying force behind keeping the wall standing during the renovation of Ravenswood into the Endicott.

When she wasn't met with any opposition to her comment, Kate continued her ranting about Finn. "All of his talks about preserving history and early American craftsmanship are just a pathetic attempt to hold on to Cordelia. I mean, how pathetic is that? Cordelia used him and then threw him away when she was done with him and he's still holding on to the idea that she's coming back."

"What if she does come back?" Bridget offered quietly. The girls eyed Kate nervously. They all had recently received tarot cards in the mail. Hannah, Bridget, Darcy, and Kate—maybe even Maddie—all of the Sisters of Misery. Everyone associated with what had happened that fateful Halloween night. "What if those cards were some kind of warning?" she said softly, as if afraid that if she spoke her fears out loud, they'd somehow come true.

"Don't you girls get it? Doesn't anyone get it?" Kate snapped, wondering if Finn was just as ridiculous as the others, thinking that Cordelia was going to return one day. That was never going to happen. Kate would never allow it to happen. "Cordelia is never coming back. If she does, she'll be sorry. Really sorry."

Worse than sorry, Kate thought as a flicker of a smile touched her lips, *she'll be dead.*

இ

"So, what's the story, Crane? You back for good?" Finn asked.

They were sitting outside the local coffee shop. Finn wanted to sit outside despite the wintry air so he could smoke. Maddie was surprised that she hadn't heard from him sooner, but when he called to meet up for coffee that afternoon, she couldn't say no. Maddie thought that he sounded hopeful for a minute, but as she watched him light up a cigarette, she realized that he'd never let his guard down around her the way he had when they were creeping around Ravenswood that terrible night. She paused for a minute.

She shook her head. "No, it's not permanent. I'm only going to be here as long as my mother needs me. She's . . . she probably doesn't have much more time left." Madeline felt strange, as if she was expected to cry or break down every time she mentioned her mother's illness. What she didn't want to admit to anyone, not even herself, was that she felt nothing. That all of her grief and sadness had been used up over all of the loss in her lifetime, and what she was left with was an overwhelming numbness.

Finn nodded and flicked the ash of his cigarette away from them. He scratched his head with his free hand. "Probably better off not sticking around here. You don't want to end up like your friends."

"You mean the members of the Junior League in training? Yeah, I know." Maddie laughed, and then took a sip of her steaming latte, burning her tongue. "It's funny, I go to school with kids whose parents own Fortune 500 companies—"

"Well, aren't you special?" Finn said sarcastically, interrupting her.

"No, what I mean is, they have more money than they could ever know what to do with and they don't have snobby attitudes half as unbearable as people around here do, you know?"

"Well, I don't really hang out with too many Fortune 500 trust fund babies, but," he said, briefly smirking, "if you're asking me if it surprises me that we have the most assholes per capita in the U.S. right here in Hawthorne, no, it does not."

THE LOST SISTER   107

"Wow, still working on that political campaign, are we?"

"Yeah, they definitely are going to be electing me mayor one of these days." They both laughed at the thought of Finn running the town of Hawthorne. "Nah, I want to get out of here, too. I'm thinking of ditching the next semester of school and taking my bike cross-country. Get out on the open road with my motorcycle and just see the world—the real world, not this pretend playhouse we call a town."

Maddie pictured Finn out on his bike, driving cross-country, with nothing but desert all around him, small broken-down motels, and the red mountains on the horizon. She had the urge to jump on the back of his bike and ride off into complete freedom. Leave everything and everyone behind and start fresh. It was a thought that both thrilled and frightened her at the same time. She could envision Cordelia wrapping her arms around Finn, pressing her cheek to his worn leather jacket, and setting off together into a new life. She often wondered why that never happened. Finn probably wished he knew the answer as well.

It was at that moment that the feeling of being watched came over Maddie suddenly like a Vise-Grip. It felt as though someone was watching her every move, paying heed to every person she spoke with, listening to every conversation. She looked around nervously and tried to continue joking with Finn, but the feeling was too strong, too overwhelming to concentrate on his words. Cars were driving by and people bundled up in North Face jackets paid no attention as they passed the teenagers seated on the bench outside the coffee shop. But still, there was this feeling she couldn't shake. . . .

"I have to—need to go," she said quickly.

"Oh yeah," he said, looking slightly hurt. "Yeah, right, well, it was good seeing you again, Maddie. Say hi to Reed and his new girlfriend for me."

Maddie wasn't sure if he was trying to hurt her feelings with the mention of Reed and how he'd moved on. She wasn't sure how much he knew about the feelings she had for her former teacher. Darcy had already told her that Reed had moved in with Bronwyn Maxwell, a girl suddenly catapulted to super social status after a multimillion-dollar inheritance from her grandparents. The former field hockey coach was now one of the It girls of the town. It made Maddie sick to think about.

"Uh, yeah." Maddie took a quick look around and stammered, "Right. I should probably say hi to him now that I'm back in town." She was worried that someone would hear them talking about Reed—that they would see the disappointment in her face.

"Don't worry," Finn snapped as she turned to walk away.

Maddie stopped midstride and turned. "About what?"

"No one saw you."

What is he talking about? Maddie wondered. "Saw me?"

"No one saw you talking to me. You're in the clear with your friends." He put air quotes around the word *friends*.

"You know that I don't care about that, Finn. You know me better than that."

"Do I?" he said sharply, and then lit a cigarette angrily, turning his back on Maddie.

Chills ran down her back, the kind that you get when you're being watched. Maddie knew that feeling all too well. She walked away briskly, trying to shake it off, but it was stuck to her like glue. Tess would have called it the Evil Eye. Abigail would have said paranoia. Cordelia would have attributed it to fairies or elves. Maddie knew it was none of those things. But the one thing she was sure of was this: it was danger.

Chapter 11

THE HIEROPHANT

The spiritual teacher, one who gives advice and guidance to those seeking it. Giving a blessing, a sign of kindness, love, and protection, the Hierophant is the one who wades in, quiets the panic, and offers good, practical advice. He symbolizes a connection to the divine, which answers with a very human voice, never oblique or mysterious. The solution is there, you just have to find it.

"You aren't really living here, are you?" Maddie joked as Reed welcomed her into the foyer of his current residence.

Seeing Reed Campbell's new digs, which were straight out of a *Better Homes and Gardens* magazine, was the last thing she'd ever expected. She couldn't comprehend how any normal person could reside in such a meticulous, picture-perfect home. The massive Colonial had a cutesy nautical theme that most houses in the area adopted. Every piece of artwork was painstakingly placed, each ribbon was expertly curled, each window treatment raised to a carefully determined height—allowing for the right amount of light in the mornings and afternoons without the threat of too much sun fading the sumptuously upholstered sofas.

Maddie wasn't sure if it was trepidation or excitement that she saw in Reed's eyes when she decided to drop in on him unexpectedly. But what did it matter? How could she compare with Bronwyn? The Maxwell family was one of the founding Hawthorne families; her trust fund was bigger than the Campbells' and the Endicotts' put together. Even though her family only recently came into their inheritance, they weren't shy about letting people know about it. Abigail had told her how it was almost vulgar the way that Bronwyn and her mother wore their Cartier Love bracelets (in both eighteen-karat gold and platinum) like cheap bangles and flaunted their never-ending supply of Louis Vuitton purses, Lilly Pulitzer clothes, and Birkin bags. If the patriarchal grandfather hadn't passed on all of his wealth that he'd kept hidden away for years, no one would have believed the transformation of the all-American girls' hockey coach to the spoiled socialite of Hawthorne. From what Maddie had heard about Bronwyn's rise to the elite, her actions would put even Kate Endicott to shame.

But Reed didn't seem to be fazed by his opulent surroundings.

"Off and on," he said about his current living arrangement. They hugged awkwardly and he stepped back, welcoming her into the house. Maddie walked uneasily over to the overstuffed couches and waited for Reed to sit across from her. Her heart was beating so hard she could feel it in the back of her throat. She was sure that the sound of it was filling the room—the space between them. Her breath was uneven.

He watched her for a few moments, as if gauging her reasons for the visit, and then sat down in the worn leather chair (obviously his one contribution to the frilly room). An uncomfortable silence settled over them, and Maddie wondered if he was remembering the last time they had seen each other and the passionate kiss they shared. She could still feel it in her knees and she had to consciously force herself not to run over and embrace him. The attraction was still very much alive on her end. She tried to gauge his feelings, if he regretted their kiss or not. Obviously, he wasn't pining away for her if he was living here with another girl.

Just as Maddie was about to speak, the front door opened and Bronwyn Maxwell swept into the hallway adjacent to the living room where Madeline and Reed sat, her head buried in the day's mail, hands cluttered with shopping bags.

"Whose car is outside, hon?" she asked as she walked into the room. Upon spotting Maddie, she pursed her honey lips for a second in displeasure before breaking into a wide, tight smile.

"Well, hello! Who do we have here?" Her annoyance was not evident in her voice, but in her cold, watery blue eyes.

"Maddie is one of my former students," he offered.

Former student? Maddie thought. She felt like a stake had just been thrust through her heart. *Is that all I am to him?*

"Well, good," Bronwyn said coolly, already losing interest in the unwelcome visitor. "It is almost seven o'clock, you know. A little late for a tutoring session, wouldn't you say?"

She brushed past them and stuck her purchases in the closet, undoubtedly more outfits from Ann Taylor or Lilly Pulitzer, similar to what she was wearing.

"This is Madeline Crane. Madeline, this is my . . . um . . . girlfriend, Bronwyn."

"Nice to see you, Bronwyn," Maddie said quietly. It was obvious that her former field hockey coach hadn't placed her. She wasn't the star athlete that Kate Endicott was, nor was she a die-hard team member like the other girls in the Sisters of Misery. Bronwyn had always treated Kate, Bridget, Hannah, and Darcy with kid gloves. Maddie wondered if Bronwyn was a former member of the Sisters of Misery, or if she was secretly afraid of the group of women that ruled Hawthorne with an iron, yet impeccably manicured fist.

"Mm-hmm," Bronwyn mumbled, passing by as if Madeline no longer existed and had suddenly become part of the furnishings.

"You're a tutor now?" Maddie asked.

"Well, if I can't teach high school classes, I can at least help students pass their SATs," he said glumly.

"At least he's putting his teaching certification to some

use," Bronwyn said. Maddie noted a tinge of harsh sarcasm in her voice. Maybe things weren't as picture-perfect here as they'd like them to appear.

Reed cleared his throat disapprovingly as he watched Bronwyn flit around the house, plumping overfluffed pillows, arranging perfectly placed decorative accessories.

"Madeline and I were just catching up. Her cousin, Cordelia, was also a student of mine." Just hearing him say Cordelia's name—the way his voice huskily wrapped around each syllable—made her feel sharp pangs of jealousy.

"Cordelia?" She turned around, her interest suddenly piqued. "Where have I heard that name? Does she belong to the club?"

Reed shook his head. "No, honey. Cordelia LeClaire. The girl who disappeared last year."

"Oh my." Bronwyn rushed over to Madeline's side, grasping her hands. "Of course, I remember that. I am so sorry, Maddie. My heart goes out to you and your family." She gave Maddie's hand a squeeze with her own perfectly manicured ones, then cocked her head to the side and looked at Maddie quizzically. "Weren't you on my team last year? You didn't graduate, did you?"

Maddie shook her head, slightly happy that she wasn't completely forgettable. That there were a few memories left of her in this town that she'd lived in all her life, other than only being known as the cousin of the girl who disappeared.

"I transferred to Stanton Prep in Maine," Maddie stated, not willing to go into further explanation.

"Really? They have a crap field hockey team. Are you on it?"

Reed interrupted. "Bronwyn, cut it out." Maddie couldn't understand what he saw in her. Granted, she was a beautiful, blond athlete who came from tons of money, and this house was a major step up from the boat he used to live in, but that didn't cancel the fact that she was a straight-out bitch. Kate

Endicott had always despised her, but it was most likely because they were too similar to like each other. But now that she had more money and a higher social status than Kate, it must be an all-out war, Maddie mused.

Bronwyn continued the interrogation. "So, if you're at Stanton now, why are you back here? Don't they have winter sessions, college-readiness programs, internships?"

"My mom kind of needs me," Maddie said softly. She turned to Reed. "My mom is pretty sick with cancer and she needs help with the house and with my aunt. Now that Tess is gone, she's all alone in that big Victorian. She could use the company."

"Well, aren't you a doll for taking care of your family like that?" Bronwyn said disingenuously. Then she looked at Reed and her mood suddenly shifted. It was obvious that she had more important things on her agenda to worry about than her former field hockey player and her sick mother. "Speaking of family, we are having dinner with my family tonight at the club and we've really got to get going." She patted Reed's knee and spun around heading toward the stairs.

Halfway up the stairs she called down to them, "It was good seeing you again, Melissa. Give our condolences to your family."

Reed waved her off as she rushed up the stairs, as if telling Maddie to pay no mind to his new girlfriend's insensitivity.

"I see we're moving on to bigger and better things," Maddie joked.

"You're hilarious," Reed said, giving the trademark grin that she remembered so well. Without Bronwyn around, Reed and Maddie fell back into their old comfortable ways. It was as if they just picked up where they had left off so many months ago.

"Seriously, Reed," Maddie said in a hushed tone. "What's with the Stepford Wife in training?"

Reed sighed and looked into Maddie's eyes for a long time.

"This is a small town where everyone wants to get into everyone else's business. And since the only interesting girls I know are under my age limit, it was suggested by my family and Bronwyn's that we start seeing each other." He seemed pained to talk about the arrangement.

"What?" Maddie laughed. "Are you in an arranged marriage or something? Is this the eighteen hundreds? Did I escape a time warp when I crossed the town lines?"

"Ha, ha," Reed said in a tone that was not amused. "Listen, you get to go out and live your life and date whomever you want. I'm stuck in this town if I want to have access to my trust—"

"And let's not forget about your new girlfriend's bust—I mean trust," Maddie joked.

Reed rolled his eyes. They both were fully aware that the merging of the Campbell and the Maxwell families was something that was desired for many years. Relationships seemed to be more of a corporate merging than anything else in Hawthorne. Even Kate Endicott and Trevor Campbell's arrangement was more of a relationship of convenience and assets than of true love. It was the Hawthorne way.

"Besides, I hear you've taken up with a Fortune 500 brat," he said. "Aren't you dating a billionaire's son? The Richard Branson of the U.S.?"

"Luke is a friend. My *best* friend. He's helped me through a lot over the past few months. He's been my rock. But really, we're only friends."

"Friends with benefits?" Reed said with a gleam in his eye.

"Ew, excuse me, Professor. Isn't that a little inappropriate for you to ask me?" Maddie said, laughing. She could put up with his taunts because there was nothing lecherous about him. If anything, he was the one to put the brakes on anything ever happening between them before she left Hawthorne. And now that she was seventeen, the age difference seemed to melt even further away. Besides, what did age matter when the feelings you had for someone were so strong?

Plus, their innocent flirtations began way after he was let go from Hawthorne Academy because of his alleged involvement with Cordelia—something to this day Maddie still refused to accept. He definitely helped Cordelia out of a hard place, either by guilt over what Trevor did to her, or by an honest caring and concern for her. Both reasons were enough to satisfy Maddie, allowing her to realize that his intentions came from a good place.

"Crane, you know I'm just joking around with you," he said as a cloud seemed to sift across his perfectly chiseled features. "I just want to make sure that you're happy and that you're being treated right. After everything you've been through, you of all people deserve to be happy."

"Me *and* Cordelia deserve to be happy."

He leaned forward conspiratorially and asked in a hushed tone, "Have you heard anything from her? Has she tried to make any contact? With you or her mother?"

Maddie shook her head. She didn't want to go into the fact that she felt like she was communicating with Cordelia through her dreams. How could she explain that to him without setting off all sorts of red flags that she was just as loony as her aunt and needed to join her at Fairview Hospital?

"But—" She stopped herself, unsure how much she should confide in him.

"But?" he asked, his voice going up an octave.

Maddie weighed whether or not she should clue Reed in to the delivery she had received prior to returning to Hawthorne and the letter that mentioned that Cordelia was back and looking for her. "Did you ever send me a letter at school?"

"Me? Write a letter? I'm a recovering English teacher. The closest I come to writing is e-mail and texting. If it doesn't come with spell-check, I'm not doing it."

"It's just that I got this letter up at school and I thought . . ." Maddie said, her voice trailing off. It must have been Finn who sent the note about Cordelia being back and coming for her. But why hadn't he mentioned it earlier? Maddie shook her head and gave up trying to ignore the stomping around upstairs by Bronwyn. She rolled her eyes to the ceiling. "Sounds like your warden is giving you the sign that it's time to wrap things up."

"She can wait a little longer. God knows how long I have to wait for her when we go on our shopping excursions. Or her new kick, going to libraries and doing genealogy and family trees."

Maddie rolled her eyes and fought back a laugh.

"Seriously, though," Reed continued, "what did you get in the mail up at school?" He sounded a little edgy, concerned even.

Maddie started slowly, giving herself ample opportunity to amend her statements accordingly, just in case it was a member of her own family—namely Rebecca—who was sending out the threatening notes and cards.

"Well, when I first got up to school, my mother wrote to me about the whole Endicott Hotel debacle and how Finn and the historical society put a halt to tearing down Ravenswood."

"Yeah, your friend Finn isn't at a loss for enemies in this town. People are losing millions, especially the Endicotts. Their investors are dropping like flies. You might want to warn your friend to watch his back."

"I think he's pretty much used to that by now. He went through the same interrogation and suspicion when Cordelia first went missing."

Reed nodded. "Guess that makes us kindred souls or blood brothers, right?"

"In this town, it's more like prisoners of war," Maddie said. "The letter was strange, but then I got something else that was even stranger."

"What was it?" Reed asked, leaning forward and listening intently, almost too intently.

Could Reed have been the one to send her the ominous note that warned, CORDELIA IS BACK AND SHE'S COMING FOR YOU? Was he the one who sent the tarot card? "I got a note that said that Cordelia was coming for me . . . and then I got a card. A weird one." Maddie spoke hesitantly. The sounds from upstairs had quieted and she wondered if Bronwyn was eavesdropping on their conversation from the top of the stairs.

"What kind of card? Was it one of those fortune tarot cards?" His interest seemed unusually piqued.

Maddie nodded.

At that moment, Reed walked over to the oak rolltop desk (a beautiful antique that obviously belonged to Bronwyn) and slid an envelope from behind a stack of papers and brought it over to Maddie.

The envelope was addressed to Bronwyn, but from the furtive glance Reed threw at the staircase, Maddie assumed that Bronwyn had never laid eyes on the note.

Without saying a word, Reed handed the envelope to Maddie with shaking hands. Inexplicably, a whisper echoed in Maddie's ear.

Run, Maddie! She could feel the cool breath on her neck and ear and visibly winced. She crossed her arms over her chest and glanced around the room; there weren't any open windows.

Damn nerves, Maddie thought furiously; she'd been spooked as she turned every corner once she set foot back in Hawthorne.

Willing her hands not to shake, Maddie opened the envelope, knowing all too well what rested inside. A tarot card. It was the Hanged Man. Maddie tried to remember the meaning of the card. She had received the Death card when she was up at school. While the Death card seemed ominous, after some research she soon learned that it also meant new beginnings and a closure on the past. Moving forward was something that she wanted to do more than anything, so she chose to focus on the positive aspects of the card as opposed to the negative.

But the Hanged Man was a different story. There were a few different ways to read the card, but none of them was very promising.

Without raising her eyes from the card, Maddie asked solemnly, "When did she receive this?"

Reed leaned closer to her. "Not that long ago, maybe a few weeks before you came back to town. You got one, too, didn't you?"

Maddie nodded as she felt a familiar flutter in her stomach, though she tried to ignore it. He was so close to her now, their knees were touching each other. It was hard to concentrate on the severity of the situation. How many nights had she dreamt about Reed Campbell? How many nights had she lain awake wondering if he was thinking about her? Once Luke came into the picture, it was easy to lock her feelings for Reed in a little box in her heart. But now it felt like the lock had sprung open and her feelings for him were swirling through her body. But did it really matter? He obviously wasn't going to wait for her as she'd always hoped.

So it was no surprise that Bronwyn had been the target of the tarot card sender. Maddie wondered if Kate was sending the cards just to stir up trouble in town.

"Do you know what it means?" Reed asked hopefully.

"It's not good," Maddie said, and then quickly added, "But I'm sure it's just some stupid joke. Someone with a flair for the dramatic."

He looked at her straight in the eye. "Do you—?"

"Do I think it's Cordelia? No. Cordelia barely even knew Bronwyn. She'd have no reason to try to scare her."

"But . . ." Reed hesitated. "What if it wasn't meant to scare her?"

"What else could it be?" She could feel her stomach drop even before he said the words that she knew were coming.

"A warning," Reed said flatly. "Maybe Cordelia is warning you both to watch your backs."

"But how would she know?" Maddie asked dumbly, understanding all too well how Cordelia might know. How was Cordelia privy to half of the things she knew? Had Cordelia told Reed about the family gift that Tess had told them about last year, before her passing? Or did Reed see it as a threat and not a warning against outside influences? Did he think that Cordelia was out to get them? That she was planning revenge?

"Cordelia is more in tune to what's going around than anyone I've ever known," Reed said in a serious tone.

That's the understatement of the year, Maddie mused as she fought the familiar jealousy that she'd felt last year. The feeling that there was something very special between Reed and Cordelia. Something that she could never come close to. Something that even Bronwyn couldn't replace.

Reed gave her a sidelong glance. They were both aware that when it came to Cordelia, no explanations were necessary. No explanations could even begin to tell the story of Maddie's magical, ethereal cousin.

Maddie treated her question as if it were rhetorical. "So where does that leave us?"

Reed sighed, brushing his hand through his dirty-blond hair. "We need to find out who sent these cards and what they mean. And I have a feeling that we need to do it fast."

"What, are you psychic now, too?" Maddie attempted a lighthearted tone. But she realized they were way past that.

"No, I've just gotten used to the feeling of when I'm being backed into a corner," he said, and then he added, "And also that awful feeling that something bad is about to happen to the people I care about. Something real bad."

Chapter 12

THE LOVERS

Often is interpreted as representing new or rekindled relationships; however, a deeper level suggests that difficult, personal choices must be made—there are usually many options to select from. Tune in to your inner wisdom: the correct choice will soon make itself known.

"I don't care what you say, Maddie, this is something that I want to do. I've been putting off my chemotherapy specifically for this occasion. And if you don't want to go, I'll just have to go out there myself. The fresh air will do me good tonight," Abigail said. "Plus, I'd like everyone in town to see that I'm fighting this cancer and I'm going to beat it."

Maddie wanted to say that the fresh sea air was just as accessible from the mainland as it was out on Misery Island—and probably wasn't as freezing—but she didn't want to get into a fight. She had agreed to come home to take care of Abigail, and her mother had refused any chemotherapy treatments until after this event, so Maddie decided to make the best of it. It would be one bright spot for her mother in what would be several coming months of pain and anguish.

Despite the fact that it was one of the coldest Decembers in recent history, the Endicotts were paying to have a huge, heated tent erected on the island. It was going to be a gala affair, right in the middle of the frosty, wintry coastal winds. It was truly the last place on earth that Maddie wanted to go. But she knew that it would raise Abigail's spirits, so she resigned herself to go.

Plus, it would be a good opportunity to talk with the Sisters of Misery—get them all in the same place, trapped on an island with nowhere to go.

The last time they were all out there together was with Cordelia, Maddie thought painfully. Perhaps the island event would trigger more memories, she mused. Or more nightmares.

&

The gala on Misery Island was the event of the year. Kate and Kiki Endicott made sure of that. They knew that if the right people from the wealthy North Shore—as well as Boston's elite—were present, it would be covered by all the local newspapers and magazines. What Kiki hadn't counted on was the appearance of Maddie Crane and her mother. Suddenly waves of whisperings rippled through the elegant affair. Just the sight of them brought up ugly memories of Ravenswood. It was hardly the type of attention that Kiki and Kate wanted. Instead of piquing the interest of the wealthy elite of Boston to invest in the Endicott, rumors swirled about the tragic events that took place at Ravenswood. Hardly an investor's dream come true.

"Did you hear about the bloody night at Ravenswood? I heard Abigail tried to kill her own sister!"

"Did that Rebecca LeClaire die? Isn't she still locked up at Fairview?"

"I heard that Cordelia's ghost haunts Ravenswood. Just what we need, another witch putting a curse on the town."

The rumors and whispers rippled through the party. To Kiki Endicott's horror, the reporters seemed more interested in rehashing the night at Ravenswood than the party they were attending.

Kate had a feeling that this would be her first run-in with Maddie since she left for Stanton; she just didn't realize she'd be upstaged by her former friend and the dark memories that clung to her like her basic black Ann Taylor dress. It wasn't even original; Darcy was wearing the same exact dress. Kate's long, pale blue Roberto Cavalli shift, which was meant to bring out the blue in her eyes, seemed to be the cloak of invisibility.

Kate looked at Darcy and made a face. Darcy turned red and slunk away from the crowd.

Serves her right for being such a slut, Kate thought. She knew about Trevor and Darcy's tryst, and she was going to think of a way to make them pay for it. But not tonight. Tonight she had other plans, ones that involved taking a certain boarding school girl down a notch. Make her remember what it felt like to be afraid.

"Mrs. Endicott, can you explain why it has taken so long for the Endicott Hotel to start construction? Is it due to the tragedies that occurred earlier this year? Can you expound on that?"

Questions were being shot at Kate and Kiki from every angle. Kiki nervously twisted her bloodred ruby ring around her long, thin finger. Kate wondered how they would explain the events that occurred at Ravenswood without turning the public—and potential investors—off about the property. But her mother was a master at spin control.

"This is exactly why we need to raise money for the Endicott and cut through the historical society's red tape so that we can officially tear down Ravenswood," Kiki spoke up to one of the reporters, her voice cutting across the party like a sharp bell. "It is a blight on this town. A town that my family— the Endicott family—helped build. The town of Hawthorne needs to move past the tragic events that occurred in that horrible monster of a place."

Kate, never one to let the spotlight stray from her for too long, spoke earnestly into one of the television news cameras there to cover the function. "That's why it's the perfect time for the Endicott Hotel. We need light and beauty and a fresh start," she said, smiling her all-American-girl smile, dimples deepening.

Finn called out behind her, "Putting makeup on a bleeding sore doesn't make it pretty, Kate."

Flustered, Kate spun around angrily.

"Who invited you here, O'Malley?" she hissed quietly so that the television crew and reporters wouldn't hear, her perfect features darkening, her cheeks appearing sunken and hollow in the dim light of the black-tie affair.

"As a member of the historical society of Hawthorne, I have every right to be here. As you know, Misery Island is open to everyone."

"Yes," Kate said through her perfectly white teeth, "but this party is not!" She turned to one of the caterers and said quietly, "Could you please escort this man out of here?"

"I'm sorry, Ms. Endicott, the next boat isn't scheduled to take people back to the mainland for the next two hours."

Finn grabbed a crab-stuffed mushroom cap off the caterer's tray and popped it into his mouth. "Looks like you're stuck with me, Endicott," he said with his mouth full.

Kate looked at him with disgust and then turned away angrily, desperate for another reporter to talk to. There was no way this lawn boy would ruin her night. Misery Island was her territory. And anyone who got in her way would risk the consequences.

Finn should know that more than anyone, Kate thought, smirking as she remembered his pathetic effort to save Cordelia. *Some people never learn.*

&

Finn winked at Maddie, who watched his exchange with Kate from afar. She blushed and nodded, silently thanking him for taking the attention off her and her mother. Once again, Finn O'Malley to the rescue. It was becoming a trend. Yet she knew that by the end of the night she and Kate would come face-to-face. It was a meeting that both excited her and filled her with dread.

೪

The party was hugely successful. Despite a few drunken outbursts and awkward questions directed toward Maddie and her mother, they enjoyed themselves immensely. Abigail may have enjoyed herself a little too much, as it had been a while since she'd had anything to drink, and the wine that evening was flowing freely.

"Maddie Crane," Kate said, handing Maddie a glass. Maddie hesitated and then straightened up a bit and took the glass from Kate's manicured hand. Kate smiled and raised her own glass to toast Maddie. "Nice to see you back home where you belong."

Maddie toasted Kate back. "Luckily, I'm not here for very long, Kate, so you can cut the Welcome Wagon act."

Kate smiled and took a sip of red wine. "Pity," she said. "I must say, there's always so much drama when you're around. I wonder why that is?" Kate never let the smile slip from her face. She served up the barbs as sweetly as slices of apple pie. From anyone on the outside looking at them, they just appeared like two girls—childhood friends—catching up on old times. No one would ever have believed what had occurred on Misery Island over a year ago. What Kate had orchestrated, what Maddie had witnessed, and what Kate had made Maddie do.

Feeling slightly emboldened by either the wine or the fact that she was no longer under Kate's thumb, Maddie said, "I guess it's just the problem with the company I keep that gets me into trouble." She was referring to the Sisters of Misery, but Kate didn't let Maddie get the last word.

"I'll say," she said. "Ever since you took up with the gas station boy, your cousin, and our teacher, you've had quite the roller-coaster ride, haven't you? Now if you'll excuse me, I have some *important* people that I need to talk to. Be a doll and make sure that you and your boyfriends"—she nodded to Reed and Finn—"stay out of trouble and out of my way. Cheers, Maddie." She raised her glass and turned abruptly, striding across the makeshift dance floor to a large group of impeccably dressed women.

∞

It was nearing the end of the night, and Maddie needed some fresh air. She made her way over to a dark, quiet spot of the tent that overlooked Marblehead and Children's Island. Children's Island didn't hold as many negative memories for Maddie as Misery Island did, but there was still the ominous presence that hung over the island like a dark, misty cloud. Tess had told her about the legends. That the island was used as a place to treat patients with smallpox in the 1700s and then became a sanitarium for afflicted children in the 1800s. Even though it had been taken over by the YMCA in the 1950s—the pool and athletic facilities built on the exact site of the hospital that had been torched in the nineteenth century—it still gave certain people the ominous feeling of being deserted, forgotten, shunned. When Maddie was a child, Tess tried to explain the sadness that Maddie often felt when she returned home from summer camp on Children's Island.

"Most people on that island knew that they would never return to their homes. They were sick with a contagious disease. They would never be accepted back into their communities," Tess said, trying to help Maddie understand why she felt a sense of despair each day when she boated out to the island and the relief she felt upon her return home. "The problem is that the children that were sent out there didn't understand why they were sent away. They couldn't understand the abandonment by their families. That's why their souls are still out there. They are waiting for someone they love to bring them home."

Tess was speaking the truth. The rumors and legends of Children's Island being haunted were known by everyone who grew up in the area. It was one of those campfire stories told over and over again, especially when the campouts were actually on the island itself. Even though Maddie never came across one of the restless spirits that so many people claimed to have seen—specter children running naked across the shore, crippled women soaking their limbs in the tidal pools, nuns wailing over the loss of the babies in their care, children with tiny crutches hobbling across the rocks—Maddie felt the oppressive nature of the place, even from a safe distance.

It was quiet on this side of the tent, the part that connected to the ruins of the old casino. Not too far from that spot was the last place she'd ever seen Cordelia. She wondered if she was the only one that night to realize the significance of the party's location.

Who am I kidding? Maddie thought. *Kate did all of this on purpose. She wants to show us all that she's moved on and feels no remorse for that night out on Misery Island.* She stared at the lights of the quaint town of Marblehead—a town so similar to Hawthorne and the other picturesque towns of the North Shore—and noted how it was lit up like a Christmas tree. She heard the waves churn beneath her at the jagged outcroppings of rock and wondered about Luke. And then she thought of Cordelia. She was lost in a slight wine buzz and the gentle warm hum of the electric heaters working at full blast when she sensed a person standing behind her. She felt warm breath on the back of her neck. If it was Finn, she decided she'd have to repay him somehow for shielding her and her mother from the spotlight. He probably expected some major sucking up.

"Maddie." The husky voice said from behind her. She could hear the restraint in the voice. The hesitation and the desire.

It was Reed.

"Reed," Maddie said quietly. She had noticed him throughout the night, moving about the party, looking uncomfortable as Bronwyn clung to his arm, laughing and chatting with well-heeled partygoers. His handsome face seemed weathered, almost defeated, as if Hawthorne had finally put him in his place and he was dutifully accepting the consequences. Every time she looked to see where he was, his eyes inevitably found hers. There was an invisible cord that seemed to tether them together as they circled each other like sharks throughout the night.

She turned to embrace her former teacher, her schoolgirl crush. Only now that he was no longer her teacher, it didn't seem so strange that she would suddenly have the urge to kiss Reed Campbell, again and again and again. But she knew he was with Bronwyn, who was somewhere in the party looking exquisite: long blond hair swept up in a chignon, designer dress, four-hundred-dollar shoes. Who could compete with that?

"I've been thinking about something you said," he said in a hushed tone.

"About the tarot cards?" She leaned in and could smell the sweet scent of his aftershave mixed with alcohol. He shifted his eyes back and forth from her eyes to her lips. He may have had too much to drink, which wouldn't have been difficult that evening. His close proximity and the look in his eyes made Maddie feel even more tipsy than she already was.

"No, something you said before you left for Stanton. About waiting . . . for you." His voice caught a bit when he said those last two words.

She inhaled sharply, suddenly overcome by emotions. Was it excitement? Desire? Fear? They all seemed to rush together.

The voices from the party swirled around her in a fog. They were tucked away out of sight, and yet for some reason Maddie felt exposed and on display. This both thrilled and frightened her. She suddenly wanted to be kissed by him, swept up in his strong embrace, and so much more.

He grabbed the back of her hair tightly and rested his hand against the back of her neck, pulling her against him. His mouth was only inches from hers, and his blue eyes peered into hers. She realized that she had missed everything about him. They were no longer bound by the restrictions of teacher and student, and suddenly she wanted him more than ever. And from the look in his eyes, Reed's thoughts weren't so innocent, either.

Slowly he leaned closer and gently kissed her. Yet when she felt the heat and passion in his kiss, mixed with hesitation, she began kissing him more passionately, letting him know that they shared the same feelings. Maddie could swear that she could feel the movement of the island beneath her feet. Everything else drifted to a faraway hum. All that mattered was right there between them. Nothing would come between them. Not the memory of Cordelia, not Bronwyn, not the Sisters of Misery, and not Abigail's disapproval.

Nothing except . . ."Maddie," Finn said sharply.

Maddie and Reed quickly pulled apart. She was flustered and looked around to make sure that no one else was witness to their impromptu display of affection.

"Hey, O'Malley," Reed said lightly. "You shouldn't sneak up on people like that."

Finn nodded and looked at Maddie, acting like Reed didn't exist. "You okay, Maddie?"

"Yeah, yes . . . um . . . sure," Maddie said nervously. She looked back out toward the ocean, where the monstrous shadow of Ravenswood sat atop Hawthorne Hill. She could have sworn she saw a light in one of the windows—probably just a contractor working after hours. But it chilled her, because it almost looked like it was winking at her, goading her.

"Your mom wanted me to find you. She's feeling tired and wants to head home. I can totally take her if you—if you're not ready to go." He fumbled over the words, while Reed shoved his hands into his jean pockets and looked uncomfortably back toward the party, noticing that Darcy—dressed in a dress similar to Maddie's—was giving him an odd stare.

"No, no, I'm ready to go. I—I guess I'll talk to you later, Reed," Maddie said, peeling her eyes away from Ravenswood and trying to keep her voice businesslike, nonchalant. Their eyes met for one more brief second; then she brushed past him and back to the party. Finn did a two-finger salute to Reed with a cocky smile and then followed Maddie through the crowded party.

"What was that for? Extra credit?" Finn joked.

"Shut up, Finn," Maddie snapped. "Just shut up."

"Looked like A-plus work to me," Finn continued to taunt. "Pity he isn't your teacher anymore."

"Enough!" Maddie said, trying to fight back a laugh. Only Finn could make a joke out of something as uncomfortable as getting caught making out with your ex-teacher, a lead suspect in your half sister's disappearance, and the current boyfriend of the wealthiest, most powerful girl in town.

"Hey, at least you're not getting graded on a curve."

Maddie swatted him hard. "Where's your jacket?" she asked, trying to change the subject and deflect any additional tauntings.

He shook his head. "Oh no, Crane, I'm not letting you off the hook that easy."

She sighed and then continued into the party to find Abigail and go home to sleep off the craziness of that night.

"Your chariot, my ladies," Finn said in a jovial manner as he helped Maddie and her mother into the launch boat. He seemed happier than he'd been in a long time. It pleased Maddie, but also made her a bit skeptical. What exactly put him in such a good mood? she wondered as the boat took them out onto the blue-black waters, heading toward home.

Chapter 13

NINE OF SWORDS
(Reversed)

Deception, premonitions and bad dreams, suffering and depression, cruelty, disappointment, violence, loss, and scandal. All of these may be overcome through faith and calculated inaction. This is the card of the Martyr and with it comes new life out of suffering.

I'm back on the island. The hum of people around me talking seems deafening. Everyone is looking at me and smiling. Why is everyone looking at me like this? I wonder. I feel different. As if I'm in someone else's clothes, someone else's skin. I try to look down, but it suddenly becomes clear that I'm only here as an observer—I have no control over my body or my actions.

My stomach drops when I see who Finn and Reed are talking to. They're talking to me! How is that possible? Am I dreaming? I try to call over to them, but my voice won't rise up over the sounds of the party.

I realize now that I'm sleeping, dreaming about the party. But why? I watch myself giggling and nervously talking to both guys. For some reason, it makes me sick.

Then I turn away and see someone hunched over the icebox right outside the tent. I see the leather jacket and wonder how Finn was able to get over here so quickly. It's freezing, but I move farther away from the tent. The waves are crashing loudly over the jagged rocks.

I close my eyes for a moment and when I open them, I see Darcy looking at me with intense fear. What's wrong? I try to ask her, but the words aren't coming out. I notice something on her face. Dirt and—what else is that? Blood?

Let me help you, *I try to say, but I can't make the words come. She shuffles away from me on the ground, looking at me in disbelief, as if I'm a monster. She inches herself closer to the edge of the island.*

I look down at my hands and notice that I'm holding a heavy, steel tent stake. It's covered in blood. Darcy's blood.

Oh my God, Darcy! With everything that's inside me, I try to move toward her and help her, but I'm helplessly stuck watching her cry and plead and beg. I can't hear her words, but I know what she's saying.

"Please don't hurt me. I don't want to die! I'm sorry!"

She's screaming now. Why doesn't anyone hear her? Why am I the only one here? Why is she screaming at me? I would never hurt her.

Suddenly, beyond my control, I move over to her.

Yes, that's right, it's over now. I'm going to help you, *I think.*

She looks at me with intense fear as I lift her to her feet. It's that intense look in her eyes that stays with me as I shove her off the cliff and onto the jagged rocks below. Her lifeless body, hidden among the rocks, looks like a broken doll thrown carelessly on the floor. Her eyes are with me as I turn back to the party and try to scream. Darcy is dead! Why can't you hear me! People nod at me as I walk back into the party. I grab a glass of champagne and fold into the crowd. I now realize that I'm trapped—trapped inside the body of a murderer. I just watched one of my oldest friends get killed by my own hands, and there is absolutely nothing I can do to change it.

I'm helpless.

I'm scared.

I'm horrified.

I'm a killer.

80

Maddie sat up straight, slick with sweat. "Darcy!" she screamed. "Darcy, no!"

Abigail came quickly into the room, and Maddie was reminded of the last time she was awoken at that ungodly hour—the night they found Rebecca at Ravenswood.

"What is wrong with you, girl? Do you want the neighbors calling the police?" Abigail scolded.

It was just a dream. Maddie sighed, relieved.

"I'm sorry, Mom," Maddie said as she sank back against her pillows. "I just—I must have been—it was just a bad dream." *But it was so real!*

Perhaps it was just nerves because today she had planned to visit Rebecca for the first time since she'd returned to Hawthorne. Maybe the haunted look in Darcy's eyes was simply an altered memory—a memory of the night that Rebecca had slit her wrists in the madhouse of Ravenswood. Yes, revisiting Misery Island and seeing Ravenswood from a distance had brought back all of those memories, twisting them together in a horrific nightmare. Maybe facing Rebecca was a way that she could put the nightmares to rest.

80

Abigail drove to Fairview, despite Maddie's offer to play chauffeur, as she had been doing ever since her return to Hawthorne.

"I'm quite capable of driving myself, although I don't know why you want to see Rebecca now. I don't think you're at the top of her list of people she wants to see."

"And you are?" Maddie scoffed. Welcome or not, a visit to her aunt Rebecca was far past due. When they arrived at Fairview, she was slightly surprised by the doctors and nurses nodding and smiling at Abigail, as if they had seen her before.

Abigail walked straight to Rebecca's room without asking for directions, then sat to rest on the bench directly across from the room. She seemed out of breath and weary, so she nodded to Maddie to continue on into the room without her.

Maddie hesitated, and then assumed that it would be less confrontational if she went in by herself. In all this time she'd never contacted Rebecca and she felt horrible about it.

She pressed the door open and she saw Rebecca lying in bed facing out toward the bar-covered windows. It seemed that Rebecca was asleep or in a drugged state. She seemed quite similar to the time that Maddie had visited her in Ravenswood. It was like she was there, but somewhere else entirely at the same time.

"Hi, Rebecca," Maddie said quietly.

Rebecca made no movement or noise, but it sounded like her breath caught for just a moment.

"I'm home for the holidays. My mom is sick. I don't know if you knew that." She continued babbling awkwardly. The blindingly white walls felt like they were closing in on her. She wished her mother had come in. Her mother's lecturing tone would have been a welcome change from this heavy silence. "Anyway, I just came to say hi." She paused. "It's been a long time, Rebecca. I'm really sorry about the last time we saw each other. I wish it had been different."

Finally she turned toward the door, promising to come back and visit her while she was in Hawthorne. "And I haven't stopped looking for Cordelia. She's still out there. I can feel it. I can't explain how I know, but I do," Maddie offered earnestly as she reached for the long, slender door handle.

"Dead," Rebecca said softly. "She's dead."

Maddie spun around, shocked to hear Rebecca's voice, and even more shocked to hear what she said. "What do you mean she's dead, Rebecca? How do you know that about Cordelia? How did you—how could you know?"

Rebecca turned her head slowly toward Maddie, her face as pale as the antiseptically white sheets. Her voice came again, almost as a whisper through her grayish lips. "Not Cordelia."

Maddie was in shock. "What are you talking about? Rebecca, I don't understand."

"Be careful," Rebecca warned. "Or you're next." And then she shut her eyes, succumbing again to the cocktail of meds being administered into her thin arm through the IV, drop by drop by drop.

Chapter 14

FIVE OF SWORDS

Insurmountable odds; the answer lies within subtle tactics; a gloating enemy. Defeat, loss, failure, dishonor, a need to curb futile belligerence, accept the consequences.

It wasn't until she returned from the hospital and got the panicked phone call from Hannah telling her that Darcy never made it home from the party the night before, and missed the first shift of her day-care job that morning, that Maddie began to realize there may have been more to her creepy dream and Rebecca's creepy rambling. Could Rebecca have been talking about Darcy? And if so, how could she know? Horrified, Maddie wondered if Rebecca had been in contact with Cordelia and if it was in fact Cordelia who was behind the disappearance of Darcy—one of the Sisters of Misery who had treated her so terribly last year.

But Abigail had a very different take on what could have happened. It was one that was shared by the police, since they had already taken Finn and Reed into custody as "persons of interest" before Maddie had even woken that morning.

"How can they be suspects?" Maddie asked her mother anxiously over breakfast.

"How can they not? You know that everyone still thinks they had something to do with Cordelia going missing. It's not that far of a jump to suspect that they might have something to do with other missing girls."

Maddie sat across the breakfast table glaring at her mother.

"But you and I both know that they had nothing to do with Cordelia's disappearance. You know the real reason she left town." Maddie was furious with her mother. How dare she blame Reed and Finn when she knew that it was the discovery of who her real father was that made Cordelia run away, the fact that she'd been lied to and treated badly by everyone? It had nothing to do with Reed or Finn. If anything, they were the only ones in the town who were actually good to her, Maddie thought.

"Of course I know! But I'm not going to go broadcasting our family's dirty laundry just to get those two boys off the hook." She fixed the scarf on her head, and then took a long sip of coffee. "Besides, how do I really know that they didn't have something to do with it? For all I know, one of them could have caught up with her after she left here and done away with her."

"'Done away with her'? Mom, this isn't an Agatha Christie novel. People don't just go around 'doing away' with other people. And you know that neither Reed nor Finn could hurt anyone."

"How? How? How do I know this?" she asked stubbornly. "How do you know this? You don't live here anymore. You don't know what people are capable of. You don't get it anymore, do you?"

"Get what? What is there to get, Mother?" Maddie slammed her hand down on the table angrily.

"Sometimes you think you know someone. You think you know them better than anyone in the world. And then one day you wake up and find out you don't know them at all. You find out that they're sleeping with your sister, or that who you think is your father really isn't or that your cousin is really your half sister. Who knows anyone? Really? And how well do you even know yourself?"

Maddie thought back to her vision of the night on Misery Island when she had thrown the rock at Cordelia's head. Abigail was right. Maddie couldn't trust anyone. Not even herself.

෯

Darcy's lifeless body was found a few days later, caught in a jagged outcropping of rocks below—waterlogged, swollen, and battered from being bashed against the rocks by the pounding surf. Instantly, suspicions of Reed and Finn being involved increased. Especially since Darcy was found wearing Finn's leather jacket.

After Maddie heard the terrible news about Darcy, a dark feeling crept over her. She and Darcy were wearing the same dress. Perhaps Darcy wasn't the intended victim. When she had gone off by herself for those few moments, she had a curious weight of someone watching her. *If Reed and Finn hadn't come by, what would have happened? What if the person who killed Darcy really meant to kill me?*

෯

At the same time Maddie was learning about the terrible fate of her friend, across town at the police station Finn slammed his fist on the interrogation table. He knew that both he and Reed were being questioned about Darcy, and that they were both innocent. The only difference was that Reed would have a hell of a lot better defense team backing him. One that all the money in the world could buy.

"Why would I give the girl I'm planning on killing my jacket?"

"Maybe it wasn't planned?" Sully said, loving the whole act of interrogation. Finn had been through all of this last year when Cordelia took off, but this was just crazy. This was murder. "Maybe you gave her that jacket hoping for something more and when she didn't give it to you, you flipped on her."

"Yeah, I'd kill a girl over a leather jacket and holding out on me. Jesus, Sully."

"Hey, I'm just saying. Some guys snap when they don't get what they want."

"I didn't want Darcy."

"Then why did she have your jacket on?"

"She was freezing. Visibly shaking. Who came up with the brilliant idea of having a party out on an island in the middle of the harbor on one of the coldest nights of the year?"

"Oh, so you were just being a gentleman. Ain't that precious?" Sully mocked.

"I was just doing what any other guy would have done if a girl had asked him for his jacket."

"Yeah, and why am I supposed to believe that she asked you out of all of the people at the party?"

Finn shook his head. This was going nowhere. "I don't know, Sully. I guess I was one step up from the caterers. Maybe she wanted a leather jacket. Maybe I was the first person to walk by her when she realized that maybe she should have bundled up a little bit better for the Winter Ball."

"So that makes you Prince Charming, I guess," Sully said snidely.

"Yeah, I guess that makes me Prince Charming," Finn said, raising his hands in the air, giving up.

"The only difference is that Cinderella didn't end up with her head bashed in at the end of the night."

Finn put his head down on the table. When would all of this end?

∞

Maddie demanded to see Finn and Reed, but no one in the police department would let her near either of the suspects. *This is impossible!* she thought. How could anyone believe that Finn and Reed would be capable of such a crime? Murder? She knew that she wasn't the town's favorite girl at the moment, but at the very least she could serve as an alibi for Reed and Finn that night. She was with them at various points of the night, and neither one of them had acted as if he had just committed a heinous crime like murder. But then again, would anyone believe all of the things that Kate Endicott was capable of without truly knowing her?

Kate, thought Maddie. She had to be behind all of this somehow.

"Ms. Crane, I understand why you are upset by this. We are all upset. Believe me, we are going to find out who has perpetrated this hideous crime."

Maddie was talking to one of the detectives brought in from Boston to investigate the crime. It was interesting how all the stops were pulled out with Darcy, but no one did this kind of investigation when Cordelia disappeared. Then again, Hawthorne had never embraced Cordelia as one of its own.

"I was with both Reed and Finn at different points of that night. Finn actually brought me and my mother home."

"Was either man acting unusual, impulsive, out of character?"

Maddie's eyes flitted to her hands. Reed. The kiss. That was definitely impulsive. But murderous, of course not. Still . . . "No, not at all."

"Did Finn mention anything about giving an article of clothing to Darcy?"

"An article of clothing?" What kind of evidence did they have? She was so confused. "Um, no."

"Did you notice him leaving without his jacket?"

"Yes, but—"

"Did you know that Darcy was found wearing Finn's jacket?"

Her dream. It suddenly came back to her. She remembered feeling like she was having an out-of-body experience: seeing herself talking to Finn and Reed and then suddenly wondering how Finn had made it across the island so quickly. And then Darcy's face covered in blood. Was she wearing Finn's jacket? She couldn't remember. Could Finn have really been involved with Darcy's death? But why? What possible reason could he have for doing this horrible thing?

She shook her head. "I know Finn and Reed very well and I know that there is no way they could have anything to do with Darcy's death," she said firmly, pounding her hand on the table.

"That's very interesting coming from a relative of the missing girl of whom both Mr. O'Malley and Mr. Campbell are still suspects."

"They had nothing to do with Cordelia's disappearance. They loved her."

"Both of them loved her?" The detective scratched some notes in his pad. "So it could have been case of unrequited love, a jealous rivalry that turned fatal?"

"No, no, no! Cordelia isn't dead. She's just . . ." Maddie's voice trailed off. She had no idea where Cordelia was or why she hadn't come back. It had been a year and still no word from her cousin—her half sister. "She just left. But I'm sure that she would be the first one to clear Finn's and Reed's names."

"Okay, well, why don't you have Cordelia give me a call when she's ready? If she'd like to come forward and officially remove their names as suspects from her case, I'd love to be in touch with her. I think we're done here, Ms. Crane."

"Yes, definitely done," Maddie sighed. She'd love to have Cordelia come back and clear their names. If only she knew where to look for the one person who held the key to answering any of these mysteries or who could give Finn and Reed a fighting chance at getting the truth out there; the one person that Maddie was both terrified and determined to find: her sister, Cordelia.

Chapter 15

KNIGHT OF CUPS

Knight in shining armor. Change and new excitements, particularly of a romantic nature. A person who is a bringer of ideas, opportunities, and offers. A person who is amiable, intelligent, full of high principles, but a dreamer who is both artistic and refined.

"You need to get out of there," Luke instructed. There wasn't a hint of humor in his voice. She'd never heard him sound this serious before.

"And what, just leave my mother?" Maddie asked. "'Gee, sorry you have cancer, Mom, and you are just about to start your chemotherapy treatments, but there's a chance that someone got me and Darcy confused. I'm the one they really wanted to kill.'" Even as the words came out of her mouth, a chill crept down her spine. What if she was saying the truth?

"How many things have to happen to you and your family and friends for you to realize that Hawthorne, Massachusetts, is not a good place for you to be right now?" The phone was breaking up. Maddie knew that Luke was still out at sea, but she also knew that it would take very little for him to be dropped at the next port and jet over to Hawthorne to make sure she was okay, if she didn't give him the reassurance he needed. But would that be such a bad thing after all?

At the very least, she'd have someone she knew that she could trust and put the mixed-up feelings she had for Reed behind her.

But this wasn't his problem. It was hers. "I'm fine, Luke.

Really," she said in a voice that she tried to make sound convincing.

There was a long pause on his end of the line. She could hear people laughing and talking in the background. He was probably surrounded by sunshine and beautiful people without a care in the world. She ached to be with him—away from Hawthorne and all of its gloom and darkness and secrets.

"You know I could be there in a heartbeat."

"I know," she said, trying not to allow her voice to waver. She could handle this on her own. She wasn't that frightened little girl that ran away from Hawthorne months ago. "But, Luke, there is something you can do for me."

"Anything," he said firmly. He loved having the opportunity to be the knight in shining armor.

"Try to find Cordelia," she said quickly. It was like pulling off a Band-Aid. The faster she said it, the less it would sting.

"Maddie," he said, his voice thick with disappointment. "We've been over this before. Some people don't want to be found. You can't blame yourself forever about something you had no control over. Cordelia can't be found."

"This isn't about me making things right with Cordelia," she insisted. "This is about saving two people's lives. Two guys that I care about very much that are going to go down for a crime they didn't commit!"

But it was more than that. It was hard for her to explain to Luke her motivation for finding Cordelia. She was like the missing puzzle piece, the lost key, the only one who could help her make sense of these dreams that made her feel like she was going crazy. Maddie needed Cordelia to be there for Rebecca, who was utterly falling apart. And she needed support while she helped her mother in her fight against the cancer that was ravaging her body. Now that Darcy had been killed, it felt like anything was possible. And since Tess was gone, Cordelia was the only other person who could offer Maddie sage advice.

"Two guys you care about? Whoa, Crane, slow down. Didn't realize that reconnecting with old boyfriends was part of your agenda in Hawthorne."

Maddie could hear a little concern—even jealousy—in his voice.

"They're friends, Luke. Just friends," she reassured him. "But they were both suspects in Cordelia's disappearance and now with Darcy—well, let's just say that all eyes are back on them. So if you could turn your underground network of informants onto this case, maybe we could convince Cordelia to come back and clear their names."

He chuckled at the thought of him having a network of minions at his fingertips. "Well, I could make a few calls, pull some strings, call in a few favors . . ." he said slowly, thinking it through. "But the question really isn't finding Cordelia, is it? It's convincing her to go back to Hawthorne. From what you've told me about her, that's no easy task."

"She'll come," Maddie said firmly. "If she knew what was happening with Reed, with Finn, even with Rebecca, she'd come back to make things right."

Maddie wasn't really sure she believed this, but there was no other way for her to fix what was happening.

"Unless . . ." Luke paused. "Unless she's already back and responsible for some of the things that have happened."

The thought hit her like a punch in the stomach.

Cordelia already back? She'd never even considered it. What if Cordelia had been here all along? What if she was responsible for Darcy's death? What if it was her form of retribution? What if that unshakeable feeling of being watched wasn't all in her head?

"That's ridiculous," Maddie said, trying to reassure herself as much as she was trying to reassure Luke. "Now, I don't need you planting creepy things in my head. I'm dealing with enough as it is. Just do your job and track my cou—sister down, okay?"

"Aye-aye, Captain Crane," he said brightly.

Maddie could imagine the sparkle in his eyes, the way his eyes crinkled at the edges when he laughed, the sun shining down on his tousled dirty-blond hair, but she quickly shook the thought away. She wasn't going to let herself go down that path right now. For all she knew, he had been with at least a dozen wannabe models and rich girls who were smitten by Luke's boyish charms and his daddy's wallet. But then again, she hadn't exactly been devoted to Luke, she thought as she recalled her passionate kiss with Reed out on Misery Island.

"And, Maddie," he said softly. "Be careful. Please. I couldn't live with myself if anything ever happened to you."

"I will," she said.

"You know I love ya," he said cheerfully, kind of the way a buddy says it. Not the way a girl wants to hear it from the boy she's secretly been in love with.

"Yup," she said quietly.

"No, really, I do," he said sincerely. "I think about you all the time."

There was a long silence between them. Maddie didn't know what to say.

"Uh, hello? You still there?" he said nervously.

"I'm here, Luke," she said. "I'm always here for you."

He breathed a sigh of relief over the phone. "Good, let's keep it that way. Listen, I have to go. I have this very important top-secret mission I need to set into action, so I need to put the call out to all my agents. We're tracking a missing girl—a runaway."

Maddie smiled. "Yes, you should go do that. Go put those people to work. And get back to me with your results ASAP."

"Copy that," he said military-style.

"I miss you, Luke," Maddie said just before she hung up the phone.

"I'll see you soon."

As she hung up the phone, a pang of regret came across her. She knew that he had a lot of connections and that finding Cordelia shouldn't be that hard for him. But at the same time she wondered if it was right to involve him in this—involve the guy she cared about most in the world in the craziness of Hawthorne and of her own life. She felt like she was leading cattle to slaughter. Dragging him down with her wasn't going to make things better. At least if he kept a good distance from Hawthorne, then everything would be okay.

But she knew Luke. If he sensed she was in trouble, he really would be there in an instant. And then she'd never forgive herself if anything ever happened to him. She knew what Hawthorne was like to outsiders. Look at what they did to Cordelia. And now, it seemed with Darcy's murder, they were turning on themselves.

Chapter 16

EIGHT OF SWORDS

Blinded and stuck in the prison of your own making. Restrictions and limitations. Hard work reaping little reward, frustration, despair, depression. Effort being exercised in the wrong place. Moving away from a problem rather than finding the solution to it.

I'm sitting in the store laughing and talking with Rebecca. The smell of cinnamon and apple cider fills the small space within the brick walls of the store. I have an overwhelming sense to reach out and hug Rebecca, nestle my face into her long red hair, almost like she is my real mother.

We are talking for what seems like hours about all of the places Rebecca has lived, the tiny villages along the French countryside, the villas in Spain, the vineyards of Italy. The joy is dizzying as we sit across from each other, our fingers nimbly creating floral works of art, raveling and unraveling tendrils of ivy and vinca, all the time laughing about the strange characters in Rebecca's endless stories. The Gypsy woman on the bleached sands of the Côte d'Azur, who showed her how to seek fortunes from rune stones and tea leaves. The milliner on Prince Edward Island, who taught Rebecca and Cordelia about the mysterious allure of textures and fabrics; how they could create a language, an entire story, by piecing together sumptuous textiles. All of these people and places seemed oddly real, as if I'd seen them myself.

But that was impossible! I wonder where Cordelia is and whether this is a glimpse into the future or a wish of what had occurred in the past.

The front door swings open, allowing the frigid December

wind to whip through the store. The candles lit all around us flicker, almost going out and then magically relighting. I turn, expecting to see Cordelia, but I'm shocked to see the face looking back at me—someone I've never expected to come face-to-face with.

It's my own face peering back at me. Not a reflection from a mirror, not a hallucination. It is Maddie Crane. I look down and notice my long tendrils of red hair. I have become Cordelia!

॰

Maddie sat up in bed with a start, trying to catch her breath and figure out the meaning of this unusual dream. Thinking back to the way that Rebecca was acting toward her, she felt it was as if she really were Cordelia. Or at least witnessing life through Cordelia's eyes. Maddie realized that this must be the psychic ability that Tess had told her she might have. The ability to look into the past through someone else's eyes. To wander around in other people's dreams and thoughts. It was so real, so accurate. She could feel, smell, hear everything from the store. And she even remembered that day of walking in and seeing Cordelia and Rebecca together. But she'd never witnessed it from Cordelia's point of view, never witnessed that conversation. Could Cordelia be trying to tell her something? Was there something in that store that would lead Maddie to wherever Cordelia was now?

If there ever was a time when she needed to find her cousin, it was definitely now. With Finn and Reed both in custody over Darcy's murder, and with the charges that they had something to do with Cordelia's disappearance, Maddie knew she had to track Cordelia down and make her come back to prove their innocence.

The light of dawn had yet to creep across Hawthorne when Maddie was pulled from her dream. There was no way she could get back to sleep. She decided that any clues as to Cordelia's whereabouts must be locked within their old store, Rebecca's Closet. The place had been completely trashed by Rebecca prior to her hospitalization and the police had combed through the wreckage, but Maddie knew that something there would lead her to Cordelia.

Maddie snuck out of the house, careful not to awaken Abigail in the early morning hours. She didn't need to be hassled about where she was going. Not now.

The plywood across the door came off easily. Maddie still had the key from when she used to work there after school and on weekends. Everything remained in shambles—just as they had found it right after Rebecca had destroyed the store.

Rebecca's voice still rang loudly in her ears, "You, you, you, *you!*" For a moment, Maddie could almost feel the tender touch of Tess as she led her out of the store last year. *Tess.* Maddie still hadn't gotten over losing her beloved grandmother. It was times like these when she missed her most. Times when she could ask her grandmother what to do, what was going on with her strange dreams. Was she really coming into her psychic powers? She couldn't talk to her mother about these things. Nor could she talk to Rebecca or Cordelia. She had to figure this out on her own. All alone.

Maddie picked her way across the store. The once-gleaming hardwood floors were now covered in dirt and filth; a broken window had allowed animals in to nest in the store. There was trash piled high and broken pieces of glass strewn about. A rotting smell pervaded the small space and it was so strong it almost choked Maddie. She felt dizzy for a moment, reaching out to balance herself and avoid falling down onto the dirt-covered floor.

A sudden flicker blinded Maddie for a moment, as if a flashlight were shone in her eyes. The place had a dreamlike quality to it, everything seemed hazy, but Maddie assumed that was because of all the dust and the bizarre actions she'd witnessed here a year ago, prior to Rebecca being committed. She could still hear the echoing blame in Rebecca's voice as she screamed in utter torment. The light in the back of the store went from dark to a soft orangey glow. Dizzy from the change in her vision, Maddie stumbled backward, knocking over an apothecary jar.

"Easy there." The voice came from the back room. She inhaled quickly, stunned by the sound. "Don't go destroying the place."

Rebecca!

How is this possible? Maddie raced into the back room of the store only to find it in picture-perfect condition. Exactly the way it had been before Cordelia disappeared, before all of the craziness had taken over their lives.

"Rebecca?" Maddie said in a strangled voice.

"Ummm, I thought we agreed that you had to wait until you were at least eighteen to call me that," Rebecca said, laughing and gathering Maddie into a hug.

"We did?" Maddie looked around anxiously. What happened? She'd heard about those rips in time and space continuum, but they couldn't possibly be real, could they?

"Let's just stick with 'Mom' for a few more months, okay? I know you're all grown up now, being sixteen and all, but could you still pretend to be my little girl, for just a little while?"

Rebecca had clearly lost her mind. But Maddie knew that already. The question was: how did she escape from Fairview? Was this going to be a repeat of that horrible scene at Ravenswood? And yet Rebecca seemed eerily calm—like the old Rebecca. The Rebecca before . . .

"I—I—where? How?" Maddie muttered incoherently, still looking around the store, trying to figure out what was going on.

"Your journal? Is that what you're looking for? You keep moving it so that I can't find it, not that I'd go looking in my daughter's private diary. I know, I know. It's not your real diary, just a journal to keep you busy while you're bored in the store. I don't blame you," Rebecca said, laughing. Maddie ached when she heard that beautiful laugh. It had been so long since she'd heard it. It was like the tinkling of bells. "I get bored out of my mind when you and Maddie are in school and I have no one to talk to."

Maddie?

Oh my God, Maddie thought. *She thinks I'm Cordelia. She's escaped from the hospital and returned to this store and cleaned it up like nothing ever happened. She's just been here waiting for Cordelia to come home, as if Cordelia was just at school and hasn't been missing for the past year.*

It was starting to make sense. Rebecca had just erased the past horrific months and had gone back to a happier time and place. A time when Cordelia was living in Hawthorne and they were one big happy family.

Maddie knew from her experience at Ravenswood that she needed to be careful with Rebecca, especially in her current mental state. She shivered, not just because of the cold December air, but because of the state of mind—and dress—that Rebecca was in. Her hair was in disarray, her clothes stained, her face gaunt. She didn't look as awful as she had that night in Ravenswood, but she definitely fit the description of a madwoman.

"Yes, my journal. Where is it again?" Maddie asked slowly, as if speaking to a child.

"Well, not that I was spying on you," Rebecca teased. "But I think I saw you over by the loose bricks on the back wall." She waited a beat. "Ahhh, you didn't think I knew about the loose bricks, did you? A perfect hiding place, I must say. I came across it when I was trying to find a good spot to hide some cash when the safe was broken. But you and your beautiful leather journal had gotten there first. Don't worry, I didn't read it. I'm not a snoop like your aunt Abigail."

As Rebecca spoke, her eyes glazed over as if she were on some kind of drug, Maddie started to feel dizzy, like the world had been turned upside down.

"Are you okay? Let me get you some honeysuckle ginger tea. Sit down, baby. Mama will take care of you," Rebecca said as she turned and started toward the front of the store.

"No!" Maddie called out. She knew that if Rebecca saw the condition of the front of the store, it would snap her back into reality and cause her to break down again. Maddie couldn't handle that by herself.

Rebecca stopped abruptly in her tracks and turned. "Honey, I'll be just a minute."

"You don't want to go in there. It's a mess. Just, just wait here while I pick it up," Maddie said, trying to push past her aunt.

"Now, don't tell me that you're becoming a clean freak like your aunt Abigail. Ugh!" Rebecca said as she continued into the front of the store.

Maddie knew she needed to get out of there fast. As soon as Rebecca saw the front of the store, she'd lose her mind all over again and who knows what she was capable of doing?

Maddie headed for the back door, but before she left, she noticed a loose brick in the wall. The journal!

Maybe there was something written in there that would give Maddie a clue to where Cordelia had gone. The original journal she found in the house had given her some information last year, but nothing definitive. Maybe this one held the answers she desperately needed. Ripping the brick from the wall, Maddie reached in and grabbed hold of the leather-bound journal. She only had a few minutes before Rebecca discovered that she had been living in a dreamworld and would completely fly off the handle. Maddie was racing to the back door when a voice called out to her.

"Where do you think you're going?"

Rebecca stood at the entrance to the back room with a

steaming mug of tea in her hand. She seemed completely oblivious of the state of disrepair that the front of the store was in. So oblivious, in fact, that she was able to make a cup of tea. How was that even possible? Maddie turned to the door and tried to pull on the handle, but it felt like it had been welded shut.

"You're not going anywhere, young lady, not when you're feeling dizzy and I need someone to help out with the store."

With the journal in hand, Maddie knew she had to push past Rebecca and get out the front door. Once she was safely outside, she could call the police or the hospital and let them handle getting Rebecca back to Fairview.

"I just—I needed some air," Maddie said quickly, her eyes darting left and right looking for a way past Rebecca in the narrow back room of the store.

"Well, why didn't you just say—" Rebecca stopped abruptly as Maddie ran past her, taking her by surprise. "Cordelia, no!"

Just as Rebecca shouted, Maddie tripped and fell to the floor. And then everything went black.

හ

Maddie opened her eyes to discover that she was surrounded by darkness. She tried to sit up and get her bearings. She was surrounded by trash, dirt, and debris. Shaking, she stood up and felt her way along the walls. The brick walls told her that she was still in the store. If she had been shoved into the basement, the walls would have been stone. It wasn't until she'd taken a few steps toward the early light of dawn streaming through the window in the next room that she realized where she was.

She was in the back room of Rebecca's Closet. And it looked exactly the same as the front of the store. Rebecca was nowhere to be found. Maddie raced over to where she had been standing in her dream, tripping over overturned pieces of furniture and moldy boxes. She ran straight to find the loose stone from her dreams and clawed at it, her finger-nails digging into mortar. She wiggled the brick until it came free. Slowly she reached inside the wall, tentatively moving her hand around until she found it. A leather journal had been shoved back into a crevice. Another one of Cordelia's journals. Maddie was elated. Perhaps this would give her more insight into where Cordelia had gone. And why she had disappeared for so long.

She then realized that Rebecca had never been there. It was all in her own mind. A sort of waking dream, different from others she'd had. She'd never witnessed this interaction be-tween Cordelia and Rebecca. But something allowed her to visit a time and place that she was never a part of. Her dreams were becoming so real that she could hardly tell where her dreams stopped and reality began. This gift she was coming into was more powerful than she could ever have imagined. The only person who could understand what she was going through now that Tess was gone and Rebecca was practically comatose was Cordelia. All roads seemed to lead to finding Cordelia, bringing her home, and making everything right again. For everyone.

∞

Abigail was fuming when Maddie slipped into the house that morning. Maddie misjudged the effects of the first course of chemotherapy and radiation treatment that her mother had undergone earlier this week. At first, it knocked her out, al-lowing Maddie the freedom of coming and going as she pleased. But now her body seemed to be stronger, and she was much more alert and aware of what was going on.

"Look at you," Abigail scoffed when Maddie softly padded into the hallway. Abigail turned the light on in the living room where she'd obviously been sitting and waiting for Maddie's return. "You're absolutely filthy! Where have you been? Have you been out all night? I've been out of my mind with worry. How dare you disappear while I'm going through my treatments! How dare you make me worry about you, especially with this Darcy situation!"

Situation. Only Abigail Crane could call someone getting killed a "situation."

"I'm sorry, Mother," Maddie said, awkwardly brushing the loose dirt and grime from her clothes. "I was at Rebecca's old store—I found this journal. I think it might be Cordelia's."

"Well, she's quite the writer, isn't she? You'd think she was trying to get her diaries published with all of that writing and waxing poetic about all her true loves and losses in this town. She definitely got that writing kick from your father—" She stopped abruptly, not wanting to go into detail about Malcolm Crane. But this was the first time she'd ever brought up the fact that Cordelia and Maddie shared a father, and Maddie didn't want to let this opportunity slip by.

"Was he a writer? My dad, I mean?" Maddie walked tenderly toward her mother, hoping that her current weakened state would soften her, would allow her to give up some of the secrets she'd spent a lifetime guarding.

Abigail snorted. "He certainly thought he was. Thought he was the next Hemingway, the next Vonnegut, the next Fitzgerald. The only thing that made him similar to those writers was his love of drinking. That's where the similarities ended. So, when he left to teach—"

"He's a writing teacher?" Maddie remembered hearing that her father taught a class up in Maine at a community college, but she had never imagined that her father—the bullish man from her nightmares, the one who was prone to smashing anything and everything that got in his way—could have the patience to be a writing teacher. She always pictured him as a shop teacher, a gym coach, anything but a professor of the arts.

"He wasn't when he lived here. He thought he was a writer. Lived off his family's fortune, until it dried out. Then when he had to get a real job, make an honest living, that's when he left us all behind. Moved up to Maine to teach writing. Last I heard he was at some community college as a writing professor. Probably taking up with half the girls and teachers on campus by now."

Maddie sat quietly, hoping to learn more about her wayward father.

"That's why I've been so hard on you taking up with Reed Campbell and Finnegan O'Malley. Nothing good can come from getting involved with the men of Hawthorne. I should have listened to Tess when she told me that years ago. But I was too stubborn—too sure of myself. You don't want to end up alone like me, do you?"

This was the first time Maddie had ever remembered Abigail showing any regrets about her life. She'd grown up believing that Abigail would never accept her or love her unless she secured her social status in Hawthorne. And here she was finally opening up to her daughter—something Maddie had waited her whole life for. "Believe me, Mom, the last thing I want to do is get involved with a guy from Hawthorne," Maddie said, laughing and trying to reassure her that she was here for one reason only—to take care of Abigail "I don't need any more strings tying me to this place."

Maddie meant it as a lighthearted comment, but it obviously struck Abigail the wrong way. The wall that had briefly come down between them quickly rose back up.

Abigail set her mouth in a grim line. "I guess, then, that I'm one of those bothersome strings keeping you attached to this godforsaken place. I suppose you'll be pleased when this string has finally been snapped." With that, she turned on her heel and stormed up the stairs.

I can't win. Maddie sighed. *I just can't win.*

Chapter 17

THE MOON

Nothing is exactly as it seems and emotions may be running high. Mystery, secrets, and a time of confusion. Visions and illusions, madness, genius, and poetry. It warns that there might be hidden enemies, tricks, and falsehoods. This is a card of great creativity, of powerful magic, primal feelings and intuition, dreams and nightmare. Trust your intuition. Prepare for an emotional and mental roller-coaster ride. Be open to inspiration from the unconscious, from dreams.

October 15
Dear Diary,

The October wind whisks along the narrow tree-lined streets, bringing a chill that foretells of the brutal winter ahead. The historic brick buildings huddle together finding strength in their unity. A strength that has pulled them through many rough winters for hundreds of years.

The trees, now stained many different shades of rust, shiver and sigh. Cars rumble past on brick-paved streets. Women and men stroll throughout the winding roads of Hawthorne. They walk slowly, taking in all of the scenery and history. Admiring the architecture of Samuel McIntyre and the stately mansions of the sea captains. They delight in the rustic atmosphere of the quaint streets that evoke images of early New England and the settlers. But in their faces it is clear that they want something more; something other than the history and the heritage. They crave something darker. An evil thing that creeps along the cobblestones at midnight when the people are tucked safely in their beds. Something that slithers like a serpentine up the trees with chameleon leaves and wails, screeching along with the howling winds. An eerie presence that dwells in dusty corners and hides among the shadows. A supernatural being that lurks behind craggy tombstones of the old burial hill. Ghosts. Magic. Vampires. Witchcraft.

The history of Salem evokes tales of mass hysteria and witch hangings and often overshadows the normal humdrum of everyday life. Hawthorne is very different. People come here to Hawthorne seeking answers. They search our faces, as if we hold ancient secrets. They wonder what has been experienced here; do things really go bump in the night? The questions are always the same when they enter my shop nestled on a quaint cobblestone street.

"Do you see witches?"

The answer to all of them is always the same. Yes. Witches are not an uncommon thing here. Definitely not something to be frightened by. I explain to them that there are many stores owned by witches in Salem that sell wands and spells, pentacles and crystals.

"One town over," I'd say. "And they will read your cards or perhaps photograph your aura.

"It's a religion," I tell them, as those who wear the pentacle have so often reminded me. "Wicca, to be exact."

I often smile at their disappointment that they do not attempt to hide.

They want more. They want the unexplained. They don't want the incense and the plastic souvenirs. Many have traveled far to experience the mysteries that New England has to offer.

I tell them to head back into Salem, to the Witch Museum in the old church or to the Witch Memorial, which lies adjacent to the old burial ground. They often sigh, grasp their hot mulled cider, and head back out in search of the red-lined Heritage Trail.

I sit in our small store housed in a brick building two centuries old and watch the tourists come in every morning eager and anxious. Then by nightfall they leave disheartened, clutching their plastic bags filled with trinkets and souvenirs. Some have their palms read, and others have bought a beautiful herbal pillow adorned with pictures of fairies or a floral creation from our store. But most are disappointed about not witnessing something eerie or unearthly. I smile as I see their faces, their mouths set in a grim line as they scurry by the arched windows, wistfully anticipating a ghoul to jump out from around an old wrought-iron fence. There is no evil presence here, they think angrily, wishing they had spent their vacation money more wisely.

They are wrong.

As I sit in this tranquil store surrounded by lavish gifts, flowers, and exquisite treasures from travels all over the world, I know of the evil and darkness and sinister tales that are just below the surface of everyday life in this town. Nobody knew how thin the veil between good and evil was in Hawthorne. That is, until I came to town.

છ

Maddie hid the journal under her pillow right before she went to bed that night. There was something in it that left her with a nagging feeling—something was unsettling about the entry. The entry was dated before the night out on Misery, so what evil events was Cordelia privy to? And the tone of the entry didn't seem like someone who was fearful or hated the town, but rather someone who had come to love it. Perhaps there was a way to convince Cordelia to return—come back to a place that so intrigued her and made her feel at home. And yet she knew from the dealings with her father that once someone left Hawthorne, it would take a miracle to bring them back. *My father,* she thought. And then Maddie was suddenly struck by inspiration. She sat up in bed and said, "Our father."

Of course! That's where Cordelia would go! She would go and confront Malcolm Crane. Confront the person who was responsible for this mess. It was all making sense now.

But how would she track him down? Contact every college in the state of Maine with a writing program? Look him up on the Internet? If he was anything like most people in Hawthorne, he would never have a published number or be easily found. Like Reed had told her out on his boat last year, some people just don't want to be found.

Lying back in the darkness, Maddie became overwhelmed with the daunting task ahead, but was somewhat relieved that she finally had a lead, a direction to point Luke in. It would be a lot easier to have him track down her wayward father than to find her will-o'-the-wisp half sister!

But Maddie also realized that if she didn't get Cordelia to return to Hawthorne, all the men in their lives, Finn, Reed, and even Malcolm Crane, were at stake. She had to figure out where to begin. And how to convince Cordelia to return. She knew that both of those were no easy task and could definitely be dangerous.

For everyone.

"Professor Crane, I have a call for you on line four," the secretary's voice buzzed over the speaker.

Malcolm Crane looked wearily at the stack of papers that needed to be graded and then sighed, "Put it through, Alice."

He was tired of dealing with other parents' children. Teenagers that didn't respect him, their parents, or each other. It was making him feel that restless urge to move forward—just to pick up and leave it all behind. It was so much easier during his youth. But now, now he had responsibilities, he had ties to a community, he had a young child. But none of that ever mattered to him before. Why should it matter now?

It wasn't a parent. It was a voice that he hadn't heard in many years. He listened for a long time as the person on the other end of the line explained what was going on. How his life was in danger, as well as everyone else in his family. Not his current family—the one he'd left a long time ago. It occurred to him that he hadn't disappeared unscathed. A person's past is always right around the corner, ready to pounce like a feral cat the moment you let your guard down. He always knew that it wasn't a question of if, but a question of when.

"What can I do?" he asked calmly.

The answer seemed to disturb him. He reluctantly agreed. After he replaced the handset, he took a deep breath.

He buzzed his secretary. "Alice, cancel my appointments this week."

He was going someplace he thought he'd never in a million years go back to: Hawthorne, Massachusetts.

It was time to finally put old ghosts to rest.

Chapter 18

THE QUEEN OF CUPS

A woman who is highly imaginative and artistically gifted, affectionate, and romantic in outlook, and creates an otherworldly atmosphere around herself. A woman who lacks common sense, but is highly intuitive and sometimes psychic and dreamy. Atmospheres, other people, and events can easily influence her.

Cordelia stopped at the Lyceum in Salem on her way back to Hawthorne. Reed had told her once about all the famous writers who had done readings there throughout the years, but what really drew her to the infamous restaurant was the legend of Bridget Bishop—the first woman in Salem wrongly accused and hanged for being a witch. She was rumored to haunt the place since it was on the site of her apple orchards. Some even said that the Lyceum was built on the actual footprint of Bridget's tavern. And from that site she was dragged through the streets of Salem, shrieking and proclaiming her innocence.

In the summer and fall, acting companies reenacted this scene over and over, but Cordelia preferred to be in the presence of the real Bridget Bishop—not the teenager dressed up in seventeenth-century clothing, sneaking cigarettes in between showtimes.

The first time Cordelia saw the ghost was when Rebecca had taken her there for lunch one afternoon not long after they moved to Hawthorne. She hadn't yet heard about the hauntings, but on her way to the ladies' room, she noticed a woman motioning for her to follow up the narrow staircase. Cordelia remembered rolling her eyes and dutifully following the woman dressed in period costume. She had heard stories of the crazies in Salem who liked to live as if it were still olden times. This was probably some new interactive play that they were trying out at the restaurant—similar to those murder mystery dinners offered at places in Boston.

Cordelia followed the woman up two narrow flights of stairs and when they finally got up to the function room, Cordelia was slightly taken aback as the woman continued up to the door and walked right through it, disappearing like a shadow into the mist. When she entered the function room, she noticed a bartender with bottled blond hair setting up. The bartender seemed uneasy and jumped at the first sight of Cordelia. The woman looked like she'd literally seen a ghost.

"Can I help you?" she asked Cordelia.

"I was . . . there was a woman—in clothes, old clothes. She wanted me to follow . . . she was dressed—"

"In old-fashioned clothing, right? That was our resident ghost, Bridget Bishop. She likes to play around with people who have the gift."

"Gift?" Cordelia said awkwardly, looking around the room with the vaulted ceilings and the staircase that seemed to wind its way up into nowhere.

"The gift of seeing what most people can't," the woman said wryly. "Ain't it a great gift to have?" She shook her head and continued drying glasses and hanging them up on the overhead rack.

Cordelia was used to people in Salem playing up their "Haunted Happenings," but there was no sense of playfulness in this woman's voice, only a slight trembling of fear.

∞

After receiving the tarot card and the strange dreams she'd been having about Maddie (almost as though they were communicating), Cordelia knew she should return to Hawthorne.

But it was only after reading the piece in the *Hawthorne Gazette* that she realized how important it was for her to return. She knew she'd have a lot of explaining to do, and possibly even be punished for wasting the town's time and money spent looking for her. But she knew that she could never move forward in her life without correcting her wrongs. How could she blame others for not taking responsibility for their actions when she was just as guilty?

She sat down at the bar, paying little attention to the early signs of Christmas decorations surrounding her. Holidays meant little to her these days. Just another way of marking the passage of time.

"Don't even think of getting served here, young lady," the surly barmaid chuckled as she washed out some glasses. "I could tell that you were underage the minute you walked in the door."

"Just some passion fruit tea, please," Cordelia said quietly.

"Passion fruit tea?" the woman laughed, saying it loudly so that the other patrons could roll their eyes along with her. "Does this look like an herbal teahouse to you?"

Cordelia looked around the beautiful bar and restaurant. She could see the ghosts of the past lingering in corners, hidden from most people's eyes. They interacting with each other as they had in their past lives, unaware of the real, live people that moved about the historic restaurant.

"I suppose not," Cordelia said quietly. "Just something warm, please."

The woman's eyes softened. She noticed that Cordelia was dressed inappropriately for the nor'easter that had come unexpectedly off the coast.

"How 'bout a hot chocolate . . . on the house?" the woman offered, winking. Then she cocked her head to the side, looking at Cordelia as if recalling an old friend. "You look familiar. Do I know you?"

Cordelia allowed her hair to slip down like a veil shielding her face. She'd long stopped dying her hair and the natural red curls were destined to call attention to her. She had just hoped she'd have a little more time of anonymity before people started to recognize her. "I—um—used to come in here a while back with my mom."

Just as the bartender started to question Cordelia further, one of the burly men at the bar yelled out, "Holy shit!"

Everyone's attention was immediately directed toward the television that hung over the bar. A news anchor was standing in front of what appeared to be a mountain of fire. The words HAWTHORNE, MASSACHUSETTS ran in the bar underneath the reporter.

"Turn it up," a booming voice called from the back of the bar.

"... we're not exactly sure how or when this five-alarm fire broke out at Ravenswood, but fire crews from four neighboring towns are desperately trying to get it under control, especially due to the close proximity to the town of Hawthorne. Residents of Hawthorne are not being asked to vacate the premises yet, but if the fire isn't contained soon, they may be encouraged to seek shelter until the fire is under control."

The news camera panned up and a huge blaze coming from four of the new buildings, almost as if they were synchronized, filled the screen. The original building seemed unaffected by the raging fire. It seemed to sit quietly in a gentle repose, simply watching the mass destruction surrounding it.

The news reporter seemed just as shocked when questioned by the anchors. The blond anchor asked, "Have they determined a cause for the fires? Isn't it strange that the four newer buildings are affected, while the original building of Ravenswood Asylum seems to be largely unaffected?"

The reporter held his finger in his ear and nodded. "Yes, it's an unusual coincidence—perhaps too unusual—that the four new buildings, which as you know have been at the center of a large controversial fight among residents of Hawthorne and the Hawthorne Historical Society, are the only buildings affected at this point." He turned back to look at the raging inferno and pointed at the old building. "As you can see, the original Ravenswood building is not affected at all. There doesn't appear to be any sign of fire within the main building, which is strange on many levels."

The blond anchor perked up. "Why is that?"

The reporter nodded again, finger still stuck in his ear. "Well, I'm being told that there is no electrical wiring in the new buildings at this point and the only way that this type of fire could have broken out on such a large scale is by some form of arson. And the fact that the main building escaped the fire is a mystery to us all."

All of a sudden, a woman came up behind the newsman, incoherently babbling. The woman was familiar, but looked as if she'd aged considerably. This couldn't be . . . Cordelia almost jumped out of her chair. Was that her mother? If it was, then she was a shadow of her former self. The woman on the television screen had hollow, lifeless eyes, a gaunt face, and a dazed expression. It was like the Rebecca she had grown up with had been replaced by this changeling of a woman.

"Yes, I'm now speaking with one of the former residents of Ravenswood—a former patient—she seems to have a theory on what caused the fire," the reporter said as he tried to keep his professionalism intact as the seemingly crazy woman continued her rant.

"It's the curse. This is hallowed land! The spirits, they're speaking to me and they are saying that they didn't want this place to be built upon. This is where many women, many souls lost their lives during the witch trials. They are stuck. They—they do not want this to be a hotel. This is their home, their sanctuary, their resting place."

Just then a woman came over and gently nudged Rebecca

away from the camera, apologizing to the reporter. But Rebecca was determined to communicate with the reporter. She clung to his arm, desperate to tell him something. "Michael, your great-grandmother Ruth wants you to know that this is not her fault. She is at rest here, but she didn't cause this! It's the Endicott—"

The woman quickly pulled Rebecca away from the reporter. He stared openmouthed at the place where Rebecca had stood and there was silence, except for the sounds of the raging inferno behind him and the rush of authorities trying to contain the situation.

"How could she know that—?" the reporter asked, aghast, when they suddenly cut back to the newsroom.

The anchors laughed stiffly and then offered, "Well, we can see that this tragic event is affecting everyone in many different ways."

The male anchor turned to his counterpart and said, "You know, there are many superstitions tied to Ravenswood, so maybe this will just add to the growing curiosity over the place."

The blonde laughed and said, "Well, this is a story better suited for Halloween, don't you think, Ron? And I suspect that plans for the Endicott Hotel will be put on hold for a while. Just another interesting chapter in the Ravenswood saga."

Ron regained his news anchor voice and said, "News Center Six will continue to keep you up to date on this developing story. When we come back Bill Baxton will be talking about how the Celtics are doing so far this season."

"And we'll have some extra tips for how to keep your cash in your wallet this Christmas season."

The two anchors continued their banter and the program cut to a commercial. Total silence had come over the bar.

"Christ almighty," Cordelia heard someone behind her say. She wasn't sure what was bothering her most. The sight of

Ravenswood being engulfed in flames, or the sight of her mother, looking frail and crazed, sapped of her former beauty and energy. Cordelia shot out of her chair and ran out into the cold winter night. She had to find Rebecca. And she had to make sure—at least for herself—that Rebecca had nothing to do with the fire that was threatening to destroy Ravenswood and everything surrounding it.

Chapter 19

SIX OF WANDS

A conqueror returns. The people walk beside him and celebrate his victory. Leadership and enterprise have been combined. This is success and advancement through labor. This is also a reminder to persevere in spite of what you may have to endure.

The fire raged through four of the new towers built at Ravenswood, the first construction sites of the Endicott Hotel. Supernatural occurrences were commonplace at Ravenswood according to local lore. Rumors of unquiet spirits angered by the new construction led people to believe that the fires that no one could trace to a source, in buildings that hadn't even been wired for electricity yet, were supernatural warnings. Townspeople speculated that the grounds filled with restless spirits wouldn't accept a building by the Endicott family—a family that had ancestral ties to the witch hangings that had occurred there centuries ago.

Despite the fact that Finn had been unable to stop the building of the hotel and that the Endicotts had swayed the state in their favor, this new setback had many people in town questioning whether or not it was a good idea to move forward with the project. Despite stipulations by the historical society that the sixteenth-century wall and fortress were to be preserved and remain intact during renovations for the luxury hotel, the Endicotts' decision to tear down the wall supposedly angered the spirits of the Pickering sisters and had set forth the curse on the town. And now Rebecca seemed to be the spokesperson for the supernatural forces that had been unleashed on Hawthorne.

Abigail muttered, "Now she's gone and made things even worse. I've always told her not to play with fire—but I never thought she'd literally do it."

"Mom," Maddie scolded. "You should be more concerned with *how* she got out than the fact that she got onto the news. If she hadn't turned up on television, we may never have known that she got out of Fairview in the first place."

"And that's a bad thing?"

"Mom, please," Maddie said, trying to reason with her. "You know that there is no possible way that Aunt Rebecca could have started those fires. She's so frail and weak, she wouldn't have it in her."

"That's not what I've heard."

"What are you talking about?" The phone rang again. Maddie checked the caller ID and it was a news station. She hit the Ignore button.

"Well, I'm not the terrible sister that you seem to think I am. I actually have been going to visit her when I go in for my chemotherapy treatments."

"Mom!" Maddie said in an elated tone. It was so surprising that her mother would take the time to visit Rebecca, especially after everything that had happened.

"Don't *Mom* me!" Abigail scolded, seemingly uncomfortable with the approval in Maddie's voice. "Fairview is connected with the hospital where I get my treatments, so I figured, why not?"

"How do you think she got out?" Maddie asked.

"Probably one of her groupies let her out," Abigail huffed.

"Groupies?" Now Maddie was really confused.

"I don't know what you call them. Fans? Disciples? Whatever. Ever since Rebecca came out of the coma, people think she's some sort of sage or fortune-teller or healer."

Maddie asked earnestly, "Why haven't you told me any of this?"

Just then, Abigail Crane did something that utterly shocked Maddie. She started to cry. "Mom, what?"

Abigail pulled the scarf off her head to reveal fluffy brown hair, like downy duck fuzz on top of her head. "I stopped the chemo after the first course of treatment. I just couldn't handle it. It affected me worse than anyone ever expected. My hair was going, my appetite gone. You've been running around so much that you haven't even noticed how quickly it sickened me. But I didn't want to burden you with this. I—I thought I could handle it myself. Then I continued visiting Rebecca. She told me that she could see the cancer. She could actually see it!"

Maddie felt the guilt creeping in. She was so preoccupied with the drama of adjusting to life back in Hawthorne that she'd nearly forgotten her mother was going through her own private hell.

"She started telling me what to do: drink different herbal mixtures, carry different stones, go to meditate in different areas near the ocean. Ridiculous things, but what other choice did I have? The doctors told me to start putting my affairs in order and that they would 'make me comfortable' when the time came. Rebecca would hold my hand and say things and . . ." She paused as if she were embarrassed to say the words. ". . . talk to my body. She was actually talking to the cancer cells. That's what she said anyway. Until one day, she told me it was gone."

Maddie opened her eyes, wide with shock.

"Of course, I didn't believe her. But then I started hearing stories from the nurses who worked with her, saying that she was helping them cure all sorts of ailments. They were bringing other patients in to talk to her and spend time with her and their diseases just seemed to disappear."

Abigail continued as Maddie sat and stared, eyes wide and mouth open. She ignored the incessant ringing of the phones.

"One woman who was diagnosed with early-onset Alzheimer's had everything just come back. I mean, everything! She asked to see her husband, her kids, and I was there for the reunion. It was incredible. It was . . . magic."

"So, what about you?" Maddie asked, wiping the tears from her eyes.

"Well, I wasn't going to take my sister's word for it that she can cure me, that's for sure. So I went back to my oncologist and they—they said they'd never seen anyone go into remission so quickly. They didn't understand it. Nothing had worked on me. Not the chemo, not the radiation, nothing! But, somehow . . . it's gone!" Abigail burst into tears and fell into Maddie's lap, soaking her jeans with her tears.

Maddie stroked her mother's newly grown hair, soft as tufts of cotton, and her own tears dropped down upon her mother. Her mother, who was no longer sick, no longer cancer-ridden. Her mother, who was healed.

℘

Cordelia let the phone ring and ring and ring, but there was no answer at Mariner's Way. She wondered if they had gone out looking for Rebecca after watching the news. Cordelia knew where her mother would go if given the opportunity. She just didn't want to face her alone. With Maddie by her side, it would be easier. She hailed a cab and headed out of Salem and back to Hawthorne. Back to where it all began. And where it would ultimately end.

℘

Cordelia picked her way down the snow-covered path. As she moved farther into the woods, the small amount of light left in the cool wintry air had been squeezed out from the branches overhead. The clean scent of pine and snow filled her senses. She clutched a bag of rosemary and quartz crystals to give her strength and protect her from danger.

As Cordelia wandered deeper and deeper into the woods, she marveled at how something as innocuous as a grouping of trees and brush could evoke such feelings of caution and mystery. The branches reached over her head, spreading their limbs and shutting out any stubborn ray of light. It was as if all color had been blighted from the earth and all that remained were different shades of brown and black and white. The sounds from the outside world disappeared and were replaced by the whispers and licks of air rushing through the trees, distant winter birds calling out to each other, as though they were chiding her for trespassing. Soon she would be home.

She couldn't be sure if Maddie was really coming through to her in her dreams. Could it be possible that Maddie had acquired this talent while Cordelia was gone? What else had changed?

When Maddie finally answered the phone, she sounded different. Hesitant, almost. It shouldn't have been a surprise to Cordelia. She *did* run off for an entire year without giving them any clue as to where she was or if she was all right. But it seemed more than that. Maddie sounded a little angry. Wounded. But at the same time, she was her family. Her sister! They shared a father. The man that she wanted to make pay for all of the deception and lies and torture he'd put all the women in his life through. But first things first. Perhaps Maddie would help her with her quest to make Malcolm Crane pay for his mistakes.

Yet why should she hold this man who didn't even know her responsible for his mistakes, when she had made plenty enough of her own? She wasn't there for her own mother—practically drove her insane with her foolish running away. And Tess . . .

Tess, she thought sadly. How could she not have known that Tess had passed away? She thought about that terrible night—the night that was recapped in the newspaper. The night at Ravenswood when her mother tried to take her own life. The night that everyone she cared about: Maddie, Finn, Rebecca, Tess, all could have been killed. The night that claimed Tess's life. Cordelia believed that Tess knew all along what was happening at Ravenswood and that she traded her life to save Rebecca's. It was the only thing that made sense.

Cordelia started to cry, coming to the realization that all of this could have been caused by her leaving. Everything. Tess's dementia and death, Rebecca's attempted suicide, Finn and Reed thought of as suspects in not only her disappearance, but now in the murder of Darcy Willett.

And what had it been for? Because she was angry that she'd been lied to for so many years about her father. Because she was treated so horribly by the Sisters of Misery, as well as Abigail. Because she felt like she was trapped in a town that despised her.

Her boots crunched through the fallen leaves, patches of ice and snow, and underbrush. Could Maddie really be waiting for her out there? She had imagined this reunion so many times in her mind, ever since she'd taken off to Maine. Once she came upon her cousin—or half sister or whatever she was to her now—Cordelia would jump out from behind a rotted stump, a crown of wildflowers in her hair, lips dyed bright red from fallen berries, yelling, "Aha! Who dares awaken Queen Mab from her sweet fairy dreams?"

They would then fall into the softness that only forest floors possess, laughing and giggling until the last few rays of sun seeped into the woods and the mosquitoes hummed greedily in their ears. Then they would trudge home along the path and Maddie would tell Cordelia of all the trouble she had caused, and what a big deal was made of her vanishing act.

Cordelia would smile wickedly, all the while concocting a remarkable tale of her adventures. She was taken away by fairies that were plotting to return a changeling to her mother instead—an evil being who resembled Cordelia, but was actually sent to do evil bidding. Or perhaps a roving band of robbers took her into captivity, forcing her to pilfer in exchange for her life. Or instead, she might say that modern day pirates nabbed her while she was collecting sea glass along the glossy black harbor rocks.

Cordelia heard rustling to her left, but realized it was only two chipmunks playing tag, scuttling from under a rock and up into a birch tree. Cordelia insisted that the stories she told Maddie about encounters with fairies and elves, spirits and magic were true, even if Maddie refused to believe. For some reason it was of imminent importance that Cordelia open Maddie's mind to the impossible. She had grown up in a town that had such a narrow view of the world that Cordelia felt it was her responsibility to introduce Maddie to fairy tales, to magic, to all the wonderful things that made every day and night mysterious and exquisite. She described to Maddie her encounters with members of the elvin world when she had lived abroad in Ireland; lithe fairies with glittery wings that beat faster than a hummingbird yet were more graceful than a butterfly. Once, Cordelia told Maddie, she happened upon a fairy ring one night and watched the fairies dance and fly up into the starlit night. Another night she had come upon gruesome gnarled trolls that lived in the gullies along the roadside, waiting to snatch a wandering child and drag him deep into the crevices of the earth.

At night, Maddie sat at the foot of Cordelia's bed as they whispered and giggled. Cordelia remembered those times fondly as she spun incredible tales of mermaids, demons, sorcery, and magic, watching Maddie's eyes grow larger with every word. Then, at the end of the tales, Maddie would creep downstairs to her own bed. Cordelia giggled as she imagined her cousin shivering all night at every strange sound and creak, trying to decipher if the stories were real or not.

Cordelia should have known at the time that they were sisters. That's what sisters do: they tease each other, they play games, they taunt, they tell stories. She was as angry with herself for not knowing, as she was at Rebecca and Tess for not telling her. Cordelia wondered if Maddie even knew. Probably not, she figured, because if Maddie had known that they were sisters, she would have gone looking for her sooner. At least, she hoped that would be the case.

It was when she finally got to Old Captain Potter's Tavern and stepped into the circle of light thrown by the lantern and saw Maddie's face that she realized what she'd done. Maddie's face was racked with a look of pain, horror, relief, and sadness. It was the look that sisters give each other when they've done something wrong. Emotions swelled within her and she started to cry.

"What have I done?" Cordelia wailed.

"It's okay," Maddie said in a comforting tone. "You're back now. We'll fix everything. We'll do it together. We're sisters, remember?"

Cordelia nodded dumbly, and repeated the word *sisters*.

Cordelia was taken aback at how strong Maddie seemed. It was as if Maddie were the older sister welcoming back the reckless, thoughtless little sister, calming her down after a tantrum. Cordelia was finally home. That was all that mattered.

Sisters.

ᚷ

Maddie knew that Cordelia was panicked when she received the phone call. She couldn't believe that after all this time—all this heartache and anguish and fear—all of it ended with a quick phone call in the middle of the night. She wanted to rush right out and get Cordelia, whisk her away from whatever demons had been keeping her from returning all these months, but instead they made a plan to meet each other at Captain Potter's Tavern—a place that was hidden and neutral—a place where Cordelia wouldn't get spooked and slip away into the night like a fairy mist. Her voice was shaking on the phone. She didn't sound like the crazy person that her mother had described her as in those last moments spent in Hawthorne. And yet there was a nagging feeling that wouldn't go away.

Now here they were, driving in Abigail's ancient station wagon, so many questions between them, so many things left unsaid. Maddie barely knew where to start.

Cordelia wasn't ready to return and face the old Victorian and all of those memories at Mariner's Way just yet. Instead they drove to the harbor, parking in a spot that overlooked Misery Island. Maddie ran into the coffee shop and grabbed two steaming cups and some muffins for the two of them. She raced back to the car, half expecting Cordelia to have vanished—for all of it to have been another one of her inexplicably real dreams.

Cordelia greedily ate the muffin and sipped at the coffee. They sat in silence, looking at the shifting waters for a little while before either of them said a word.

"I always thought you blamed me," Maddie said quietly. "I thought that you would hate me forever."

"You're the one who should hate me," Cordelia said with a laugh, but there was a sadness in her voice. "I had no idea all that would happen—how everything would just get so messed up when I left. With Tess, with my mom . . ." It seemed like she was trying to fight back tears. "I just thought that my leaving this town and making our father pay for what he had done—I don't know, that somehow it would make things right again."

"And what would killing our father have done to help any of us?" Maddie asked, almost scolding her half sister.

Cordelia shrugged. "I was just so angry. I wanted someone to pay."

"If anyone should pay, it's Kate Endicott," Maddie said, and then added, "y'know, an eye for an eye?"

"With Kate it should be a heart for a heart," Cordelia offered. "If she even has one." They both laughed.

"Still, I was there that night. I could have stopped things. If there's anyone to blame, it's me," Maddie offered quietly.

"No, no, not you. I've never, ever blamed you, Maddie. You have to believe that."

Maddie wanted to head back to the house, but Cordelia was worried about facing Abigail. Maddie assured her that the coast was clear. Abigail was going to be tied up at Fairview for hours, trying to figure out how Rebecca had escaped from the facility, as well as fill out additional paperwork to make sure that it never happened again.

"How can you not blame me? I mean, they were my friends. I invited you," Maddie insisted.

"You had no idea what was going to happen out there. Believe me, I probably knew more about the situation than you did."

"But I . . ." Maddie couldn't bring herself to say that she had struck Cordelia in the head with a rock—the horrific image that would remained burned into her memory forever. Perhaps Cordelia didn't even remember.

They continued driving toward the house, an awkward silence hanging over them for a few minutes.

"You were doing what you had to do for your own survival," Cordelia assured her. "I know that you're strong, but there's no way that you could have survived that night. I made the choice to be in your place. It was my choice, not yours."

"But it was a choice you should never have had to make in the first place."

Cordelia smiled as she looked out the window. "I know, but sisters have to make sacrifices for each other once in a while, right?"

Maddie smiled as she looked over at Cordelia.

Sisters. That's what they really were. It seemed like she almost knew from the start. Tess knew. Maddie wondered if that was why she was so adamant that they stick together . . . "no matter what."

They pulled into the driveway and Cordelia hesitated before unlocking her seat belt.

"Don't worry, my mom isn't here."

"That's not it," Cordelia stammered. "It's—it's just . . ."

"Too many bad memories," Maddie offered.

"Yeah," Cordelia said, stilted. "Too many bad memories." What she didn't tell Maddie—or couldn't—was that the pictures in her mind were not of things that had already happened, but of what was yet to come.

Chapter 20

THE WHEEL OF FORTUNE

Unexpected opportunities. Good fortune that is unexpected. Coincidences. Luck. The beginning of a new cycle. Advancement. Positive upheaval. Change. A card of good fortune, the appearance of destiny and karmic change.

The night of the fires also marked another local tragedy. Bronwyn Maxwell was missing.

It was all over the news the next evening. It happened a week and a half after Darcy was killed and at the exact time Cordelia returned to Hawthorne. So, obviously, Abigail scrutinized Cordelia upon her return.

Even Maddie had her doubts. Could it have been just a massive coincidence that Ravenswood—now thought to be the result of arson—went up in flames the very night that Cordelia returned home? Had Cordelia sent those tarot cards? Was that some type of warning of what she planned to do?

"Why don't you just come out and say it, Abigail?" Cordelia snapped at her aunt when she received a very bristly, cold shoulder after Abigail returned from her visit with Rebecca. Maddie noticed that Abigail's demeanor had softened quite a bit since she began visiting Rebecca—only now with Cordelia back, all of her anger had a new target. "You think I'm to blame for all of this—for my mother's institutionalization, for Darcy, for Bronwyn. Hell, you probably also think that I torched Ravenswood."

Abigail held Cordelia's gaze firmly. Neither one was going to back down. Maddie could feel it. They were like two dogs baring their teeth at each other, each taunting the other to make the first move.

"Don't be silly," Abigail scoffed. "I don't blame you for any of those tragic events. What I do hold you responsible for are your actions. I just don't think you realized how many people you hurt by taking off like that."

"How many people I hurt? Me?" Cordelia yelled. "That's hilarious coming from you. I guess the view must be pretty nice for you up there on your high horse. Or maybe it would better be described as a glass castle."

Abigail smirked. "I wasn't the one to throw the first stone."

Maddie froze as her mother suddenly eyed her. What did her mother know about that night? Did Rebecca tell her? Could she have heard it from one of the Sisters of Misery? Maddie's face turned red and she turned to leave. Cordelia grabbed Maddie's arm protectively.

"If anyone is to blame for setting the wheels in motion of all that has happened, it's you—and Kate Endicott. That's some wonderful company to keep, by the way."

Abigail smiled in a Cheshire cat sort of way. "If memory serves me right, it was your mother that really started all of this about seventeen years ago."

Cordelia turned bright red. If steam could actually come out of someone's ears, it would be happening right now. She turned on her heel, grabbed her coat, and raced out the front door.

"Mother!" Maddie scolded. "Cordelia had nothing to do with who her father is. You know that."

"All I know is that the apple doesn't fall far from the tree. I'd keep your Luke fellow far from Cordelia if I were you. Like mother, like daughter." With her mouth in a grim, straight line, Abigail turned into the kitchen and started angrily slamming the cabinets.

Maddie took off after Cordelia, struggling to keep up with her, which was no easy task as Cordelia's gait was much longer and faster than her own. She was a girl on a mission.

Her hair flew wildly behind her as she hurried down the street.

"Wait, wait," Maddie said, out of breath as she reached for Cordelia. "Where are we going?"

"We have to talk to Finn."

"They won't let us in to see him. You know that he and Reed are being held for questioning."

Unfortunately, the prime suspects—Reed and Finn—were brought back in for questioning when Bronwyn disappeared. Only this time, the police weren't as quick to release them. They were being held indefinitely and—from the looks of it—the police weren't looking too hard for another suspect in the crimes. Cordelia hadn't even had a chance to reconnect with them, but that wasn't deterring her from getting in to see them, or from finding out the truth.

The walk to the police station wasn't that far, but the sight of Cordelia back in town spread like wildfire. Maddie could hear the murmurs of surprise and anger and disbelief as the two girls whisked through the crowded streets of the annual Winter Festival.

Cordelia, dressed in her long black coat, hair now returned to its natural shock of red curls, stood out among a sea of washed-out onlookers.

Is that the girl who disappeared last year?

Yes, the one who drove her mother to try to kill herself.

I heard she had an affair with Bronwyn's boyfriend. If you ask me, I think she had something to do with the girl's disappearance.

I think she set Ravenswood on fire to get back at Kate Endicott. You know how girls can be. So catty. So vicious.

She's a witch, you know. You can tell by just looking at her. She was sent to bring a reign of terror on this town. She can't be stopped.

Maddie heard the women in town talking, so obviously

Cordelia heard the harsh words being spoken about her. But she never seemed to let any of it bother her. She even seemed to enjoy it. In fact, she made a point of looking straight into people's eyes when their paths crossed. Maddie had never been so proud.

ॐ

"Let us in to see them, Sully," Maddie demanded.

"Not happening," he shot back in his typical smug manner. "Out of my hands now that they've called in the big guns from Boston. No one gets to see O'Malley or Campbell until the big bosses give the go-ahead."

Cordelia asked, "Why are they even suspects?"

"Well," said Sully, scratching his goatee, "Reed is Bronwyn's fiancé, despite what you might think, Maddie."

"What is that supposed to mean, Sully?" Maddie snapped. Sully held his hands up in the air as if to say he wasn't going to get involved.

"And Finn?" Cordelia asked impatiently, ignoring Sully's taunts to Maddie. "What about him? Why is he a suspect?"

"Well, because the last dead girl in town turned up wearing his jacket and if I recall correctly, he was held as a suspect in a missing girl case last year. Do you remember that, Cordelia?"

"Obviously, he's not responsible for kidnapping me, Sully. I'm standing right here in front of you!" She stamped her foot angrily.

"Well, go on and plead your case to the Boston officers. I'm sure they'd love the chance to talk to the girl that wasted all the taxpayers' dollars on a bogus statewide manhunt last year. I'm sure you're at the top of their list right now."

Cordelia glowered at him. "Well, you did a bang-up job at tracking me down, didn't you?"

"Wouldn't go down that road if I were you, Miss LeClaire.

You and your mother aren't exactly the toast of the town these days," he said.

"Like we ever were," Cordelia muttered. Realizing that they weren't going to get anywhere with Sully, Maddie grabbed Cordelia's arm and convinced her to leave. They would come back when the Boston police were available to take Cordelia's statement.

"See you ladies later. Don't go disappearing on us again," he mocked.

Cordelia spun around ready to snap at him, but Maddie just pulled her out of the police station. "Come on, Cordelia," Maddie said loud enough for Sully to hear. "We'll come back and talk to a real policeman. Not an overgrown boy with a badge, playing cops and robbers."

Sully started to protest and yell at them, but they were already out the door.

They walked back home, ignoring the Christmas carolers on the street corners and angrily stomping past the tree lot that remained unattended now that Finn was in custody.

"Looks like we'll have to go about talking to them a different way," Cordelia stated.

"How?" Maddie asked. "You heard Sully? We can't ask the police again. We—you will get in trouble. We can't risk that, Cordelia. Not now. Not after everything and all this time."

"Whoever said anything about asking them to let us do anything? You're going to take a catnap and I'm going to astral project into his cell."

"Astral what? And how do you know about my dream—my whatever you call it?"

"I know about a lot of things that I can't exactly explain. Let's just say that you and I are coming into our powers, just the way Tess described to me. She didn't say it in so many words—I mean, she didn't draw me a detailed diagram of what we would be able to do. But the gist of what she said has come true for me. Hasn't it for you?"

"Whoa, whoa, whoa, wait, this is crazy, Cordelia," Maddie said hurriedly. "I don't think I have enough control to just jump into anyone's dream whenever I want. How do I even know that he's sleeping? I can't control this dream jumping— or whatever you call it—anyway."

"You're right," Cordelia said.

"Thank you!" Maddie said, hoping that Cordelia finally understood that she wasn't as keen on all the magic stuff that Cordelia seemed to be born into.

"He's probably not asleep yet. I'll do my astral projection first and then later tonight, you go and visit him in his dream."

"Okay, wait—no!" Maddie shouted. This obviously wasn't sinking in for Cordelia. "I have no way of even knowing how to get into his dreams."

"You got into mine."

"How did you . . . ?" Maddie hesitated. She just assumed that it was Rebecca's dream she was tapping into, but perhaps it was Cordelia's memories that she had somehow infiltrated. "We're related. That's probably why it was so easy for me. And even though I did before, who knows if I can do it again? Maybe it was just a fluke?"

"It wasn't," Cordelia said firmly.

"How can you be so sure?"

Cordelia turned. "Because it's what you were meant to do. Besides, you can't tell me that was your first time ever jumping into someone's dream before. Haven't you ever done it to someone that you weren't related to?"

Maddie didn't want to tell her about the nightmares and her vision of Darcy's murder, but she knew she couldn't keep that information to herself for too much longer. Why should she? If there was anyone who could help her control this weird power she seemed to possess, it was Cordelia.

Or Rebecca. But after she had jumped into Rebecca's dream— something that she would never tell Cordelia—she feared going into the heads of people she cared about. Sometimes, seeing a person's innermost thoughts and dreams gave you a whole new perspective. It allowed you to see things that should stay hidden. Things that no one should ever see or know about. Secrets that could change everything.

The girls bypassed Mariner's Way and headed to the town library. It was empty because of the holiday celebrations taking place across the town. A murder and a missing girl wouldn't get in the way of Hawthorne's annual Winter Festival. "Maybe my power isn't as strong as yours," Maddie said quietly. Cordelia was busily flipping through the pages of the book in the Hawthorne historical archives. "And what exactly is— astral projection or whatever you called it?"

Cordelia looked up at Maddie in exasperation. "I can't really explain it. I don't know how to control it right now. It's not something as easy as jumping in a car and taking off somewhere. It's a defense mechanism of sorts." Her voice trailed as her fingers ran across the pages of text in front of her. "It happened out on Misery Island. It's the only way I survived."

Maddie looked down at her hands, silently cursing herself for forcing Cordelia to recall memories of that night. But now that they were opening up, she asked another question. "Did it help you survive what happened with Trevor?"

Cordelia raised her eyes from the page and stared blankly ahead of her, as if weighing what she was going to say. She didn't make eye contact with Maddie and then said quietly, "You know about that?"

Maddie nodded. Words failed her.

Cordelia inhaled deeply. "So now I guess you know all my secrets, don't you, Maddie? Who told you? Reed?"

Maddie nodded again. The pain in Cordelia's eyes was almost too much to take. But Cordelia quickly shook it off, choosing to busy herself in her research. "Well, it shouldn't come across as too much of a shock how much of an asshole Trevor Campbell is. Not exactly breaking news, is it?" she said with a slight smile passing across her lips.

"Trevor Campbell? An asshole? Bite your tongue!" Maddie teased.

"Now if you could just tap into his dreams and we could get some proof that he's responsible for Darcy and Bronwyn, then we could really nail him. It's up to you, Maddie."

Maddie felt butterflies in her stomach. It was magical and scary and made her feel completely off-kilter. She knew in her heart that what Cordelia was saying was right. She had a power. They both did.

But the million-dollar question was: how could she use it to her advantage, and how did she get it in the first place? Had she always had it? When she dropped off to sleep as a toddler and dreamed about playing with her friends, had she really been bouncing around in their dreams the night before? And even worse, the nightmarish dreams of seeing Darcy Willett being killed, was that from the mind of her actual killer? Did Maddie actually "witness" Darcy being murdered? And could she actually use it to help find Bronwyn? Did she even want to?

It would make perfect sense if she had tapped into Trevor's dreams. He'd have good reasons for both Darcy's death and Bronwyn's disappearance. Plus, both she and Cordelia knew what kind of a violent streak ran through Trevor. That, coupled with an overwhelming sense of entitlement and privilege, could turn even the most timid person into a monster.

Maddie chose not to tell Cordelia about her recent nightmares, although she knew that she'd eventually have to come clean. But what if the dreams were really coming from Reed or Finn? What if her knowledge of the crime (something that would never be allowed in court, thankfully) let her know that one of the two guys she cared most about in this town was actually a killer?

Cordelia seemed oblivious of all of Maddie's inner turmoil and was running her fingers nimbly along the ancient texts they'd uncovered.

"Ha! I knew it!" Cordelia held out the antique book triumphantly. "One of the first families in Salem, the *Endicott* family, was responsible for making the witch trial laws that sparked the witch-hunts in the sixteen hundreds. An Endicott!"

Maddie furrowed her brow. "And that helps us how?"

Cordelia looked at her half sister in exasperation. "It gives us ammunition. Knowledge is power!"

Maddie shook her head, still not understanding.

Cordelia pushed her long, tangled strands of red hair behind her shoulders, tucking stray pieces behind her ears as she began her explanation. "You see, if we can point to Kate Endicott's family as having unjust reason to tear down Ravenswood, a place where so many wrongly accused women were tortured and buried because of these unjust 'witchcraft' laws, then maybe we can use it to sway popular opinion against the Endicotts. I mean, it says right here that Rebecca Nurse, one of the wrongly accused witches, had a property fight with the Endicott family. That was probably the reason she was accused of witchcraft in the first place."

"Just because they were related to tyrants doesn't make them guilty." Maddie knew once the words were out of her mouth that she sounded ridiculous. The smirk on Cordelia's face gave it away. "I mean, yes, they are awful people, and yes, Kate and her mother and all the Sisters of Misery have done hideous, terrible things to more people than any other person I know, but still . . . how does that keep them from getting their way?"

"Karma," Cordelia said flatly. "They may have money and powerful people and laws on their side, but we have something even better."

Maddie shook her head, waiting for the answer. She watched as Cordelia's face lit up before she said knowingly, "Magic." And then added with a wink, "And witchcraft. Real witchcraft."

Chapter 21

ACE OF CUPS

*This is the time to consider how the past is connected
to the present. Look for ways in which you can begin
to connect with others. This card announces the beginning
of great possibility in this area of life. It can mark the
start of a new relationship, or a deeper connection to
an existing one. While this may be a romantic
relationship, it can also signify a friendship.*

"You need to relax." Cordelia had chosen this spot for
its "magical" properties. The two girls looked like any
other teenagers enjoying the rare New England sun, walking
by the ocean's shore on an unseasonably warm December
day. But the difference between what Cordelia and Maddie
were doing and the others who were enjoying this break in
the winter chill was worlds apart. They were both wearing
quartz crystal necklaces, cleansing them with the sun's rays
as well as soaking in the spectral power from the powerful
stones. Cordelia instructed Maddie to wear the necklace whenever she was trying to channel her powers.

"So, seriously, how did you learn to astral project? Who
taught you?"

"This amazing woman I met on my way up to Maine.
She's actually the one who gave me the car."

"She *gave* you a car?" Maddie asked incredulously. Only
Cordelia could win someone over so much that they would
give her a car.

"Well, technically, I borrowed it. I'll give it back to her as
soon as I save up enough for my own."

Maddie shook her head, stifling a laugh. In many ways,

Cordelia led a charmed life. But then she had a vision of Cordelia being tied up out on Misery Island, and of what she herself had done to her own flesh and blood, and she held back any further comment. She looked at Cordelia and wondered if she felt any lingering anger or resentment for Maddie. Just then Cordelia turned and looked Maddie straight in the eye, as if she could hear her thoughts.

"We're sisters, real sisters. Not that stupid club you're a part of. We will always have each other's back no matter what."

Maddie eyed her suspiciously. Had she been able to read her thoughts? What other powers did Cordelia have? Maddie smiled and hugged Cordelia and then the two girls continued down the beach to their destination.

The rock was in Swampscott and supposedly had mystical powers—it was captured in a poem by Whittier and its proximity to the land and sea was the perfect bridge between the natural and the supernatural worlds, according to Cordelia. The ocean had properties that were not only healing, but essential to harnessing their powers. This was why Cordelia often swam in the ocean by moonlight—the rays of the moon coupled with the power of the ocean helped her draw upon her spectral visions.

They would be returning later that night for their astral projection and dream jumping missions, but Cordelia felt it was important to clear their minds and relax their bodies completely before attempting the ritual.

Maddie had just about perfected her yoga breathing that Cordelia had showed her how to do, when she noticed that the air around her felt different. The energy suddenly changed. It was like a negative charge of electricity disrupted the peaceful setting. Sitting up quickly, she knew the cause of the change.

Kate Endicott was marching toward them like a woman possessed.

"What the hell do you think you're doing?"

Cordelia didn't move a muscle. Maddie wasn't sure if she

was really asleep or if she had relaxed herself into a trance that not even Kate Endicott could rouse her from. Or, more likely, she was ignoring Kate. They had yet to confront each other since that night out on Misery, and Maddie wasn't sure what would happen.

"We're lying out on the beach. It's the perfect winter day to lie out for a tan," Maddie said sarcastically. "What are *you* doing, Kate?"

"Well, it's nice to see that you're back to try and fix things. Is your little drama-fest over? Have you come back to take responsibility for your little running away act?" Kate directed her comments to Cordelia, who continued to ignore her.

Cordelia kept her eyes closed. Maddie could feel the anger growing inside her and she was sure that Cordelia was feeling the same.

"Kate, leave her alone," Maddie instructed.

"Well, I'm not here to reminisce about old times, that's for sure. I just came from the police station. Trevor called me and said that the Boston officials are ready to take Cordelia's statement now. It would be nice to get Trevor's brother out of jail and finally take the spotlight off of our families."

"But I thought you loved the spotlight, Kate?" Cordelia said, sitting up and glaring at Kate. "Isn't that why you held that big party out on Misery Island? It wasn't to celebrate the hell that you put me through, was it? If you had let me know about it earlier, I could have cleared my schedule and made an appearance as the guest of honor."

Maddie was about to ask Cordelia how she knew about the Winter Gala, but then realized that the news of Darcy's murder had given the event more publicity than Kate could ever have wished for.

"No, but perhaps if you were there, Darcy wouldn't have been the one fished out of the ocean wearing your boyfriend's jacket. By the way, I thought that you would be interested in knowing that your *mother*"—she stretched the word out and wrinkled her nose—"is now the talk of the town. People are coming from all over to see her. News is spreading all over about her. It's turning this town into a freak show."

Maddie was confused. "Why would they want to see my mother?" Maddie knew that people were aware that her mother's cancer had gone into remission, but why would that pique anyone's interest?

"Ugh, not your mother, *her* mother—the nutcase," Kate said, visibly annoyed.

At the mention of Rebecca, Cordelia jumped to her feet. "What about my mother?"

"Oh, you didn't know?" Kate said coyly. "Seems she's a healer now. After Maddie's mother's cancer went into remission and she did her little television appearance at the fire, word spread that just being in Rebecca LeClaire's presence is enough to heal any illness or affliction. People are coming in droves just to see her, like she's that picture of the crying Virgin Mary or the potato chip that looks like Jesus."

Cordelia looked at Maddie with an accusatory glare. "What's going on? How can this be happening? People don't honestly believe that Rebecca is a healer, do they?" Maddie looked down, guilt creeping across her face. She knew that she should have told Cordelia about this new development with Rebecca, but it was such a far-fetched notion, she didn't want to spook Cordelia and send her running off again. Maddie just hadn't realized how many people were privy to the information.

"How do you know this?" Cordelia demanded.

"How do you not? Don't you watch the news or read a paper? It's become national news, soon to be international news. And it's royally fucking up my family's plans to finish the Endicott Hotel."

"How so?" Even if Rebecca had become labeled as a healer, what did that have to do with the fate of Ravenswood? Maddie wondered.

"Because Rebecca is saying that the site is filled with magic and healing properties. People are starting to treat it like it's the freakin' mecca."

Cordelia was in Kate's face in an instance. "How do you know so much about my mother?"

"Oh," Kate said in mock innocence. "You didn't know about your mom's newfound fame? Pity she's never asked for you. Guess you're not her golden girl anymore, Cordelia. That's what happens when you run away and destroy people's lives."

Maddie grabbed Cordelia as she started to lunge for Kate. Cordelia could withstand the harshest words, but she'd never allow anyone to talk to her about her family that way. If Maddie hadn't grabbed her arm, she knew that Cordelia would have punched Kate squarely in the face—not that she didn't deserve it, of course.

Cordelia pulled out of Maddie's grasp and raced down the beach away from them. Maddie knew that Cordelia had been working up the courage to go visit her mother all week. But now that Kate had rubbed it in her face, Cordelia was hell-bent on proving Reed's and Finn's innocence down at the station and then continue on to Fairview to see Rebecca. It was time to right her wrongs. It was the only way to move forward.

"I wouldn't get my hopes up!" Kate called after her, and then turned to Maddie to finish. "They're only letting people in that Rebecca wants to see. My guess is that Cordelia isn't on that list. Not anymore."

Maddie wished that Cordelia was at her side at that moment when she did what she should have done a long time ago—slapped Kate straight across her face. Kate screamed in agony as she fell to the sand below. Maddie had even surprised herself at the force of the blow; the base of her wrist seemed to have connected with Kate's nose, which now had blood streaming from it.

"You fucking bitch. You broke my nose! It's bleeding, for Christ's sake! You are so going to pay for this, you bitch!" Kate screeched.

Maddie smiled down at Kate's blood-smeared face and said, "You were right, Kate: karma *is* a witch."

∞

Before going to see Rebecca, Cordelia went straight to the police station and made a statement to officially clear Finn and Reed from having anything to do with her disappearance. Now she and Maddie wouldn't have to rely on their powers to get them out. At least the Endicotts' influence was good for something. They didn't want to be associated with a prisoner in any way. And luckily for Finn, he got to ride along on Reed's coattails out the prison door.

Maddie waited for Cordelia in the police station waiting room as she gave her statement. She worried that Cordelia would be fined or sentenced to some sort of community work—or even worse, imprisoned, because of the chaos that her disappearing act had caused. But luckily, the police department was too concerned with Darcy's death and Bronwyn's disappearance to punish Cordelia. They weren't really ever that concerned with Cordelia's disappearance or reappearance. They were just happy to be able to clear Finn and Reed—especially because of the pressure being put on them by the Campbell and Endicott families—so that they could look for the real killer. Maddie was shocked at how quickly the whole thing blew over.

Maddie waited patiently with Cordelia while they released Finn and Reed. She wondered what would happen when Cordelia came face-to-face with the two most important men to her in Hawthorne. What would her reaction be? What would theirs be?

Maddie felt an uncomfortable wave of tension as the two girls sat under the flickering fluorescent lights in the waiting room at Hawthorne County Jail.

Reed was the first one to enter the room. He gave the girls a tired smile. He seemed stressed and tired and worried. Maddie realized that he must be so concerned about Bronwyn's disappearance. He walked over to Maddie and gave her a hug and then turned to Cordelia.

"So the wandering traveler returns," he said as he softly brushed her cheek. Maddie felt a twinge of jealousy as they held each other's gaze.

"I'm sorry," Cordelia said, her eyes welling with tears. "I really didn't mean to cause all of this—"

"Hey, hey, hey," he said, still smiling. "It's okay. You went through more than anyone should have ever gone through. I would have taken off by now, too, if I was in your position. Everything is going to be okay."

Just as Maddie was starting to feel like a third wheel, the look on Cordelia's face changed suddenly. The air seemed to vibrate with electricity and Maddie was convinced that Cordelia had stopped breathing. She followed Cordelia's line of vision and saw Finn standing there. They were staring at each other intently. Finn didn't even look down at the paperwork he was signing and in an instant, Cordelia was at his side.

They kissed so passionately and so intensely that it seemed like the rest of the world had dropped away. It was only Cordelia and Finn. Finn and Cordelia. Nothing else seemed to matter. He grabbed on to her tightly, squeezing her into his chest as if he couldn't pull her any closer without devouring her.

Reed let out a long low whistle. "Wow," he said. "That's pretty intense."

Maddie looked at the two and wiped tears from her eyes. "That's love."

Reed grabbed Maddie's hand, squeezing it and looking at her intensely.

"I'll see you later, Maddie," he said, his voice filled with emotion. "I—I need to go." He turned away from her quickly, almost like he was afraid of his emotions for her surging forward to the surface. Right now, as the boyfriend of the missing girl, it wouldn't look good if he was too affectionate with anyone. "Take care of Cordelia."

Maddie laughed. "I don't think I need to."

Reed turned back and looked at the two, who were kissing through tears, whispering softly to each other, and laughing as they touched each other's face, and Maddie detected a hint of sadness or jealousy or longing. She wasn't quite sure. And then he turned and walked out the door into the unseasonably warm afternoon.

Chapter 22

TEMPERANCE
(Reversed)

*Naïveté, helping others to their own detriment,
imbalance. Volatility. Poor judgment. Fickle decisions.
Conflicting interests. Physical stress. Disagreements.
Restlessness and instability. Trying to combine too many
or the wrong elements in too short an expanse of time.*

After they finished up the paperwork to free Finn, Cordelia
knew that there was one last person she needed to see:
Rebecca.

"I'll be right by your side," Finn assured her, holding her
hand like he never wanted to let it go. He seemed so completely awestruck being back in Cordelia's presence that his
brief stay in jail didn't seem to faze him.

"I'm coming, too," Maddie offered, though she still felt like
the third wheel. Finn and Cordelia were so consumed with
each other that Maddie didn't think they even heard her.

"What if she doesn't want to see me? What if Kate's right?"

"When has Kate Endicott ever been right?" Finn said
glumly.

Just then, Maddie's phone started beeping. She got a text
message.

"What's going on back there?" Cordelia said, looking into
the backseat. "You have a pager now? What are you, a drug
dealer now? Jeez, I leave town for a little while and the whole
world goes crazy."

"No, it's a text message from Luke."

"Oh, Luuukkkeee," Cordelia said, drawing out his name
for effect. Maddie had told her a little about her best friend

at school that she was not-so-secretly in love with and how she'd given up the chance to spend a winter break on his beautiful cruise ship to come back to Hawthorne. What she hadn't told Cordelia was that she had asked Luke to look into bringing Cordelia back and finding out the whereabouts of Malcolm Crane.

"Who's this Luke guy? I thought you and Reed had a thing going?" Finn asked. Maddie was about to yell at him for saying something so inappropriate, especially after Reed's girlfriend was missing, but then she remembered when Finn interrupted their kiss at the Misery Island Gala.

"Never mind," Maddie said, flipping open her phone to read the text message.

> Maddie, ur dad is on his way to Hwthrne. Do u want me 2 come? xoxo always, Luke

"Good sweet Lord," Maddie said under her breath.

"What's going on?" Cordelia said, bending over the seat to try to peek at Maddie's phone.

"Not much," Maddie said, a state of shock settling over her. "Just the family reunion from hell."

&

When they got to Fairview, Cordelia knew that she should go in to see Rebecca alone. Maddie and Finn agreed to wait in the waiting area. Maddie frantically tried texting and phoning Luke, but he wasn't returning her messages.

How had he tracked down her father? When? With everything that had been going on, she had forgotten to inform him about Cordelia's return. Was Malcolm Crane coming to see Abigail? Rebecca? Did he even know what had gone on in the past decade? And if so, why was he choosing now, when all hell was breaking loose, to come back to town? Just to fan the flames?

Finn sat patiently next to Maddie and watched as Cordelia hesitated briefly and then entered her mother's hospital room. He wanted desperately to get into that room and be part of the reconciliation, but he knew this was something that they needed to be private.

Cordelia pushed the door open and gasped as she saw her mother lying in the hospital bed. This was a woman who never got sick, never caught a cold, who was filled with energy at every moment of the day and night. Rebecca LeClaire was light and energy and happiness personified. How could this shell of a woman be her? Despite seeing her mother on the television news, Cordelia was unprepared for this face-to-face reunion.

Rebecca's eyes lit up as soon as she saw Cordelia. Her mouth opened as if the words were there, but couldn't come out.

"Mama," Cordelia cried, her voice breaking. "I'm so sorry. You have no idea how sorry I am." She wanted to run over to her mother and hug her, but Rebecca appeared so frail that she might break.

Rebecca shook her head and widened her eyes as if Cordelia were simply a mirage in front of her. It was clear that this was the day she'd been waiting for—that she'd been living for—ever since Cordelia left Hawthorne. Suddenly Cordelia became overwhelmed by guilt and felt foolish for running away and causing so much grief, so much pain.

"You are my beautiful angel, Cordelia," Rebecca said, her voice filled with emotion. "The past doesn't matter. What's happened has happened. You're here now and that's all that I care about. You are my entire world, and now you're back where you belong. Come here, my baby girl."

Cordelia raced into her mother's open arms, curling her

body next to Rebecca's on the narrow hospital bed. Rebecca showed remarkable strength for someone who appeared to be in such a fragile state. She embraced Cordelia so tightly that it almost took her breath away. The two rocked together, sobbing and laughing, oblivious of the world around them. It was as if no time had passed. All feelings of betrayal and abandonment and fear were put to rest. Cordelia was home. That was all that mattered.

Maddie and Finn were surprised when the door suddenly opened and a nurse motioned them into Rebecca's room. It was filled with beautiful flowers—almost like being back in Rebecca's Closet. There were huge arrangements, baskets of baked goods, balloons, and a huge assortment of candies strewn around the room. Obviously, Rebecca's "healing powers" did not go unnoticed. Maddie wondered how many people had been helped by her aunt, and if it was frustrating for Rebecca to heal so many other people's pain, but not her own. She got her answer when she looked at the hospital bed.

Cordelia was curled around her mother, sobbing. Rebecca was whispering into her hair, shushing and rocking her as if she were a small child. Rebecca looked up at Maddie and Finn and mouthed the words *Thank you.*

Finn and Maddie knew that they should let them have their private time to start mending their relationship. Maddie was overjoyed when she saw the sparkle back in Rebecca's eyes. The dead, glazed-over eyes that she'd been accustomed to had been replaced by a dazzling flicker of life. Rebecca had her baby girl back and she was holding on to her tight, like she never wanted to let her go.

When visiting hours at the hospital were over, Maddie and Cordelia returned to Mariner's Way. Maddie had a feeling now that Cordelia had officially returned and was here to stay, Rebecca wouldn't be staying in the hospital for much longer. It was obvious that the only medicine she needed was the return of her daughter.

The girls were talking over each other, their voices trilling like birds, filled with happiness, when the shock of seeing the man sitting calmly with Abigail in the living room literally took their breath away.

It was Malcolm Crane.

He looked a lot older than Maddie remembered, but he hadn't changed much in the ten-plus years since she'd seen him. He seemed a lot smaller, less powerful. But then again, she was just a toddler when he took off. She remembered his drunken rages around the house. He seemed so powerful, larger than life back then. She was shocked to see that he was just a man. A regular, everyday man.

Cordelia, on the other hand, bristled. She looked at him with pure disgust. Maddie was afraid that the overwhelming emotions that were inside Cordelia after her reconciliation with Rebecca would turn to pure rage at the sight of their father.

"Hello, girls," Malcolm Crane said, standing up formally and putting his arms out for a hug. "It's been a long time." Abigail looked as though she'd been crying. He cocked his head to the side when he looked at Cordelia, appearing to be slightly shocked that the girl who had waited on him for so many months at the college coffee shop was his own daughter.

"Not long enough," Cordelia said under her breath.

"Hi, Dad," Maddie said curtly, not making an attempt to move toward his open arms. He held his arms out for a few beats and then awkwardly let them fall to his sides.

"I know that there are a lot of things that I need to make amends for and apologize to all of you, Maddie, Abigail, Rebecca, Cordelia."

Cordelia dropped her gaze down to the floor. It was almost as if she couldn't bear to look at him. The happiness that was brimming inside her was replaced by something much darker.

"You mean me and my sister? Your wife and your lover?"

Maddie spat the words at him. How dare he come here and try to make everything all right? All she needed him for was to track down Cordelia—that was all. Why did he even bother coming back to Hawthorne? Why now? "Isn't it nice of you to finally meet your daughter face-to-face? And me, I'm surprised you even remember my name, considering how long ago you left us behind!"

Abigail had a stony look on her face. Maddie could tell that her mother was steeling her emotions against this dysfunctional family gathering. "I'm just happy that Tess wasn't here to witness this," she said quietly.

"Maddie, I don't expect you to welcome me with open arms. I realize it will take time—" He stopped short as Maddie cut him off.

"Time is the one thing I don't have for you, for any of this. I'm here for my mother and Rebecca and Cordelia. The people I care about. I have no time for someone like you!"

Defeated, Malcolm turned to Cordelia, and a look of recognition came over his face. "You, you're the girl from the coffee shop," Malcolm offered, almost like an olive branch to Cordelia. "I should have known—now I see the resemblance to your mother."

"You can't see anything," Cordelia spat. "You're oblivious to the world around you. You're a narcissist, a callous womanizer, a waste of a human being, and I am disgusted to be related to someone like you."

Cordelia began sobbing and ran up the stairs to her bedroom. Maddie never stopped staring at her father, curious to see how he handled Cordelia's outburst. He looked deflated and saddened. He was wringing his hands uncomfortably and shifting his weight back and forth.

"I guess I deserve that."

"Yeah, you do," Maddie deadpanned. "Listen, I don't know why you chose now to come back to Hawthorne, or what you want from us, but Rebecca will probably be released from the hospital soon, and I don't think she's in the right frame of mind to handle this. I don't think any of us are, quite frankly. Especially Cordelia," she said, motioning toward the staircase. Maddie wondered if Cordelia was listening at the top of the stairs.

"Yes," he said, nodding and sitting back down, looking up at Abigail with a look of guilt washing over his handsome face. "I'm aware that she didn't take the news well when she learned that I was her father."

"Didn't take it well?" Maddie laughed, practically shouted. "Didn't take it well? Hmm, let's see, she took off for a year in a vendetta to try to track you down to kill you. She cut off all ties with us all, making us think that she was dead. Made her mother—your ex-lover—so crazy that she tried to kill herself and has been locked up in a mental facility for a year. So yeah, I guess you could say she didn't take it well."

Being the narcissist that he was, Malcolm seemed to hear only the part that concerned him. "She wanted to kill me?"

"Yes," Maddie snapped. "Too bad for her that she failed."

He winced and then said, "I came here to make things right."

"How are you going to do that, Dad? Do you have a time machine? Don't you realize that when you burn bridges, there's no traveling back over them?"

Maddie was shocked at her mother's silence. After all of the years of hearing her mother's rants about Malcolm Crane, she was simply sitting there like an obedient housewife, unable to look at anyone or express anything. This filled Maddie with even more rage. She could almost feel Tess standing behind her, giving her the strength to carry on.

"If you are so filled with hatred toward me, then why did you send for me?"

"Send for you? I never sent anyone for you. Truth be told, I would have paid or done anything to keep you out of all of our lives—the lives you so royally screwed up!"

The only reason she ever wanted to track down Malcolm Crane was to find Cordelia. And now he had come back to Hawthorne thinking he was going to right his wrongs. But that wasn't going to happen. Maddie wasn't giving anyone any more second chances. She'd already learned that the hard way.

"I wanted to bring Cordelia back. I didn't want *you* back here. But now that you are, maybe you can make good use of yourself and support my mother—something you've failed to do for most of my life. You did know about her cancer, didn't you?"

He looked down sadly, guilt-ridden.

"Besides, I'm heading back to school, away from Hawthorne, away from all of this, so maybe now you can help pick up the pieces of this family that you shattered years ago," Maddie shouted, deciding that she'd spoken to her father more than she wanted to, more than he deserved.

Maddie still had questions, like how Malcolm knew to come back to Hawthorne, who was the little boy that Cordelia thought was his son, and how he could abandon his family, but she was too tired for all of it. Too many things happening at once. Her whole world was spinning at such a rapid pace that it felt as though the ground beneath her feet were actually off-kilter.

"Nice seeing you, Dad," Maddie said, excusing herself. "Why don't you check in with us in another ten years?"

And with that, Maddie stormed upstairs and went to bed.

∞

After Malcolm left the house and Abigail retired to her room, Cordelia crawled into bed with Maddie, eager to talk about her reunion with Rebecca—and to discuss the man that they both equally despised.

"Thank God you were standing next to me or else I would have completely lost it and just grabbed the nearest, heaviest thing and knocked him out," Cordelia said. Maddie knew she wasn't kidding. "But seriously, why would he come here? What does he have to gain by coming here now?"

"I don't know," Maddie said sleepily. She looked at the clock; it wasn't even eleven and she felt like she hadn't slept in days. "Maybe he read about everything that was going on and thought, 'Hey, their lives aren't messed up enough, why don't I go add more insanity to the mix?' Who knows? All I care about is that you and Rebecca have made amends. That's what's most important."

Cordelia beamed. Before they all left Fairview, Cordelia spoke to the caseworker to see what needed to be done in order for her mother to be released. Now that Cordelia had returned, Rebecca's mood was visibly improving so rapidly that the caseworker seemed to think she could be released with outpatient care and medication sometime in the near future. Cordelia was beyond thrilled and wanted to make it happen right away. She was obviously choosing to focus on the positive events of the day and ignore the fact that Malcolm Crane had come back into their lives so unexpectedly and without good reason.

"I know. I can't believe I did that to her. I'm so selfish. It must be a Crane trait," Cordelia said, giggling as Maddie threw a pillow at her and it narrowly missed her head. The pillow knocked some books to the floor. But then the knocking came again.

Cordelia stopped giggling. "Is there an echo in here or do you have a ghost knocking on the walls?"

Maddie sat straight up in bed, shushing Cordelia.

There is was again. A slow knocking sound came from downstairs.

"Someone's at the door, I think," Maddie whispered.

"Okay," Cordelia whispered back. "Why don't we go see who it is?" She was obviously still giddy and acting playful. "And why are we still whispering?"

Maddie shoved Cordelia off the bed playfully and the two girls went downstairs. When they opened the front door, Cordelia's jaw dropped. Maddie kept her composure and asked, when she saw who was standing in their doorway at that late hour, "Since when does Kate Endicott make house calls?"

ॐ

"A favor?" Cordelia seemed upset that she hadn't slammed the door in Kate's face when she showed up at Mariner's Way that night, which was obviously what she wanted to do.

The girls sat together whispering in the living room, trying not to awaken Abigail. Maddie was shocked that Kate had even come to the house. *She must be really desperate for answers,* Maddie thought.

They decided to hear Kate out. Kate quickly explained that the Endicotts didn't believe in the supernatural or curses or anything of that nature, but they were unhappy with all the setbacks that were related to Ravenswood: the fires, as well as Bronwyn's disappearance and Darcy's murder. Kate Endicott would never admit that she was cursed, but she was concerned that her family had a string of bad luck following them and anyone around them.

"So I'm coming to you—for help," Kate said quickly. Maddie could tell that she was at the end of her rope, which would be the only reason that she would ever ask for help—especially help from Cordelia.

But Cordelia wasn't so quick to believe that Kate, of all people, would be turning to her for help. "Yeah, so, why do we need to go to your house to get answers? Are you planning on doing another 'initiation ritual' for me and Maddie once we get there? How are we supposed to know that we're not walking into one of your traps?"

"Because I'm scared," Kate said, her bottom lip quivering. Maddie had never seen Kate like this before and she was hesitant to believe it herself. "My family is about to lose everything. One of my best friends was murdered and the killer is still at large. Bronwyn is missing. Ravenswood was burned to the ground. There just seems to be so much happening around my family—I'm afraid that I'm going to be next."

"Why should I help you after everything you did to me?" Cordelia shot back. "You had a big hand in destroying my family; why should I help yours?"

"Because it's not just me that's at risk," Kate said flatly. "It's all of the Sisters of Misery." She turned to look at Maddie. "Which includes you, Maddie."

ಬಿ

On the road over to Kate's house, Cordelia had to be reminded several times by Maddie why she was going along with this.

"If she wants our help so badly, why can't we do it at our own house? Why do we have go to Kate's?" Cordelia felt like they were following a poisonous spider back to her web.

"I don't know, but it's just as well. My mom has been through so much today, I'd rather not have her get angry with me on top of everything else. I can't take any more stress."

"You're telling me," Cordelia added. Maddie realized how much Cordelia must be going through. Coming back to Hawthorne, reuniting with Finn and her mother, coming face-to-face with two people she despised: Malcolm Crane and Kate Endicott. She was handling it very well. Almost too well.

Maddie sighed. "Let's just get this over with and see what she wants us to do."

"Fine, but if I see a boat or a blindfold or anything that reminds me of my initiation ceremony, I'm out of there."

Maddie was in awe of Cordelia's courage. She'd been facing the ghosts of her past all within such a short period of time and taking it all in stride. Maddie wondered if she'd hold up so well under such intense pressure.

"Humph," Cordelia said, and then reluctantly smiled. "The only reason I'm heading over there is for your sake. And so that I can get a better look at her bruised face, courtesy of my awesome sister."

The two girls broke into hysterics as the car wound its way down the wooded path to Kate's house.

∞

Kiki Endicott answered the door and looked at them with disdain. "Yes?" she asked rudely. Kate obviously hadn't informed Kiki of the late night visit.

"Mom, it's okay, I invited them over," Kate said, opening the door wider to allow the girls to enter. Kiki stumbled backward. The ruby-red wine in her crystal goblet sloshed over her hand and slid down her arm. She shook her arm angrily, swearing at Kate for being clumsy, and stumbled down the corridor.

Kate laughed. "Looks like she's going to be down for the count pretty soon," she said as she motioned to the direction her mother went. "Just as well. I don't need her to know that I've enlisted the help of psychics."

The girls walked into the grand living room. Maddie could see the lights twinkling across the harbor from the large wraparound windows. They sat down and Cordelia pulled out a Ouija board from her large canvas bag and set it on the glass coffee table.

Kate laughed snidely. "My God, are we back in junior high

or what?" she said, and then spoke directly to the board in a little girl's voice. "Oh master Ouija, who am I going to marry?"

Maddie gave Kate a withering look—one of Kate's trademark facial expressions given right back to her—and snapped, "Listen, Kate, we're doing this for you as a favor. Cordelia doesn't even have to be here, but she is, and the least you could do is be civil. Don't you want to find Bronwyn? And figure out who killed Darcy? Jesus, Kate, what do you want?"

Kate sniffed toward Cordelia and said, "I'd like for your cousin to admit to how much she's screwed up this town with her disappearing act, and I'd *really* prefer to not be playing a Parker Brothers game and expect a real answer. And I'd like you to apologize for hitting me in the face! That's what I really want."

Just as the words came out of her mouth a large crash sounded outside, reverberating through the room. The lights went out and they were thrown into darkness. Something pushed the three girls backward and Maddie felt something whiz by her cheek. Another smaller crash, only this time it felt closer.

The wind picked up outside suddenly, as if a storm was coming off the sea. It could only be described as a moan. The hair on Maddie's arms stood up and her skin prickled. Kate must have experienced a similar feeling because she snapped, "Damn electrical storm."

Then Maddie felt Kate stand up and start calling into the darkness. "Rosalinda, can you get the electric lanterns and some flashlights?"

There was a scurry of movement in the adjacent rooms. Kate's staff was quick to act.

And then instantly the lights came back on. Maddie and Cordelia still remained in the exact positions they were in prior to the lights going out. The Ouija board still rested on the table, but the plastic eye was missing. Kate was standing in the doorway, still calling out to the help, when she turned and started back into the room.

"Ouch, for Christ's sake," Kate whined, grabbing her foot and hopping up and down. There were streaks of dark red blood that matched her perfectly manicured toes. She started plucking pieces of glass from the arch of her foot. A crystal picture frame lay shattered at her feet; the plastic eye of the Ouija board lay next to the broken frame, as if hurled by unseen hands at the pictures.

"Thanks, Cordelia," Kate snapped. "Throwing that piece of crap toy at me was real mature."

"I didn't do it," Cordelia said honestly.

"Whatever," Kate mumbled angrily as she hopped over to the couch and grabbed an old blanket to sop up the blood.

Maddie looked at Cordelia curiously. She had felt Cordelia next to her the entire time. Neither one of them had moved. Who threw the Ouija board eye across the room? And with enough force to knock over a heavy, lead-crystal picture frame?

"What picture was it?" Cordelia asked calmly.

"It doesn't matter," Kate snapped. "Anyway, if you wanted to hit me, you'll have to improve your aim."

"Believe me, Kate, if I was going to throw something at you, it would be a lot heavier than a crappy piece of plastic," Cordelia said. "Now, I'll ask you again, who's in the picture?"

"Why do you care?" Kate asked.

"Because whoever is in that picture is either responsible for Bronwyn and Darcy—or is the next to die."

Kate flipped the picture over and Maddie realized that it had been taken that afternoon at the Crestwood Yacht Club right after Cordelia disappeared. There, smiling on the deck of the yacht club with the afternoon sun glinting off the harbor, were five girls that made up the Sisters of Misery: Maddie, Kate, Hannah, Darcy, and Bridget. If Cordelia's predictions were accurate (and they usually were frighteningly so), that meant that any one of them was the murderer, or one of them was the next in line for a gruesome fate.

"What, are you saying that I'm the murderer? Sorry, I don't do manual labor and I'm not in a hurry to do hard time. And I don't think that I'm being stalked by some psycho predator."

"From the looks of things, I'd say you're looking at plan B."

The girls turned and were horrified to see that above the doorway there appeared to be an inverted cross crudely painted in blood.

"What the hell is that and where did it come from?" Kate insisted.

"All I know is that when people are trying to protect a house from evil, they make the sign of the cross over doorways in holy water. So—"

"Meaning?"

"Meaning that instead of keeping evil forces out, someone or something is inviting evil forces into your picture-perfect life."

"Why do you think it's me? There are five of us in that picture," Kate said defensively.

"Darcy's already dead. That pretty much counts her out. And the mark of Satan just appeared on your door. Plus, the fact that your family is the one directly descended from the witch trial judges pretty much makes you the number-one target, I'd say."

"Cordelia," Maddie interrupted. "Do you really think that one of us is in danger?"

"Well, that picture is associated with someone who is in trouble—real trouble," Cordelia said in a knowing way. It reminded Maddie of when Tess had a hunch about something. There was no need to question it, because you knew she was speaking the truth.

"What about the person who took the picture?" Kate said stoically.

Maddie suddenly remembered clearly the day that the picture was taken. She'd been so concerned about Cordelia's disappearance that Maddie hadn't even remembered Bronwyn Maxwell being there. But she was. And she had taken the picture of them.

"Bronwyn," Maddie said hurriedly.

And after she said the name, a dream she'd had weeks ago suddenly came to her as if it were a movie playing out in front of her.

&

I open my eyes and see Bronwyn gagged and bound on the dirt floor. She's in a cellar that looks straight out of the turn of the century, which could be any of the older houses or historical properties in Hawthorne, Salem, Marblehead, or anywhere on the North Shore. It seems familiar, but I'm not sure if I've ever been here before. Bronwyn's face is tear-streaked and dirty, and etched with fear. Somehow I've stumbled into this dream, and yet is it a dream of the past, the present, or what is yet to come? Is Bronwyn still alive? Or is the killer simply having a sadistic remembrance of the thrill of keeping Bronwyn captive?

She's looking at me in fear, and there's so much inside me that wants to help her. But I'm at the mercy of the person who is keeping her captive. I'm looking through his eyes, not my own. I am only a watchful participant, with no ability to alter the consequences. I fear that I'm going to see Bronwyn murdered right in front of my eyes, the same way I witnessed Darcy's death. This can't be happening, not again. I try to reach out to her, but I feel as though I'm paralyzed. I have no control over my body. All I can do is watch. Suddenly my arms are moving—though I have no idea what is going to happen next. It's like watching a scary movie and trying desperately to tell the victim to run, get out of there, save your-

self! The monster is going to get you! But in this instance, I am watching the events play out through the monster's eyes. I am watching a girl recoil in fear for her life, and there is nothing I can do to stop it.

୬

"Bronwyn, no!" Maddie screamed. When she opened her eyes, she realized she was on the floor, and Cordelia and Kate were looking down at her anxiously. She must have passed out. The back of her head hurt where it struck the floor.

Cordelia knelt down next to her and asked, "What did you see? What happened? Could you see where Bronwyn is? Is she still alive?"

Kate skeptically looked down at Maddie like she was a freak, as if they were putting on a show for her. "What the hell was that, Crane?"

"I saw Bronwyn. I don't know who has her or where, but she's definitely in danger. I—I couldn't do anything. . . ." Maddie started crying. "I tried to stop it. I really did."

"Stop what?" Kate asked, her interest piqued.

"Stop her from being killed," Maddie said stoically. "I watched her die."

Chapter 23

THE QUEEN OF PENTACLES
(Reversed)

A person who enjoys the company of sycophants to shield her from criticism and uses her wealth to do this. She is unable to see beyond material possessions or rise above them. She can be highly changeable with a suspicious and narrow-minded outlook toward things either that are new or that she misunderstands. Fortune used for displays of grandeur and opulence.

"Why would Bronwyn be a target?" Maddie asked Kate pointedly. She had returned to the Endicotts' house the following day at Kate's insistence. After the episode that had occurred the previous night, Cordelia was adamantly against it.

"That place is pure evil, and so is Kate," she warned. "If you can't see that, especially after your episode last night and the whole Ouija board fiasco, then maybe you need to be in Fairview more than my mother."

Cordelia told Maddie to be careful and that she was going back over to Fairview to see what kind of paperwork needed to be filled out for her mother's release. "Seriously, call me if you see anything strange," Cordelia said. "Well, anything strange besides Kate Endicott groveling for help," she added, smiling.

This gave Maddie the opportunity to get some real information from Kate, one-on-one. Maddie knew how to get Kate's guard down, or at least get under her skin a little.

Kate looked at Maddie with a withering look and began speaking to her slowly, as if she were talking to a small child.

She was curled up on a luxurious leather chair next to the fireplace, sipping hot cocoa spiked with Baileys. She looked like one of those girls curled up in a J.Crew winter catalog—all innocent, blond, sipping a mug of hot chocolate. But Maddie knew the evil and ugly monster that was beneath the porcelain doll exterior.

"Bronwyn knew too much, and around here, knowing too much and sticking your nose into things that don't concern you can get you into trouble." Kate continued by explaining that Bronwyn knew of the sacrifices that the Sisterhood had to make throughout the years. She knew of the legends and the curse. She was never part of the Sisters of Misery because she wasn't originally from the town—had no local or ancestral ties.

Maddie did.

Kate explained to her that the reason that everything bad that had happened to her—Cordelia running away, Rebecca being committed, her mother's cancer, her father's disappearance—all of it was due to the Sisters not being able to sacrifice one of their own to keep the curse of the Pickering sisters at bay. Maddie tried to understand what Kate was saying to her, but it seemed too far-fetched—too Stephen King for it to be really real.

"Every group of Sisters has to sacrifice one of their own. It's a fact. It goes back for hundreds of years, ever since the Pickering Witches cursed the women in the families of Hawthorne. The Sisterhood was created to protect us from the evils that exist if we don't fulfill our end of the deal."

"So Cordelia was supposed to be sacrificed?" Maddie said indignantly.

"She's your family, Maddie, but to the rest of us, she was a complete stranger, which made her the perfect person. She had the original ties to Hawthorne—and to a member of one of the Sisters—but wasn't someone that meant anything to us."

"To you!" Maddie snapped. "To me she was my family, my best friend, my own flesh and blood, my—"

"I know that she was all of those things to you, but look what happened when we didn't follow through with the sacrifice. Your family was torn apart, your mother's sick, your aunt has lost her mind. My future brother-in-law Reed has become the laughingstock of the town and his only chance at happiness, Bronwyn, has pulled a disappearing act, much like Cordelia. My family—as well as many others in this town—is on the brink of financial ruin because of the unexplained fires at the Endicott, which just so happened to be the site of Ravenswood. And I don't have to remind you that the broken-down asylum—in addition to being your aunt's living quarters for a short period—was also the place that kept the Pickering sisters when they were accused of witchcraft."

"So what are you saying?" Maddie asked as she was trying to take all of it in. "That instead of just torturing Cordelia that night, you were planning on killing her to keep the pact of the Sisterhood fulfilled?"

"Not killing, sacrificing," Kate insisted as if there were a real difference between the two.

Maddie was so angry that she couldn't even begin to speak. She could feel the bile rising in the back of her throat. Maddie shook her head in disbelief. "Okay, okay, just how many *sacrifices* are we talking about?"

"There have only been a handful that you and I know of. I mean, it's not like a weekly thing."

"How often does it take place?" Maddie asked, cringing.

"Every ten years or so," Kate said with about as much emotion as if she were reading from an almanac.

Maddie thought back to the premature deaths that she had known of—the parents and friends who'd died unexpectedly or simply disappeared.

"Who?" Maddie was insistent on knowing.

Kate hesitated. As if she'd said too much already. "I can't

give you everyone. That's a complete betrayal of the Sisterhood."

"But killing a member is totally acceptable?" Maddie said
incredulously.

"They don't always have to be part of the Sisterhoo—"

"But it helps, right?" Maddie interjected. "Unless it's someone who's getting too close to figuring out what's going on.
Someone like Bronwyn Maxwell."

Kate was getting visibly uncomfortable with where the discussion was headed. Maddie had never witnessed Kate
squirm.

She must be really desperate to open up to me like this,
Maddie thought.

"Yes, I mean, no . . . I mean, if it's someone that's one of
the Sisters—a descendant of one of the ancestors of this town—
then we don't need as many, as many . . ." She searched for
the right word as she gazed into the crackling fire.

Maddie helped her out. "Murders."

"Exactly."

Maddie looked Kate straight in the eye. "If you want my
help, you'd better give me at least one person that was vic-
timized by you."

"You know, you're just as much a part of the Sisterhood as
the rest of us. Even if you switched schools, you'll always be
a member of the Sisters of Misery."

"Yeah, well, I guess I didn't read that part of the hand-
book," Maddie snapped. "A name, Kate."

"Fine," she said uncomfortably. "Eleanor Putnam."

"Mrs. Putnam, as in Kevin Putnam's mom?"

Maddie remembered the shock that rippled through their
fifth grade class when Kevin's mother overdosed on pills in a
surprising, and unfortunately successful, suicide attempt. It
was the first time that Maddie had ever been subjected to a
tragic death happening to someone she knew so well.

"Kevin's mom was part of the Sisters of Misery?"

"Yes, back when my mother was the head of the group."

"Oh, so your mom decided that Mrs. Putnam should take one for the team. Or did Eleanor volunteer like she was baking a freaking cake for a fund-raiser?"

"It wasn't like that," Kate insisted.

"Really? Well, tell me what it was like, Kate, because after seeing Kevin and his family go through such a traumatic event, it would really surprise me if Eleanor Putnam would raise her hand and say 'Pick me, pick me. Kill me to get rid of the curse.'"

"That's not the way it works—or worked. My mom explained it to me. If your mother had been a part of the Sisters of Misery, then it wouldn't seem so strange to you. Not when you grow up knowing that it's a part of you, part of your destiny—a responsibility to your Sisters, your town, to everyone." Kate continued trying to rationalize the murder spree that had been going on for decades unbeknownst to most of the residents of Hawthorne. "You see, everyone going out to Misery Island knew there was a chance that they could be the one selected. It was part of our legacy. Things just cooled down. Things had been going well for everyone, so there wasn't a need to—to . . ."

"To kill," Maddie said bluntly. "So you guys just got rid of that whole giving someone a fighting chance option—giving someone the choice *not* to go along with the sacrifice." Maddie waited a beat and then asked, "Why didn't any of you volunteer, seeing as how you are all card-carrying members of the Deaths R Us Club?"

"We were, but then . . . things changed."

"Meaning?"

"Meaning Cordelia came into town and she just seemed like the obvious choice. She had the ties to the town, the right ancestry, and, well, we all hated that bitch. It made it a lot easier to take out someone that you can't stand than one of your best friends."

"Wow," Maddie said, shaking her head in disbelief. "It must have been just like winning the lottery when Cordelia came to town. She certainly turned your luck around."

"Obviously not, because she's still alive."

"The nerve of her!" Maddie said in mock horror.

"Maddie, I wouldn't be so cocky. Just so you know, your name was tossed around a few times before Cordelia entered the picture. I kept you out of it. I convinced the girls that we could pick someone outside of the Sisterhood. Someone like Emily Johnson or Sarah Charles. But then Cordelia came to town and the opportunity just presented itself."

"Wrapped up in a pretty bow, wasn't she?" Maddie said harshly.

"For someone who has probably been hit the hardest by the curse, you seem to be pretty glib."

"Well, maybe I just don't take much stock in village stonings or sacrificing virgins to appease the war gods."

"Well, Cordelia was hardly virginal."

"You know, Kate, you would have done everyone a huge favor if you had been the one to volunteer. I can honestly say that the world would be a better place without Kate Endicott to manipulate, taunt, blackmail, and generally destroy people's lives. It's a pity that option never occurred to you."

"Maddie, silly Maddie," Kate said in a mocking tone. "If I weren't here to continue the tradition, who would?"

Chapter 24

THE TOWER

Disruption. Conflict. Change. Sudden violent loss.
Overthrow of an existing way of life. Major changes.
Disruption of well-worn routines. Ruin and disturbance.
Dramatic upheaval. Widespread repercussions of actions.

A week before Christmas, the buildings ravaged by the fire at Ravenswood were finally secure enough for investigation. The main building of Ravenswood, the one that had been built centuries ago right after the terror of the witch trials, remained inexplicably untouched by the fire. It was almost as if a protective bubble had formed around the original building. The authorities assumed it was arson, either an accidental fire from a homeless squatter, or someone with a grudge against the Endicotts. Either way, there was no possible way that the fire could have started on its own, especially since the four towers mainly affected by the fire hadn't even been wired for electricity yet.

It was during one of those initial sweeps that one of the firemen came across the body. He called in a local officer—Officer Sullivan—to see if it was, in fact, the missing girl.

At first, they weren't sure if it was a prank: a wax dummy or one of those blow-up dolls left over from a Halloween party. But as they got closer to the heap of a body sprawled on the dirt floor of the basement of Ravenswood, the realization that this was a person became gruesomely real. Her hair was cut short, as if angry hunks were torn out. She was facedown and sprawled toward the entrance, one leg coagulated with blood and bruised from the archaic metal shackle coming from the center of the floor. It was Bronwyn Maxwell.

Sully looked at the frail body in horror. Despite his burly frame and reputation for bar fights, a thin sliver of fear crept under his skin and made his body visibly shake.

"Hey," he called softly, as if he were afraid to disturb the spirits that clung to the moss-covered stone walls. "You okay?"

Silence.

"Oh, shit, she's dead," he said to the firemen.

He crept closer to her, silently cursing the pathetic lighting they had within the chamber.

Her body was clad only in undergarments and the pale skin had a blue hue interrupted by darker blue bruises and crimson bloody scrapes.

Sully inched forward and then drew back suddenly as a large sound clapped through the chamber. His heart leapt into his throat and he directed his flashlight to where the sound emanated from. There was a plate of food left on the floor, now covered with remnants of ants and cockroaches; the plate was left just out of her arm's reach. Whoever locked her up here left the food there to taunt her, knowing how she would strain and struggle for just a small mouthful of insect-laden sustenance. Next to her body was a large bottle of water. It became clear that the person who locked her up wanted her to live, yet suffer every moment of that life.

"Looks like whoever did this to her wanted to cover their tracks," the fire official said.

"You think?"

"Why else would they want to torch this place down? Stupid fools didn't count on this old building being the only one left standing," he said in a gruff laugh. Sully could only focus on Bronwyn, the girl that all the guys he knew growing up had fantasized about at one point in their lives—the golden girl who could stop a guy in his tracks with one flip of her hair and a sidelong glance. One of Hawthorne's great beauties reduced to a broken and battered body on the filthy floor of Ravenswood. Shudders ran down his spine and he turned away quickly to vomit.

Once the EMTs had arrived, they declared Bronwyn dead at the scene. And the statewide manhunt for her killer was under way. There was no way that this was going to remain unsolved like Darcy's murder. There was a kidnapper and murderer among them and the Maxwell family would not rest until he was found and brought to justice. They would spare no expense. They were dead set on finding out who was responsible for the death of their only child. They would be relentless.

But only a select few knew that the Maxwells were up against something even more powerful than all the money in the world. The Sisterhood.

Chapter 25

THE MAGICIAN

One who represents the potential of a new adventure, chosen or thrust upon one. A journey undertaken, bringing things out of the darkness into the light. Exploration of the world in order to master it. There are choices and directions to take. Guidance can arrive through one's own intuition or in the form of someone who brings about change or transformation. The card represents a beneficent guide, but he does not necessarily have our best interests in mind. The card represents the intoxication of power, both good and bad.

After hearing about Cordelia and Maddie's adventure at the Endicotts', Finn decided to head out to Misery Island. He knew there had to be a clue, something that connected Darcy's and Bronwyn's murders. And he knew that if he didn't discover the connection, then the next people on the list would be Cordelia or Maddie. It was his responsibility to figure it out in time. He didn't tell the girls where he was headed, because he knew they would want to tag along. He needed to do this alone under the cover of darkness. They'd already done enough to help him clear his name. Now he needed to do something for them—to possibly save them from their intended fate.

He dragged his boat up onto the shore of Cat Cove and wandered over to the site of the Winter Gala. The ruins of the old casino looked monstrous in the moonlit night. He headed over to where the tent was erected the night Darcy was murdered. He knew his way around the island pretty well from working for Hawthorne's grounds department. He walked over and looked down at the jagged outcropping of rocks where Darcy's body was found. If someone had pushed her off the rocks where he was standing, she would have been able to crawl back up and save herself.

"Unless she was unconscious when she was pushed off," he said to himself. The police reports said that she had several blunt traumas to her head, neck, torso, and legs, and that they believed these were consistent with her body being bashed against the rocks repeatedly by the waves. But what if she had been struck prior to being pushed into the water? Finn decided to look around in the overgrown sections of the island for any evidence that would point to it. It was then that he found it. A tent stake with dried blood. Darcy's blood. It had been thrown deep into the bracken behind the old casino. But what shocked him even more was what he found lying next to it. When he shone his flashlight around the tent stake, resisting the temptation to move anything so as not to disturb any useful fingerprints, something caught his eye. Something familiar. Something that could connect the assailant to the crime. It was just so unbelievable.

Finn had grabbed the evidence and was running back to his boat, eager to get back to the mainland and notify the police, when he realized that he wasn't alone on the island.

"Hey there, lawn boy," Trevor said with disgust in his voice. He and his friends had pulled up onto the shore and Trevor had a baseball bat in his hands. "Taking a moonlight stroll on Misery Island, are we?"

Finn knew that he was outnumbered, so he chose to walk past them and get into his boat. He pushed the boat along the sand into the water while Trevor continued to taunt him.

"Yeah, I come out here sometimes to think about last year out on Misery Island. That was going to be an awesome party until someone had to come out here and ruin all the fun," Trevor continued when Finn refused to respond. Finn knew Trevor was referring to the night when Cordelia was tortured and almost gang-raped by Trevor and his friends. It might have happened if Finn hadn't heard about it ahead of time and showed up with his gun.

"If I recall, you and your friends needed a change of underpants after I showed up with my gun," Finn muttered.

"Yeah, well, you don't have a gun now. Guess you're not so tough after all," Trevor taunted while the others laughed.

"Guess so, Trevor. I'm the wimp. You got me." He continued shoving the boat toward the water. The sooner he was out to sea, the better off he'd feel.

"Going out on a late night boat trip, Finn? You should have brought Cordelia with you. I remember one night out on my brother's boat with your little slut girlfriend. Boy, did she make the boat rock that night! She's a firecracker, that one is. Hoo-eeyy!" He yelped with glee and high-fived his friends.

Finn couldn't take it anymore. He could handle the taunts about himself, but hearing Trevor gloat about the night that he violently raped Cordelia, possibly impregnating her, was too much for him to bear. He lunged at Trevor, who was waiting for him. All Finn remembered was the sound of a crack of the bat as it connected with his skull.

❧

Finn woke up when a shock of cold hit his body.

"Self-righteous prick," Trevor said as he looked down at Finn flailing helplessly in the freezing water. Finn felt like the world was moving in slow motion. The words and the sounds were garbled like a worn-out tape recorder and the freezing water sapped his energy, making him feel like he was paralyzed. His body hurt to even move, let alone tread water to keep his head above the waves.

He was going to drown.

Out in the middle of the harbor, Finn began calling out for

help. It was starting to come back to him as he gulped mouth-fuls of salt water. They had beaten him severely and then taken him out onto the boat. Once they were out on the water, they dumped his body on their way back to the mainland. He started floundering and then seemed to be pulled under. The guys on the boat were yipping and hollering. Finn had a flash that this was how his life was going to end. Battered and bruised and being taunted by Trevor and his crew while he slowly slipped under the surface. As he went underwater for what felt like the hundredth time, he felt the sharp pang of irony that he was going to die—something he prayed for every day that he was away from Cordelia to ease the pain. And now that she was back, he was finally going to get his wish.

∞

With the noise and shouts echoing off the harbor, Reed Campbell came out of his boat. He'd been there almost every night since Bronwyn's disappearance, drinking himself into a stupor, not caring if he fell overboard and drowned. He de-served it. If he had only paid more attention to her—if he had only given her the affection that she so desperately wanted from him, then maybe he could have prevented all of this from happening. And now that she was dead—he knew it was only a matter of time before he was brought in again as a suspect. They always look closest to home when crimes of this nature occur. He had finished a bottle of Jim Beam and was ready to crack open a bottle of Stoli when he heard the shouting and splashing.

In the bright moonlit night, Reed could see his brother and his friends laughing at someone desperately trying to keep his head above the freezing ocean water. He heard them yelling:

"Swim, Finn, swim!"

"Run, Forrest, run!"

"Come on, Finn, use your fins to swim back to shore!"

Reed dove into the oily blackness of the waves to save him. He came up sputtering and coughing; the icy water took the wind right out of him. Finn resurfaced behind him, screaming and gasping for air. Before Reed could make it over to him, Finn had sunk beneath the glassy shoal once more. Reed started yelling to the guys on the boat for help.

"Jesus Christ!" he screamed. "Pull him up, you assholes. Trevor, do something! He's gonna drown!"

A few of them seemed to want to help Finn, but Trevor wanted to wait it out a little longer. Just to see what would happen.

Reed quickly realized that if anyone was going to save Finn, it was going to have to be him, despite his own inebriated condition. Just as Reed was about to dive under again, Finn came up a good ten to twenty feet in front of him, heading toward the shore. Before any of them could figure out how Finn had made it all that way, Reed began swimming furiously toward the dark figure.

By the time Reed reached him, Finn seemed to be at the brink of death. Reed used his lifeguard training and was able to float on his back and keep Finn's head abovewater all the way back to shore. The other boys watched from the boat, still enjoying the show. When they got up to shore, Reed dragged Finn onto the beach and started screaming at Finn to wake up; then he yelled to the others that he was unconscious. The boys quickly pulled their boat up to shore and jumped out to assess the situation.

"We have to call an ambulance," Reed cried. "He's going to die."

"No way," Trevor snapped. "If you call an ambulance, the cops will come and we'll get busted for kicking his ass."

"He needs help! Don't you fucking understand that?"

"Just relax, Reed. He'll be fine. He just needed to be taken down a notch. He needed to learn to stop poking his nose into places where it doesn't belong." Trevor tried to calm his brother down.

Standing there dripping and looking from face to face, seeing them dark and grotesque in the pale glow of the streetlights above, Reed became enraged. "You guys did this to him?" He looked down at Finn's beaten and bruised body. The lumps on his face were the size of lemons, his eyes were swollen shut, and his mouth was gushing blood. "He could have died! Would that have been a cool enough show for you guys if he had drowned out there?"

Kate made her way to the edge of the shore out from the shadows, her eyes lit up ecstatically. She'd been watching the whole time.

"Definitely," she said enthusiastically, her breath turning the cold air into smoke. "Now, that's what I call a fun night."

Reed looked over at Kate angrily. "You knew about this? You knew what they were going to do to Finn?"

"Why do you care anyway? Did you guys become soul mates while you were cell mates?" Kate asked as she laughed.

"Kate, he could have died."

"Just like your girlfriend! Or did Bronwyn stop making your heart go pitterpat when your little girlfriends came back to town? Don't you think it's a little gross to be going after underage girls who also happen to be related!"

"I'm not going after anyone," he said angrily. He refused to let Kate get under his skin. She was like one of those tapeworms that once you let get into your system, you can never get it out.

Reed grabbed a sweater and a flannel shirt out of his backpack. Even though his entire body was shaking uncontrollably from the frigid harbor water, he knew that Finn's life was at stake. He covered Finn up, trying to get some warmth back into the boy whose lips were blue and trembling.

Kate went over to her car and grabbed a big flannel blanket and handed it to Reed. "Here," she said offhandedly. "A prize for the hero of the day."

Reed pulled the blanket around his shivering body and ordered Kate to call 9-1-1. He then turned to yell at his brother and his friends, who were still laughing like hyenas. "Laugh it up, but you're going to have to explain this to the police when they get here."

"Boys will be boys, won't they, Reed?" Kate purred. "Now, if I were you I'd stay away from your new best friend, Finn, as well as your little girlfriends Maddie and Cordelia. Because that would put you in a very awkward situation, considering what happened to Bronwyn and with all those people that frown upon old, lecherous men and underage girls." She turned and looked at Trevor, who was now rolling on the ground in a drunken stupor.

She wrapped her arms around Reed's neck and continued. "Luckily I'm all for those kinds of relationships." Before he could stop her, she started French-kissing him and pushed her tongue so far back into his throat he started gagging. He pushed her away in disgust.

She narrowed her eyes and pulled his arm back around her, only to yell out, "Get off me, you pig. Trevor!"

Trevor lifted his head up and saw Kate struggling to get away from his brother and before he knew what was happening, did a running tackle and took his brother down.

Kate sat back watching the brothers beat the crap out of each other and said, "Boys, boys, I hate to see you fight over little old me." Her grin grew wider as the other guys circled the brothers, cheering them on. Reed definitely was a better kisser than Trevor, she'd give him that much.

The police sirens and ambulance lights broke up the fight between Trevor and Reed. The paramedics started loading Finn into the back of the ambulance, placing an oxygen mask over his face, starting an IV, and putting heated blankets over his shivering body.

Kate turned and started to head back to her car, pleased with what she'd accomplished. It wasn't until she passed by where the ambulance had been parked that she saw something on the ground. It must have fallen off Finn when they were getting him into the ambulance. She glanced around to make sure no one was looking before picking it up and slipping it into her pocket. Very lucky that it was in her possession.

"If anyone found this, then there would be a real problem," she said to herself. Then she wondered just how much Finn knew and if he would be able to make anything of this puzzle piece. Because if he could, then the rest of the puzzle would fall quickly and easily into place. And that would be a very, very bad thing.

Chapter 26

DEATH

The end of a phase in life which has served its purpose. Abrupt and complete change of circumstances, way of life, and patterns of behavior due to past events and actions. Alterations. Change that is both painful and unpleasant. A refusal to face the fear of change or change itself. Agonizing periods of transition. Physical or emotional exhaustion.

Bronwyn Maxwell's and Darcy Willett's funerals were set one week apart. The news media were crawling all over Hawthorne. The Darcy incident evoked some suspicion, but many believed that she had simply had too much to drink at the Winter Gala on Misery Island and ended up drowning. There was no evidence of foul play.

Bronwyn's discovery was something altogether different.

Someone wanted her dead and did everything they could, even arson, to cover it up. And the people of Hawthorne wanted answers. No one more than the Endicotts and their investors who'd poured millions into the development.

"You know, now that you're back in town, you might want to keep a better watch on your boyfriend," Kate snapped at Cordelia when she ran into them at the Christmas Holiday Walk. Despite the frigid weather, Maddie could feel the collective heat of anger emanating from Maddie and Cordelia. The girls entered one of the stores on the walk.

Cordelia went immediately to the back of the store, obviously too upset about Finn's hypothermia and hospitalization to get into an argument with Kate. "How's the ice diver doing anyway?" Kate called over Maddie's shoulder.

Maddie shoved Kate backward. "Leave her alone."

"Wow, Maddie. Look at you," she said, smiling. "It's the new and improved fighter Maddie doll. Where can I get one?"

"Why in the world would Finn do that to Bronwyn? He didn't even know her," Maddie hissed. "And burn down Ravenswood? He's been fighting to keep that place around for years through the historical society. Why would he throw that all away?"

"Exactly," Kate said, inspecting the jewelry in the glass case in front of her. She stared at the shopgirl until she felt so uncomfortable, she turned away, red-faced. "He wanted to preserve the original Ravenswood. Not the new structures that were part of the new hotel. And, wow, what a coincidence, the only part of that monstrous place to survive the fire was the original building—the place that Finn so desperately wanted to save. Isn't that ironic?"

Maddie shook her head, and turned to see if Cordelia was in the proximity, listening to Kate's madness.

"So, Miss Detective, if you're right—that in addition to being a landscaper, student, and member of the historical society, Finn is also a brilliant arsonist—why would he leave Bronwyn in the one place where the evidence wouldn't be destroyed?"

"Maybe he wanted her to be found. Maybe it was a message to us to back off of the construction. Or maybe he's just a sick twisted bastard. Now I see why he fits in so well with your family," she said with a light tinkling laugh.

Suddenly Kate fell forward against the case, causing a Waterford crystal bowl to fall to the floor, shattering into millions of shards of glass.

"Oh my, I'm so sorry about that, Kate. I must have tripped," Cordelia said lightly. "Come on, Maddie, let's go." And then she turned to the shopgirl. "You can just put that on the Endicott tab; I'm sure they can afford it. Happy holidays."

Maddie followed Cordelia out the door only to hear Kate shouting after them, "This isn't over!" The shopgirl raced around to start cleaning up the shards of glass and Maddie watched as Kate angrily ground them into the floor with her boots.

"You're going to get us in so much trouble," Maddie said, giggling.

"Trouble doesn't even begin to describe what's going to happen when I get done with Kate," Cordelia said dryly.

Maddie knew that this was no laughing matter.

This was revenge.

∞

"You really shouldn't be out of the hospital so soon," Cordelia said as she helped Finn out to her car.

The girls had received the message once they got home that Finn was signing himself out of the hospital. Cordelia jumped into her VW Bug the moment she heard that Finn was going to be released.

The girls walked on either side of him, Cordelia with her arm around his waist.

"I'm not going to break. You guys can take off the kid gloves," Finn said, attempting to be lighthearted. His voice was still raspy from the hypothermia and the treatment he'd received in the hospital. His memories were so clouded from that night. He knew that there was something important he found on Misery Island, but during all of the craziness, he had forgotten what it was and how it related to Darcy and Bronwyn. It may have been nothing at all. But, still, it nagged at him. The only reason it bothered him was that he feared that whatever happened to Darcy and Bronwyn could just as easily happen to Cordelia and Maddie. That's why he wasn't going to let either girl out of his sight.

When they got back to Mariner's Way, Maddie busied herself in the kitchen making hot chocolate for everyone. Cordelia bundled Finn in blankets, despite his good-natured protesting that he was fine. They lit a fire in the fireplace and all huddled around the warmth, bracing themselves against the cool icy winds coming off the ocean that still seemed to find their way through the cracks and slats of the old Victorian.

"Do you remember why you went out there that night?" Cordelia asked.

Finn shook his head. "There wasn't a real reason. I just had a hunch that I'd find something out there."

"Great, just what we need, more psychics in this house." They heard the stern voice come from the hallway. Abigail had just returned from visiting Rebecca and didn't seem pleased to see the gathering in her living room.

Cordelia let Abigail's snide comment slide and quickly asked, "Are they letting my mom out soon? What did the doctors say?"

"They want to make sure that Rebecca is coming to a safe, calm, and normal home. No craziness, no antics, no stress."

Finn said under his breath, "That counts out Hawthorne."

Abigail continued, ignoring Finn's remark. "We need to make sure that she doesn't have another episode, so that means that everyone has to agree to make this place as stress free as possible. No running off on a whim, no disappearing acts, no night swims on the islands, none of that."

Maddie knew that Abigail had conveniently pardoned herself of any blame as to what had happened to Rebecca. It was a convenient, self-preservation technique. In her mind, she was blameless. And the rest of the world should be held responsible. It was something that Maddie had become accustomed to when dealing with Abigail Crane.

"Don't worry, Mrs. Crane. I'm going to watch out for these girls," Finn said staunchly.

Abigail gave him a sharp look. "And who is going to look out for you, Finn?" She smiled for the briefest moment and then headed upstairs, leaving the three of them to return to their discussion.

"You don't really think we're at risk, do you, Finn?" Maddie asked. All of it seemed surreal. Darcy's death and then Bronwyn's kidnapping and murder. The fire at Ravenswood. There had to be a connection to it all. Who was doing this and why?

"Well, you all realize that I'm the main suspect," Cordelia said dryly. "I'm the one who disappeared for a year. I'm the one that people think is crazy. I'm the one that drove my mom into a nuthouse. And all of this insanity started right when I got back to town."

"Plus, the tarot cards," Finn said to no one in particular.

"What did you just say?" Cordelia asked, her voice suddenly shaky. "Who said anything about tarot cards?"

Finn looked back and forth between Maddie and Cordelia. They both were staring at him strangely. This was the first time that tarot cards had ever been mentioned among the three of them.

"I—uh—I thought you guys knew," Finn stammered. "When Reed and I were being held as suspects, he told me that Darcy and the rest of the Sisters of Misery got some weird tarot cards. And then he mentioned that Bronwyn got one, too. And you," he said to Maddie. "He said you got one up at school. I found one with my name on it shoved into the stone wall with faces of the Pickering sisters."

Cordelia's eyes glazed over. "I got one up in Maine. I didn't know how anyone found me. I'd been hiding for a year and all of a sudden, the same day I read the paper about the mess I'd left behind here—all of the craziness that happened at Ravenswood, Tess's passing . . ." She stopped talking, her eyes welling up with tears. "Someone knew where I was. I got a tarot card. The Death card. I thought it was some kind of message from the Sisters of Misery. That they found me or something. That they'd been watching me the whole time. That's when I knew I had to come back here. Not only to clear Finn and Reed as suspects, but also to find out who had been keeping tabs on me for all that time."

"Who do you think they're from?" Maddie asked quickly.

Finn answered solemnly, "Whoever sent those cards is probably the same person responsible for all the recent tragedies." He paused and looked at the girls with a mixture of fear and anger. "And that person is giving us a warning."

"What kind of warning?" Maddie asked, afraid that she already knew the answer.

"That one of us is next."

Chapter 27

THE WORLD

*A culmination of events. A sense of repleteness.
Frustration. Completion delayed. Inability to bring
something to a satisfactory end. Resistance to change.
Lack of trust. Hesitation. Despite appearances to the
contrary, an indication that events have not yet come
to a conclusion, but are nearing completion.*

The phone rang at 3:00 a.m.

Finn lunged for it and instantly regretted it when the searing pain went up his back. He remembered the last time he got one of those 3:00 a.m. calls, and how that night ended up.

The voice on the phone was barely a whisper. "I know what you found and I think we need to talk."

Finn didn't recognize the voice right away, but when he did, a sickening feeling fell across his body. It felt even worse than all the bruises and cuts on his body from his near-death experience off the shore of Misery Island.

"What the hell do you want?" he growled.

"You wouldn't want to live with the fact that you could have saved Cordelia and Maddie's lives, and you did nothing to stop it, would you?" the voice hissed. Finn could picture the person and the bile rose up in the back of his throat. How could this be possible?

"Like I said, what do you want?" he said in a resigned manner.

"Meet me at Ravenswood. You know where."

Click. The phone line went dead. He stared at the receiver for a minute and then slowly lowered the phone back onto his nightstand. He felt winded, like he'd had his last breath punched out of him.

Jesus Christ, he thought, *what the hell am I going to do?*

The haunting voice stuck with him as he drove to Ravenswood. He debated about calling Maddie and Cordelia, just in case something happened. He knew that if he called them right now, they'd want to go with him, which was the last thing he needed. So instead, he sent an e-mail that they'd get in the morning. That way, if he never made it home, at least they'd have a place to start looking.

଼

Maddie was lying in bed, trying to process everything that had gone on in the past few weeks. It seemed like such a short time ago that she was up at school—her only concern was that Cordelia was out there somewhere lost. Every night before she went to bed she had the same wish, to find Cordelia. And now she had gotten exactly what she had been praying for. But at what cost? Darcy and Bronwyn were killed—the killer still at large and most likely someone she knew well. The fire at Ravenswood. The threats on all of their lives. The tarot cards. Finn almost drowning. Malcolm Crane returning to Hawthorne just to make things even more insane.

But then there were the good parts. Getting Finn and Reed off the hook and removing any suspicion that they were involved with the disappearance of the girls. Cordelia and Rebecca reuniting. Abigail's cancer going into remission. Luke checking in on her and making her feel like despite all the craziness in her life, he would remain a constant—he'd look out for her.

But there was something nagging at her. Something just wasn't right. There was a connection there that she felt should be obvious, but it still eluded her. She heard knocking downstairs and sat up. It was probably just Cordelia getting a glass of water, but it reminded her of the night that Reed showed up. That first night that they went sailing together.

Reed.

He was the connection. He was involved with Bronwyn, and yet he obviously didn't have any real feelings for her, or else he wouldn't have kissed Maddie that night out on Misery Island. He knew about the tarot cards and gave Finn just enough information about the cards so that Finn could be implicated. He was there that night that Finn was almost killed. Bronwyn was missing and instead of tirelessly looking for her, he was spending his time drinking out on his boat? None of it made sense. And yet—he was there all along in plain sight. Blending in and yet never really proving his innocence. Could he have discovered where Cordelia moved to and sent her that tarot? Or perhaps he was just covering up for his little brother again?

There was a soft tapping at her door.

"Oh, good, I'm glad you're up," Cordelia said, rushing over to the bed with a glass of water in her hand. "I think I know who is at the center of all this."

The girls locked eyes and said at the same time, their voices overlapping:

"Reed."

"Trevor."

"What?"

"No!"

"How can you possibly think Reed has anything to do with this?" Cordelia asked. "If anyone had a motive it would be Trevor."

Maddie considered this for a moment. Trevor had dated Darcy last year and ended things with her abruptly to return to Kate. Maybe Darcy threatened to go public with their affair that night out on Misery, and that was Trevor's way of quieting her.

"Think about it," Cordelia said. "He raped me and got

away with it. Their family is superrich and could have easily tracked me down, making sure that I never came forward to press charges. But instead of silencing me with cash, Trevor sends me a tarot card, knowing that I would see it as a sign— a sign to keep my mouth shut and to stay away."

"Why would he burn down Ravenswood? Why kill Bronwyn?"

"Maybe Bronwyn was onto him about the Darcy thing? Maybe he was jealous that she preferred Reed over him. Who knows? With Trevor, anything is possible. And Ravenswood burning down could have been his way of getting back at Kate and showing her who's boss. He knew that all the Endicotts' money was tied up in that place. What better way to take down a rich ex-girlfriend than by hitting her where it hurts the most? The very thing that defines her. Her money."

Maddie chewed her fingernail thoughtfully. Cordelia did have a point. It could have been Trevor.

"Or . . ." Cordelia's voice trailed off. "Maybe Reed was just cleaning up after his little brother. Just like last time."

There were so many possibilities. But each one seemed to point to the Campbell brothers more and more.

Just when Maddie was about to agree with Cordelia about her theory on Reed and Trevor, her phone went off.

"Oh God, another text from lover boy?" Cordelia said, trying to lighten the mood. "Doesn't he know that booty calls don't work at three in the morning when you're separated by an ocean?"

Maddie flipped open her phone. It wasn't from Luke. It was an e-mail from Finn. She'd had her e-mails filtered into her phone while she was up at school. It was just easier to keep track of assignments that way. But Finn didn't know that. *Which is probably why he sent it,* Maddie thought. *Hoping that I wouldn't get the message until the morning.*

"Oh, crap," Maddie said, and then said to Cordelia quickly, "Get dressed."

"Why? What's going on? Where are we going?"

Maddie's stomach dropped as she said the name. It was just like last year all over again. "Ravenswood."

ॐ

Finn cut across the sloping hill to Ravenswood. He left his car parked far enough away so that no one would know he was there. Granted, no one in their right mind would be out and around Ravenswood in the middle of the night, especially in light of all that had happened there. But Finn knew he was dealing with someone who definitely wasn't in their right mind.

As soon as he passed the yellow CAUTION tape that criss-crossed the area surrounding Ravenswood and the charred remains of the newer buildings, it occurred to him that the only reason he was being summoned out here in the middle of the night with no one around for miles was that this person had one goal in mind.

To kill me, Finn thought as he stopped in his tracks, unsure of what he was getting himself into. He'd brought a knife, just in case, but he was starting to wish that he'd brought additional protection. After last year's nightmare and having been held as a suspect for both Darcy's and Bronwyn's murders, Finn wasn't allowed to go near a handgun, let alone be in possession of one. And even if the police hadn't enforced it, his father certainly would have.

He silently cursed himself as he picked his way along the darkened overgrown path, around the charred remains of brick and mortar—the smell of a dampened fire still clinging to the air, as if the scent had sunk into the trees that surrounded Ravenswood like a fortress.

The desolate monster lay in front of him. He thought he detected some movement outside the building, but the flashes of light on the main floor let him know that someone was waiting for him. He suddenly wished he'd called someone to go with him. But he knew that Cordelia's and Maddie's fate rested in his hands, so he went in alone. It didn't matter what happened to him; he wouldn't be able to live with himself if he allowed any harm to come to those girls.

He walked up the snow-covered path, shaking not only from the cold, but from what was about to happen. When he walked in the front door to Ravenswood, which was left ajar, he wasn't at all surprised to see Kiki Endicott sitting calmly waiting for him, like a spider waiting for its prey. Waiting for him to enter the madhouse to meet his death, so that she could continue her web of lies and deceit. She was dressed for a cocktail party—at complete odds with the crumbling surroundings. She seemed so out of place, her hair perfectly coiffed, strings of expensive pearls wrapped around her neck, a designer coat and dress suited more for an elegant evening out than a night committing murder in an abandoned insane asylum. And yet she seemed oddly calm—comfortable even. It was as if she were preparing for a dinner party, waiting for the guests to arrive. As he moved closer to the ring of light that surrounded her, he noticed her crocodile pumps and was amused by the woman's serpentlike qualities. It was like being in the presence of the devil—only one that wears thousand-dollar shoes.

What did surprise him was that she was alone . . . and that she had a gun pointed right at him. When he looked at her hand, he saw the ring. The bloodred ruby ring that he had found near the tent stake that was used to kill Darcy and then hidden in the bracken on Misery Island. The one that he almost lost his life trying to bring back to shore. The piece that tied Kiki Endicott to Darcy's murder. The ring he thought he had lost when he was trying to keep from drowning in the icy Atlantic Ocean. It was all coming back to him now.

"So happy that you could come to see me, Finn. You and I have a lot to talk about," Kiki said with a grin spread wide across her face. The lantern light surrounding her made her face glow eerily, as if she were an escapee from an asylum. Ravenswood was the perfect setting for this meeting. She looked more like one of the inmates than the wealthy matri- arch of Hawthorne. And she held the gun unwaveringly at his head, as if she knew exactly how to use it. As if she'd used it before. "And thank you so much for finding my ring! I thought I'd lost it forever."

"Mrs. Endicott, please." Finn edged into the main foyer. The light was playing tricks on his eyes. He kept seeing shad- ows darting around him, but it was just the flicker of the old kerosene lantern. Yet he couldn't shake the feeling that there were others around him, watching, waiting. "I don't know what this is about, but whatever it is, we can fix it. I'll do whatever you want."

"Now you'll do whatever I want?" she laughed gaily, as if he had just told her a joke at a cocktail party, and not in this scene straight out of a horror movie. "Now? After all of the nonsense that you've put me and my family through, you lit- tle weasel? Now you want to play nice? I don't think so."

"Honestly, I have no idea what you're talking about. I had nothing to do with Darcy or Bronwyn or the fire here at Ravenswood. Please, you have to believe me. I—I know that I made it difficult for you to turn Ravenswood into a hotel. And I'm sorry. But you won. There's no one stopping you from rebuilding this place into the luxury resort that you wanted."

"Silly boy," Kiki said, looking and speaking to him like he was a toddler. "You don't get it, do you? There's never going to be a resort. The Endicott was never going to happen. The money is gone."

"Mrs. Endicott, I had nothing to do with the fire. Anyway, the money that you lost—it'll be covered by insurance. You'll get the money back and you can start over." He was trying to reason with her, but he was unnerved to see that her hand holding the gun was steady as a rock. She had it pointed directly at his head.

"The money is gone because we spent it. All of it. All of the hassle that you put us through last year caused us to lose most of our investors—we had no choice but to live on the money from the few people who stuck with us. The few who wanted to invest in the idea of a beautiful, luxurious resort—the only one of its kind on the North Shore of Boston. And one with stories! So many stories that you and your girlfriend and her family contributed to! I thought that my own family played a big part in Ravenswood. The fact that the Endicott family was responsible for the witch hangings that took place on this very spot—you knew that, didn't you? That this place was built on top of the graves of so many people accused of witchcraft. Well, it's true. And all of those thrill seekers who come to New England each year to get a taste of horror, of witchcraft, of evil, they would pay any amount to stay here to relish the ghoulish experience. Don't you see how what happened last year only added to the deliciously evil story?"

She was taking care to hold the gun steady on her target as she spoke.

"But then you and your little friends in the historical society had to come along and tie things up. By the time we cut through all that blasted red tape, the money for the resort was gone. We'd gone through it all."

"How?" Finn asked weakly. He thought that if he could keep her talking, he would be able to find a way out of this mess.

"You have no idea how much it costs to be an Endicott, do you? Of course you don't. When you have nothing, you don't realize how much it costs to be rich. It's a chore, really. Keeping up appearances when you're flat broke. Ha! So we knew we had to torch this place for the insurance money. It was the only way to avoid getting caught."

"You burned this place down?" Finn asked, horrified at what he was hearing.

"Of course," Kiki answered in a matter-of-fact tone, as if it were the most natural thing in the world. "Unfortunately, this building was stubborn—like you. It just refused to give up the ghost, so to speak. Which is why tonight, you, my friend, are going to help me burn this place down for good. And do you know how I'm so sure it will work this time?"

Finn shook his head. She had clearly lost her mind and was now involving him in her crazy games.

"Because you are going to stay here and watch it burn—make sure it burns to the ground."

"You want me to get in trouble for arson? I'm not going to just stand outside and watch this place burn down."

"Of course you aren't," she said sweetly. "You're going to watch it from the inside. It's a pity that since you killed Darcy and Bronwyn and are so consumed with guilt, you have no choice but to take your own life." She stopped talking and smiled as the realization hit his face. "Yes, Finn, this is your last night, your grand finale, your big good-bye. It's quite fitting that it's taking place right here in the place that you fought so hard to keep standing, don't you think?"

"You're crazy," he said, his voice cracking. "I had nothing to do with what happened to Darcy and Bronwyn. I didn't kill them. I swear!"

"Of course you didn't kill them, darling Finn," she cooed. "I did."

Chapter 28

THE CHARIOT

*A war, a struggle, and an eventual, hard-won victory;
either over enemies, obstacles, nature, or the beasts
inside you. This card represents the struggles we have
with ourselves and with life. It promises that with
diligence, honesty, and perseverance we can overcome
the most insurmountable of obstacles.*

"Do you think it makes sense for us to go out there by ourselves?" Maddie asked Cordelia as she drove the VW Bug so fast it almost tipped over as it took every corner. Maddie was rocking back and forth in the passenger seat, rubbing her hands together trying to get the icy, numbing sensation out of her system. The heat in the old car wasn't working, and the girls were shaking out of fear, adrenaline, and the bitter cold of the wintry night.

"Finn is there. Wasn't he the one who saved you the last time?" Cordelia asked. When Maddie nodded, Cordelia then said, "Well, now it's our turn to return the favor."

"But we have no idea why he's going there. Who is he meeting? Why in the middle of the night at Ravenswood? Why go alone?"

"Those are all awesome questions. Really awesome. So why don't we go and ask Finn ourselves, shall we?"

Maddie realized that nothing was going to stop Cordelia—nothing could make her turn back from saving Finn. After everything he'd done for them, there was no way she was going to back down from this challenge. Which was why Maddie left the note for Abigail about where they were headed. Cordelia was adamant that they tell no one for fear of getting Finn hurt, but Maddie had been at Ravenswood in the dead of night and she knew the madhouse feel—the fact that spirits were more alive there than probably anywhere else in the world. It would be too much for them to take, and she didn't want to risk their lives again. So when Cordelia was searching for her keys, Maddie took the time to leave the note for her mother, shoving it under her bedroom door. She knew that once Abigail saw the note, she'd call the police and they would be safe. Unless, of course, it was the police who had called Finn to meet them at Ravenswood that night. In Hawthorne, anything was possible.

Finn's old car was parked at the front gate of Ravenswood.

"Why wouldn't he drive up to the building?" Cordelia asked.

"I don't know, but I'm not walking, so pull up to the front of the building," Maddie said. Her hands were blue from the cold.

"Sorry, sister. No way. Whoever called Finn out here in the middle of the night obviously wanted him to come alone. I'm not going to risk him getting killed just because it's too cold for us to walk a few hundred steps."

When Maddie started to protest, Cordelia snapped, "Come on, Maddie, it'll warm you up. Get the blood moving. Let's go!"

The girls raced up the winding road, the snow crunching beneath their feet. The monstrous Ravenswood seemed to be grinning at them.

Welcome back, Maddie, it seemed to say to her as a shudder went down her back. *Let the fun begin.*

&

"You killed Darcy and Bronwyn?" Finn said incredulously. "Wh—why?" Everything was happening so fast, he couldn't wrap his mind around it.

Kiki seemed to be happy to finally tell someone the truth. As she spoke, it appeared as though a weight was being lifted off her chest. She seemed almost giddy, like a little girl sharing a secret with her best friend. "Well, I didn't mean to kill Darcy. It's actually your fault, come to think of it."

"My fault? How could it possibly be my fault?" Finn asked.

"She was wearing your jacket that night out on Misery Island. She was all hunched over—now I know she had gotten her heel stuck in some rocks—that silly thing. Serves her right for sneaking out behind the tent to go look for my daughter's boyfriend. Oh, you thought I didn't know about Darcy and Trevor? You underestimate me and my daughter. In any case, since that little tramp had your leather jacket on, I thought it was you. It was only after I struck her with the tent stake that I realized my error. But at that point, there really wasn't much I could have done. She'd been knocked unconscious, blood was everywhere, so I just nudged her over the rocks and into the ocean. I figured that when and if she was found, your leather jacket would get you put away. I had some sympathy for the poor girl, but I thought it was a win-win situation. Since I wasn't able to kill you as I'd planned, I'd at least be able to frame you for murder. And there were other reasons that her death was—how shall I put this?—convenient."

She inspected her nails in the dim light that surrounded them and seemed annoyed that her polish was chipped. She looked up and obviously saw the confusion in his face mixed with horror. "I can't really explain why it was convenient." She whisked her hands upward in a *Why bother?* manner. "Some things are better left unsaid, don't you agree?"

Finn's jaw dropped open. She was talking about her murderous actions as if she were discussing a PTA meeting or a luncheon event. "Why kill me?"

"Oh, well, you know I was really angry with you. You

were royally screwing up my plans. I just—I just didn't want you around anymore. And there you were at the Winter Gala—stirring up even more trouble—and I just couldn't help myself. It wasn't premeditated. It was pure rage. I wanted you dead. It's as simple as that. But then, of course, I made that little mistake and things got messy. It's a pity I didn't just hire someone to do it. I learned from my mistakes, you know. Murder is a task best left to professionals," she said with an evil grin.

Finn noticed a stirring at the entrance. It was Cordelia and Maddie. They were sneaking in, trying not to cry out in shock as they saw the situation unfolding in front of them.

Finn knew he needed to keep Kiki's attention firmly on him, so that she didn't notice the girls entering the building.

He walked around to the other side, appearing like he was pacing, trying to understand what she had done and why she had done it. He knew from watching television shows on psychopaths that they reveled in discussing their crimes at length, especially if they knew they would get away with it. "So you hired someone to kill Bronwyn. Why? What did she do?"

"She saw me," Kiki said flatly. "The night of the gala." She looked down at her shoulder and brushed away a hair or stray piece of lint. "Or at least I thought she did. In any case, I couldn't risk having someone out there knowing the truth about what happened to Darcy. And then it hit me. I could have her kidnapped. Hire a professional to kidnap her and use her to extort money from her family. Do you have any idea how much money that family has?"

Finn tried to keep his eyes firmly locked on Kiki, afraid that if he looked away and dropped her gaze for even a moment, she would turn and see the girls creeping along the shadowy walls. He moved to the opposite wall from where the girls were now hiding, so that Kiki had turned completely in his direction.

"There was never any ransom request for Bronwyn," Finn said.

"Actually, yes, there was. But once we got the money, we realized that we couldn't let Bronwyn go. She knew all about my involvement. That was my stupidity, really. Once the man I hired found out how much money was involved, he got greedy and told Bronwyn who he was working for. That was a big mistake on his part. But one less groundskeeper at our house was never going to be missed."

Finn continued to stare at her in disbelief. The way she was talking about having people killed, extorting money, torching buildings for insurance money, it was obvious that she had no conscience.

"So I had to kill her. There really was nothing else to do. But I hadn't planned on her being found here. When I had the fires set, my intention was for the entire place to go up in flames. But unfortunately this stubborn building"—she held a fist up in the air as if she were challenging Ravenswood to a fight—"it just wouldn't burn the way it was supposed to." She cackled, her voice echoing off the walls. That's when Finn noticed the gasoline tang in the air. She must have already set the place to go up like a firecracker. All she needed was to light the spark.

"So why burn the place down now? I'm sure that you got all the money you needed—from the original insurance claim, from your investors, and from Bronwyn's family. Why do you need to burn down Ravenswood? And why do you need me to go down with the place? It sounds like you've got your story set in place. Obviously, you have the best lawyers that money can buy. Why not just frame me for everything? For Darcy's death, for Bronwyn, for arson? Why kill me?"

"Because you're a smart little bastard, Finnegan O'Malley. Somehow you would find a way to screw all of this up for me again. And this time, I'm not taking any risks. Bronwyn's family isn't going to give up until they find out who killed their precious little girl, so I need to hand over an explanation to them tied up in a nice, tidy little bow."

"How will killing me and burning this place up possibly clean things up? Won't it make you look more suspicious? All of these deaths and tragedies happening around you?"

"Here," she said, holding a piece of paper. "It's a suicide note. As soon as I leave here, it will be sent to the police, to the newspapers, to Bronwyn and Darcy's families. It explains how you were so tormented and angry with everyone in town. How you blamed everyone for Cordelia's disappearance, for the terrible things done to her on Misery Island. So you killed Darcy and then when Bronwyn confronted you about it, you kidnapped and ultimately killed her. You burned down Ravenswood the first time to cover your tracks, but when the part of the asylum that contained her body remained unscathed, you knew it was only a matter of time before the evidence pointed in your direction. In a final fit of desperation, you admit to your crimes in this suicide note and douse yourself and this blasted building in kerosene and Poof! You have paid for all of your sins."

She laughed gaily at her well-thought-out plan, waving the letter around like a victory flag.

"Who else knows about this?" Finn asked. In the dim light of the lantern, he could see streams of tears on Maddie's and Cordelia's faces. He needed to get them out of there.

"No one," Kiki said. "It's too tiresome to get more people involved. So much cleaning up to do, you know?"

Realizing that he wasn't buying it, she sheepishly added, "Well, maybe Kate had an inkling of knowledge, but you know that nothing is stronger than a mother-daughter bond."

"Which is why you deserve this!" Cordelia screamed, barreling out of the corner at Kiki, throwing her whole body weight against her, causing them to fall to the floor. The gun was knocked loose from Kiki's hands as Maddie ran to retrieve it.

"No!" Kiki screamed.

"Cordelia, don't!" Finn yelled.

Kiki threw Cordelia off her and managed to wrangle the gun out of Maddie's hands. Kiki appeared thrown for a moment, but was able to regain her composure, waving the gun back and forth at them.

"You stupid boy," she snarled. "I told you to come alone."

"I did," he pleaded. "Kiki, this is between you and me. Let the girls go."

"No, no, no," Kiki said, scratching her chin with the tip of the loaded gun. "You know that I can't have any loose ends. Let me see, why would the three of you be here together? Aha! A lovers' triangle. Of course. It makes it that much more dramatic. Maddie discovers Finn's secret and tries to talk him out of killing himself, while Cordelia arrives here in a jealous rage—furious that Maddie and Finn are having a clandestine affair. After all, she's still angry about everything that happened last year, and she still blames Finn and Maddie for not being able to save Rebecca from the asylum. It's perfect. Cordelia, clearly unbalanced, decides that they are all going to go together. A suicide pact. It's brilliant. I don't know why I didn't think of it in the first place. That way, I don't have you girls digging around trying to figure out why and how Finn could have done such a terrible thing. Ah yes, three birds, one massive stone. Perfect!"

&

Kiki's voice was echoing through the abandoned hallways, curling around pockmarked corners, and swirling into the void in the monstrous belly of Ravenswood

Maddie tried reasoning with Kiki.

"You don't know what you're doing. You can't do this!"

Finn angrily shouted, "Leave the girls out of this. I'm the

one you have a problem with. I'm the one you want. Let them go!"

"How can I possibly let them go now?" Kiki asked, her eyes wild and maniacal. "They know my secrets. All my secrets. The secrets of the Sisterhood. The secret of my crimes, my misfortunes."

Cordelia started to weep. It all seemed helpless.

Kiki moved the gun back and forth at each of them. If anyone made the slightest movement, one of them would get shot.

Maddie looked at Cordelia and Finn and realized how much they had put themselves at risk for her, how much they'd done for her. She knew what she had to do, what she was meant to do. It was as if Tess were there whispering in her ear. *You can make up for how you've wronged Cordelia in the past. This is your chance. You are strong and now it is time for you to show your strength.*

With a growl and a surge of energy that seemed to emerge from her very core, Maddie lunged at Kiki, knowing full well that the moment she did it, the gun would go off and possibly end her life. None of it seemed to matter anymore. As she leapt into the line of fire, images of Luke, Reed, Finn, and Cordelia, of her mother and Rebecca, and even the horrible night out on Misery Island—all of it flooded her brain. The bullet seared through her skin with such intense heat she felt like her body was on fire. She knocked into Kiki, hurling them both to the floor, but it wasn't enough to keep the gun from firing the bullet deep into Maddie's shoulder. She heard Cordelia scream and Finn shout, "No!"

But it was too late. Maddie fell to the floor, swallowed up by dizziness and the feeling of blood rushing from her body. Kiki stood up and looked down at her, laughing.

"You stupid, stupid girl. You'll never learn, will you? Never, ever learn."

Her voice sounded hollow and Maddie's body suddenly

felt very cold, as if there were hands reaching up through the floor and pulling her downward. She thought she imagined a large hulking figure coming out from the shadows. Was it a spirit? Maddie could see the shadows coming closer. Spirits of those who had been tortured or abused or killed within the confines of the asylum were coming closer—crowding around Kiki, unbeknownst to her. She continued to cackle and laugh at her good fortune. But no matter how hard they tried, they were ineffectual. They could not manifest themselves—they weren't strong enough to distract Kiki from her mission. In the corner, she saw Darcy and Bronwyn, clinging to each other—helpless and in shock. Maddie knew that she was close to death because the veil had been lifted so that she could see the spirits on the other side.

One of the figures lunged at Kiki from behind, throwing her back onto the floor. The gun went off accidentally this time. Maddie felt the bullet graze her head. She didn't have the energy to even try to shield herself from the blow. The room was swirling and her body was numb. She wondered how the spirit was able to attack Kiki and save them. It was so curious.

Cordelia ran over to Maddie and tried to stop the blood that was gushing from her left shoulder. Maddie tried to speak, but the air felt like it was sucked out of her. She moved her mouth wordlessly, choking on the copper taste of blood that seemed to be filling every part of her. She was drifting away. The gentle spirits were surrounding her, letting her know that everything was going to be okay. Even Tess was there, smiling down at her. She just needed to close her eyes for a moment. *Just a moment and everything will be okay.*

Finn pushed Cordelia out of the way and started CPR. Maddie could hear him say, as if he were down a long, dark tunnel, "Stay with me, Maddie. You stay with me."

Cordelia turned in amazement to see Malcolm Crane knock Kiki off her feet, her head slamming onto the cold cement floor. He ripped the gun from her hand and steadily pointed it at Kiki as she was shrieking in pain and fury.

"Finn, try to stop the bleeding any way you can," he shouted as he tossed a cell phone to Cordelia. "Call 9-1-1, the police, anyone! She's losing a lot of blood. We need to get her to a hospital right away." And then he looked at Kiki. "I should shoot you right now for everything you've done, but death is too good for you. You deserve every humiliation in the world for all the pain that you've caused. And I know you, Kiki. Death won't be as painful as being torn apart in public for what you've done."

Cordelia pressed down on Maddie's shoulder, trying to keep the blood from squirting out. She leaned over Maddie's chest, listening for a heartbeat. "Maddie, don't go. Don't leave me," she cried.

Suddenly a flurry of activity descended upon them. EMTs and police swiftly moved through the cavernous room. A stretcher was brought in for Maddie. As they strapped her down and tried to control the bleeding, an oxygen mask was placed over her mouth. Cordelia wept and had to be dragged away from Maddie—from her sister. Finn held her as she shook and cried out for Maddie, as she watched Maddie's eyelids flutter and her eyes roll back in her head. Orders were being barked left and right. Officer Sullivan was right behind the EMTs, cuffing Kiki, shoving her through the entryway and reading her rights as she laughed hysterically.

"I own this town! I own you! Get your hands off of me, you mongrel! I'll have you fired. I'll have you killed! I'm an Endicott, goddammit! Let me go!"

Malcolm Crane brushed the dirt and debris from his clothing. Cordelia remained in Finn's arms, sobbing, realizing that he'd put his life on the line for her once again. He truly was her white knight.

"How did you—?" she asked Malcolm through her tears. "How could you know?"

"When Rebecca called me while I was up teaching in Maine, she told me she saw this happening. She needed to warn us all—she said she sent tarot cards to everyone that she felt was in danger, or who was involved in this crazy plan. It was her only way of reaching out to us all. I don't know how she found me, or how she knew what was going to happen. But I think we all know by now to listen to Rebecca when she has anything more than a hunch about certain things."

He smiled sadly and then continued. "That's why I needed to come back here. Plus, I read about Tess and Rebecca and everything that happened here at Ravenswood—and then with Abigail's cancer, I knew it was time for me to make amends. So I came back here. I was going to try to make things right as best I could."

Cordelia was sobbing into Finn's shoulder as Malcolm continued. "I knew that it would be a while before you girls would forgive me, which is why I stuck around a little while longer. And then out of the blue, Abigail calls me and tells me about some note that Maddie left. She felt that I was the only person to help—the only one to stop this. As soon as she called, I knew that you were in trouble. That Rebecca's visions were coming true. I knew I had to do everything in my power to save you kids. I've caused enough pain in your lives—it was time I did something right. Even if it meant putting my life at risk."

Cordelia smiled sadly and nodded, realizing that her mission to track down Malcolm Crane ultimately saved her life and Maddie's. It was too much for Cordelia to take. Her head was spinning. The spirits of Ravenswood were crowding her, all trying to be heard, to be seen, to be remembered, to be avenged.

She turned to Finn and said, "They're happy now. The spirits will finally be at rest here, because of you."

Finn grabbed her just as she collapsed and the two men carried her outside, bringing Cordelia back to Mariner's Way. Bringing her home.

Chapter 29

THE STAR

A card of healing, hope, joy, and illumination. Peace and calm. Regeneration, vision, and new life. When this card appears, you know somehow that life is just about to become easier and brighter. The Star is a card that looks to the future. It does not predict any immediate or powerful change, but it does predict hope and healing. This card suggests clarity of vision, spiritual insight.

Maddie's eyes fluttered open. Her last memory was of darkness and pain, Kiki standing over her like an evil witch cackling. Blood everywhere. Freezing winds howling in her ears. Scorching pain consuming her body. Spirits crowding around her shrieking in pain. Now her ears were filled with a void, a silence, eyes blinded by the lights, and a numbness that enveloped her body. She was floating. Was she dead? Was this what death felt like? An overwhelming sense of peace and of letting go? Of not caring anymore and succumbing to the light? She saw Luke's face hovering over her, worried and stricken. Would she be able to say good-bye? Faces crowded above her. She tried to focus on the people she loved—to let them know that she was going to be okay. They looked down at her: Finn and Cordelia, Rebecca and Abigail, Luke and Reed, and even Malcolm Crane, all were vying for her weak stare.

"She's coming out of it," she heard Luke say. But it sounded like she was underwater and he was speaking from dry land.

Then Cordelia spoke. "Easy, don't try to talk. We're here

for you, Maddie." She could hear the fear and the sadness in Cordelia's voice.

A blinding light suddenly filled her eyes. This was her good-bye. She got to see them all before she left and now she was heading into the light. It was so beautiful and peaceful and bright. Just when the light became overwhelming, a man pulled his head back and she realized that she was looking into a doctor's face. His headlamp had caused her temporary dip into the light and now he was moving a flashlight back and forth between her eyes. It was as if he were looking deep inside her mind—into her dark memories: the pain, the misery, the secrets of her soul.

"Looks like the computer's working in there," he said as a collective sigh of relief ran through the sterile hospital room. "Just give her some time to readjust. She's been through a lot mentally and physically." He turned back to Maddie and smiled down at her. "You had a pretty close call, young lady. You've been out for a few days. Welcome back."

Maddie tried to speak, but the words wouldn't come. Her mouth was dry and her throat hurt.

"Don't try to talk," the doctor said kindly. "We've had a tube down your throat keeping those lungs working while you fought to come back to us. It'll be a few days before you'll be comfortable enough to speak." And then he turned to the rest of the people in the room and said, "But the rest of you are welcome to give her words of encouragement and love right now. You came pretty close to losing this little lady. But she's a fighter, that's for sure."

Rebecca leaned in and looked at Maddie. Her beautiful eyes were filled with life once again—they were no longer vacant and haunted. "She's going to be just fine," she said. "She's stronger than any of us ever realized. I don't even think she was aware of her strength." Then she whispered to Maddie, "Thank you for saving my little girl. For bringing her back and for risking your life for hers. Tess is very proud of you."

Then Cordelia shoved her way into Maddie's line of vision. "Why would you jump in front of a gun? I can't believe you did that for us! I just can't believe that we almost lost you."

Luke was the next person to lean over her and a feeling of warmth rushed through her body as he smiled at her. He held her hand and gently kissed her mouth. "Next time I invite you to go with me on a trip, I'm not taking no for an answer."

Maddie's mouth hurt as she tried to smile, but her eyes filled with tears, letting everyone know how happy she was to be alive; how thankful she was to have all these wonderful people in her life. And how blessed she was to have survived.

Chapter 30

JUSTICE

A very wise card that literally means justice and fairness have been achieved. There is a balance in all things. The scales of justice are in equilibrium. A return to the natural order. Logic and reason have been restored.

"Where are you going?" Maddie asked. "Can I come with?" She was almost afraid to let Cordelia out of her sight for fear that she'd slip away again, disappear like she was kidnapped by an elvin king and dragged underground for another year. She sat up anxiously in her bed.

"No," Cordelia said firmly. "You know that the doctor said you needed at least a few weeks of bed rest before doing anything that could drain or exhaust you."

"Well, what are you planning on doing that's so exhausting? Hiking a mountain or something?" Maddie laughed as she flopped back down on her pillows. She could hear the flurry of activity going on downstairs. Abigail was preparing breakfast for her houseful of guests: Reed, Finn, Rebecca, Malcolm, Luke, and his father.

"No, I have to thank someone. I have to return something. It's something I have to do alone. And if I go now while grub is being served," she said jokingly, "I might be able to sneak out undetected and without a chaperone." She leaned over and kissed Maddie's forehead and promised that this time she wouldn't be gone for long.

Maddie understood that Cordelia needed to thank Sophie, the strange woman who helped her escape from Hawthorne, who taught her astral projection, and who took her in when she needed the most help. Maddie wished she could thank that woman in person as well. Maybe she would when she was up on her feet again. But for now, she was going to enjoy having Luke, Reed, Finn, and her father waiting on her hand and foot, Rebecca and Abigail happy and healthy and under the same roof, and Cordelia returning back to them safe and sound. It was the happy ending she'd been craving for as long as she could remember.

෨

Cordelia guided the car onto 95 North and headed toward Ipswich and Wolf Hollow, the place where she had hitched a ride over a year ago. Once she arrived at Wolf Hollow, she walked over to the pen and looked at the magnificent creatures. One poked its head up above the others, perked up its ears, and howled. That must have been her friend who helped her stow away.

"Can I help you?" a man said as he lumbered across the field. It was the guy who drove the truck.

"Oh, um, I'm just trying to find a little place near here. It's called the Crow's Nest. I wanted to talk to Sophie, the woman who owns the place."

A strange expression came over his face. "You mean Sophie Pickering?"

Pickering—the name hit her with a full force. Of course, she was a descendent of the Pickering sisters. Now it was all coming full circle, as Tess used to say.

"Yes, I guess. I only knew her first name," Cordelia continued, trying not to show her shock. "I was here about a year ago and she helped me out. I just wanted to thank her." She turned, motioning to the thick woods that surrounded them. "I remember it was near Wolf Hollow, I just don't remember exactly where."

"Well," he said slowly, "the old cottage called the Crow's

Nest is about fifty feet off the road that way." He motioned toward a thick stand of trees.

"Oh, thank you—" she said, before being cut off.

"But the place is in shambles."

"Oh no!" Cordelia raised her hand to her mouth. "What happened? Is Sophie hurt?"

Cordelia couldn't bear to think of what could have transpired over the past year. The woman had been so helpful, so wonderful to her in her time of need. A wave of guilt passed over her.

"No, I'm sorry," he said softly. "She's not. She passed on."

Tears filled Cordelia's eyes. She felt selfish and awful. If she had only returned within the year, perhaps she could have seen Sophie and thanked her before she passed away. The emotions swirled within her, bringing the pain of losing Tess and not being able to say good-bye to her beloved grandmother. It was all too much for her to take.

"Excuse me," the man said quizzically. "Do you mind my asking how old you are?"

Cordelia sniffed. "I'm almost eighteen, why?" She brushed the tears from her cheeks. The cold air was now stinging the spots on her face that were wet.

"Well, Sophie died about twenty years ago. I was just a kid working here when she was in her eighties. So I don't think it's Sophie Pickering you're looking for."

"Does she have a daughter or a niece or someone that's been living there since she passed away?" This didn't make any sense. Why would that woman lie to her about her name?

"No one's been over there in years, best I can tell. Sophie had a friend that lived in Hawthorne that used to check in on her. But I haven't seen her in years. What was her name again?" The man rubbed his chin as he looked down and kicked the dirt, deep in thought.

That woman was from Hawthorne? she thought incredulously.

"Tess," he said suddenly.

Cordelia snapped her head up. "Excuse me? How do you know—?"

"Sophie's friend from Hawthorne. Her name was Tess— uh, Tess . . ."

"Martin?" Cordelia said slowly.

"Yeah, that's it. Tess Martin," he said proudly. "But she's got to be in her eighties by now, so I don't think that's the woman you saw at the Crow's Nest. I don't even think the place has been touched since Sophie passed on."

"Th-thank you," Cordelia said, dumbfounded. "I think I'd still like to see it, though." She turned and headed in the direction that the man pointed and she heard him call after her.

"Be careful, now! Don't stay too long in those woods. And get out of there before it gets dark. I'll be watching for ya!"

His voice disappeared behind her, meaningless. She was so confused. Sophie died twenty years ago? Then who was the woman who had helped her?

She walked into the forest until she came upon the tiny cottage. The sign with the freshly painted black crow was now rotted and hanging off the rusted wrought-iron hanger. The windows were covered in newspapers and the brush had grown up so thick around the window and doors that there wasn't any way to get close to the front door. Cordelia looked up and saw that the roof was rotted and had a large hole in the middle. It looked as though no one had been inside for decades.

But that's impossible, Cordelia thought. *I was just here!*

She turned and walked away from the house, afraid that she was losing her mind, trying to put the pieces together and trying to make sense of it all. She saw something bright on the ground. A shock of color on the blanket of white snow. It was a tarot card—worn and tattered. Cordelia leaned over to pick it up. It was the same as the cards the woman had used to read her fortune. Despite its weather-beaten and aged look, she could recognize the same artistic design—the one that had intrigued her so much on that night that hadn't seemed so long ago. She smiled when she realized which tarot card she'd found. It was Justice.

Cordelia called to the man who was in the wolf pen throwing a bucket of food into the troughs to let him know that she was leaving. He raised up one of his hands to say good-bye. The wolf that she had ridden along with came running up to the gate. It looked at her knowingly. She held its mysterious gaze for a moment before turning back to the car.

Epilogue

"So what do you think is going to happen to this place?" Maddie asked Reed as they walked toward Kate's house. Even though the Endicott family had relocated to a smaller place in town during Kiki's arraignment, the mansion still possessed that smug, better-than-the-rest feeling. Maddie held the cup of hot chocolate in her hands, hoping that it would warm up her shivering body. She knew it was time to head back to school. They wouldn't give any additional extensions, especially now that Abigail's cancer was in full remission and she was being cared for by both Rebecca and Cordelia. Plus, her doctor had given her a clean bill of health. Her war wounds had healed nicely and she had made a full recovery. It made Maddie a little sad to return to boarding school. Even though Luke would make the transition easier, she felt like she would be missing out on her home. Her real home.

Just then the door burst open and Kate appeared, struggling under the weight of the last of her suitcases. This time she didn't have the hired help to do the work for her. "Great," she said when she saw Maddie and Reed. "Are you here to throw a celebration or something? Can I get a little help? Please?"

Maddie rolled her eyes and turned to Reed, ignoring Kate's demands.

"Like I said before, what's going to happen to the infamous Endicott house?"

"I don't know," he said, stifling a smile. "You should ask the new owners." Reed nodded toward the end of the driveway. Maddie and Kate turned quickly to see Luke Bradford strolling up the walk.

"Oh my God," Maddie said, rushing over to Luke and giving him a big hug. "Is this for real?"

He smiled and grabbed her hand and continued walking to the former Endicott house—now the summer home of the Bradford family. "It's for real, all right."

"But, why?" She couldn't imagine that he was moving to Hawthorne just to be near her, could he? Even that was too far-fetched to believe.

"Well, my dad has always had a soft spot for Hawthorne—this is where he learned to sail and actually met your dad. I know, small world, huh? Plus, Marblehead Harbor is where we'll be storing our boat, since it's the deepest natural harbor in the country. It's the perfect place for the Bradfords to summer, don't you think? Bet you didn't think I did my research, did you?"

Maddie heard Kate say to Reed, "The Bradford family? As in the Billionaire Bradfords? The Fortune 500 Bradford family? That's the Luke that Maddie was talking about?"

Maddie shook her head. This was too good to be true.

"But why Hawthorne? Why now?"

"Well, I've always thought that life in New York City was interesting, but *nothing* compares to the craziness that goes on here. This is my kind of town," he said wickedly.

Kate, never one to lose an opportunity to hit on a wealthy guy, pushed between Maddie and Luke.

"Well, you should know that before this whole 'debacle,'"

she said, wrinkling her nose and gazing angrily over her shoulder at Maddie, "my family practically built this town. If there's anyone who you should come to for a—an extra-special, private tour of the town, I'm your girl."

Maddie felt physically ill. She turned to Reed, only to have him shrug his shoulders. Luke couldn't possibly fall under Kate's spell, could he?

"You know, since this is your old house and you are familiar with the area, it would make sense for you to stick around for a while, darlin'," Luke said, tipping her head up with his finger. Maddie felt like she was going to scream. He was using his smoky voice that she'd grown to hate when he talked to other pretty girls.

"I'd love to stick around and get to know you better, Luke." She smiled and then flashed her eyes wickedly at Maddie. Maddie could see the wheels turning in Kate's head. If she could nab Luke Bradford, then she could return to the lifestyle she was accustomed to.

"Great," he said, clapping. "Then you can move your things into the maid's quarters, because I really don't know the first thing about getting good help in this area. I'm actually quite at a loss. Plus, you know the house better than anyone, I would assume, and you'd know how to keep it tidy, yes?"

Kate's jaw dropped open. "You can't be serious."

"Well," he said with mock sincerity, "you do need money for school, yes? And your family has lost everything. I just assumed you'd be looking for work. You could share the quarters with your mother if she's looking to be in our employ. Oh, wait. She and your father are incarcerated, isn't that right? Well, in any case, why don't you talk it over with your family? If they—how did you put it? Built this town, you say?—then they would be the ones to go to for assistance as a newcomer. And I need all the help I can get."

"Yes, you do. Starting with your attitude, you asshole. I am an Endicott, you know."

"Oh, I know." He leaned in closer and whispered, "But I won't hold that against you."

He turned and winked at Maddie, and she knew that—finally—everything was going to work out just fine.